CRAZY BEACH

DISC II-CRAZIER BEACH© 2019

L.R. WELBORN

The events and conversations in this book have been set down to the best of the author's ability, although some names have been changed to protect the privacy of individuals.

First paperback edition April 2019
Published by Federal Point Books
Wilmington, NC

Book design by L.R. Welborn and Steffany Welborn
Author photo by Lance King

ISBN-1795453265
Other books by L.R. Welborn
Crazy Beach Disc I
Crazy Beach Disc III-Craziest Beach

www.facebook.com/CrazyBeachNovel.com

Dedicated to my wife Steffany, whose love, encouragement, and support I treasure. She was the reason these stories finally escaped my mind. I love you.

To those of you who see yourself in these pages and those of you who have been a part of my life, I know I have failed you along the way, some more so than others. For that I am truly sorry. I hope any joy or laughter I brought your way will enable you to forgive me.

"I wanted a perfect ending. Now I've learned, the hard way, that some poems don't rhyme, and some stories don't have a clear beginning, middle, and end. Life is about not knowing, having to change, taking the moment and making the best of it, without knowing what's going to happen next."- **Gilda Radner** (1946-1989), actress, comedian, original Saturday Night Live cast member.

Track 1-Raindrops Keep Falling on My Head-B.J. Thomas (2:57)

The clock on the wall in the school office struck three. The same time as when Paul Newman, as Butch Cassidy walks into a bank at the start of *Butch Cassidy and the Sundance Kid*. Butch, obviously casing the place for a potential robbery, notices a lot of new security devices have been installed since the last time he robbed the same bank. He asks the security guard why all the changes, noting it used to be such a beautiful bank.

"People kept robbing it," the security guard said.

"Such a small price to pay for beauty," Butch said.

We had all been through a lot of changes in the year since Darlene moved to Durham. One thing that hadn't changed was mine and B's propensity to get into trouble. We were waiting to be called into Principal "Bossy" Mossy's office again. School had only been in session a little more than a month and we were already on our third visit to start our junior year of high school off right. We were approaching double-digit visits over the course of less than three high school semesters.

"Ok," Bossy Mossy said, entering the school's office door. "Not you two idiots again. Well, get the hell in here."

We followed the skinny, 5'10", 150 pounds or so ex-Marine drill sergeant into his cluttered private office. He was sporting a bad light blue 1970s leisure suit. He shuffled some papers around on his desk looking for our "sent to office" paperwork as we grabbed our familiar spots across from his desk. He looked us over. We were wearing green doctor's scrubs and coalminer's lighted helmets. We kinda looked like we flunked out of a try out for 80s tech-pop band Devo. "Whip It" real good indeed. He pressed the intercom button.

"Miss Rhodes," he started. "What have these two jackasses done this time?"

"Uh, oh, oh my," Miss Rhodes stammered. "I'd rather not say."

Miss Rhodes, basically a stick-person with giant Harry Carey-like black coke bottle glasses, served as a librarian in the county school system for over 30 years. Her eyesight had gotten so bad they had to move her into the front office that year because she could no longer tell Dewey where his decimal was.

"Ah, aww," she hemmed and hawed some more. "Will you just ask them sir?"

Bossy Mossy raised his combat-tested brow at us and grimaced.

"Ok, let me have it," he started. "It can't be any worse than last time. You two are really leaving skid marks on history here."

As the spokesperson for our modern Butch and Sundance crew, I started to speak.

"Shut up motor-mouth," Mossy ordered. "Let's hear from the jolly silent giant one time."

B had grown another couple inches and was now near 6'2". Our Nigerian soccer coach Mr. Nwsou called him "Big One". B had a thin black mustache making him look like a villain from a bad silent film or an actual member of Butch and Sundance's "Hole in the Wall" gang of old west outlaws. He looked at me. I shrugged my shoulders.

"Well," B started.

"Whaaa-Whaaaa, riiiing-riiiiing" the sound of the fire alarm blasted across the school grounds and throughout the buildings. It sounded like World War III had begun. Mossy just glared at us. He pointed up.

"Let me guess," he said slamming both hands down on his desk sending papers flying everywhere. "One of your flunkies from the cornucopia of bozos that follow you around?"

I shrugged my shoulders as Mossy stormed out to handle the required fire drill procedures.

"I'm not done with you two," he yelled from the office lobby. "Not by a long shot."

"Let's roll," I said.

We got the hell out of there and walked quickly to the parking lot, shedding our costumes along the way. We got to my car in seconds flat. Hal was leaning on the left rear quarter panel.

"Thought I would delay the execution for a bit," he smiled.

Good ol' Hal, you could always count on that boy. I opened the door and pulled my seat up to let him in the back. David clamored in on the other side. It was Friday, a glorious last week of summer in late September. The temperature was low 80s, nice soft breeze. We had a bye week, so no Friday night lights or practice, just a free day and night.

"Let's go down to Knotty Beach and drink some beer," Hal said.

"Nah," I said. "Cops down there are all over this car anytime I show up cause of that crap last spring. How bout we go to Munchies and drink a few?"

"Hell yea," David said. "You should have seen the look on ol' Foss, the drama maestro's face when he tore down your sign. Boy was he pissed. Everyone else was laughing."

Everyone was laughing because B and I had set up an impromptu doctor's office outside of the drama department's exterior door facing the sandy back courtyard. It was in a near-perfect spot for our little afternoon of fun. No other classes nearby, just the area behind the cafeteria. Doors on each end of the walkway connected the cafeteria and classroom buildings, so lots of traffic.

I had stagecraft that year, helping with the lighting and sound for thespian activities so I knew where all the props were. The drama kids were practicing in the auditorium that day so I had free reign even though I was supposed to be doing inventory. We set up an old dentist chair with a scantily clad female dummy in it, posted a lab skeleton hanging from a display mount, and had a card table with a couple of chairs out front with a tacky hand-made sign:

"Welcome sophomores! Guys join the Amateur Gynecology Club, GIRLS-FREE EXAMS today only!"

B would stand there "examining" the skeleton or the dummy while I pitched the virtues of our "club" to students. Lexi and Sabrina came by and took some pictures. Sabrina had developed into quite the camera buff over the summer and was on the yearbook staff. Our photos as "doctors of delight" didn't make the cut. Lexi had a copy on her bedroom bulletin board for a long time.

We made it to Munchies in just a few minutes. It was the joint where many of us had our first beer at a bar. My fake ID (remember, Wonder of Boyhood number six?) had arrived in the mail right after Labor Day and was a boon to my burgeoning illegal enterprises. I was buying booze for tons of my friends and making some good money. I had talked our way through only me having to show my ID at Munchies that week, telling the owner we were college students at the university just down the street.

You only had to be 18 to buy and consume beer back then so it wasn't a big stretch. Munchies was mostly a college hangout, and real cool. We got to know some of the regulars, but most importantly we could go drink a beer at a bar and talk to college girls. I was still several weeks from 17 and the others about the same. Their size, B and David being tall, and Hal being big all over made it a little easier.

We spent many cool hours during our junior and senior years drinking away at Munchies, laughing, joking, and trying to get college girls to notice us. That was sometimes, but not totally a bust. That day was a good time, one of the best in late summer and fall at the joint. We drank a couple of pitchers of ice cold beer and headed back to our little island.

"Man, you see that stupid name, Pleasure Island, they are starting to put on everything around here?" Hal asked. "What a joke, makes us look like a poor man's Fantasy Island or a cheap hand-job town."

We all busted out laughing. No one under 30 thought the new marketing term for our little island was any good. It didn't represent who we were or what we wanted to be. In fact, we thought it sucked. I still do.

"Let's go camp out at Boy Scout Lake or Sugarloaf tonight," Hal said.

B looked at me. I nodded ok. David said he was in.

"The Scout won't be ready until next week," Hal said. "Guess we'll all have to pile in B's Jeep."

"Ok, you guys get your crap together and we'll pick you up after supper," I said.

Track 2-The Song Remains the Same-Led Zeppelin (6:00)

I know those of you who have read Crazy Beach-Disc One (and if you haven't, please stop, go read it first, this will be a lot more fun, and make a lot more sense) are waiting to hear what happens between me and Darlene, what happened to all the other people you got to know, and all that stuff. We'll get there. But first, you remember when Darlene said my life's ambition was to see Led Zeppelin? She said it the night of Ike's party at Knotty Beach. Well, this is how I fulfilled my life's ambition. Bucket list check mark number one and at such a young age.

Zeppelin's concert film, *The Song Remains the Same* was released the fall of our senior year in high school. We kept waiting and waiting for the film to be shown in our coastal market, but things sometimes took a bit longer to reach us. Plus the Wave Theatre had burned down a few years before, leaving us islanders with no local cinema. We had to head to town on the mainland to watch movies. We sure missed the Wave. I still do. Every time I go to Britt's I look at the space next door and remember some of the good times I had at the Wave. We saw several great concert films at the Wave. I remember Melissa always wanted to see Zep as well. She said to be patient, they would get to us. So we'd been waiting patiently for Zep to tour nearby, but they never came around. Well, all of that changed a few weeks before I graduated.

"Yo," my buddy Ken said. "The Zeppelin movie starts today, want to cut last class and catch the first showing at two."

"Hell yea," I said. "I'll see if B or Gregg wants to go."

Well, I couldn't find B, but Gregg was in. Ken had been my football teammate our 10th grade year and Gregg was my soccer teammate the last two years. I'd given up football after 10th grade to concentrate on soccer because I thought I had a better chance of earning a college scholarship on the pitch or the diamond. My dad wasn't thrilled with my choice, but I did get the baseball scholarship. Of course, I screwed that up as well by tearing the rotator cuff on my throwing arm on a super cold March day my sophomore year in college. I didn't warm up properly due to being a little drunk and a lot stoned, but that's a tale for another day.

"Ok, fire one up," Gregg said as I drove toward the theatre.

We got really high, bought a ton of popcorn, some other goodies, and headed in to see Zep rock. The film was really trippy great. We snuck in a pint of rum, so between the herb and the rum we were feeling pretty tight. The movie was quite long, almost two and a half hours with a dozen extended Zep performances from their summer of 1973 shows at Madison Square Garden (MSG) in New York City.

There were wild, sci-fi fantasy sequences with each of the four members having their own little mini-film within a film. There's also lots of footage of the band members and their associates hanging out, their interactions with MSG personnel, and others. As the credits rolled over another playing of "Stairway to Heaven" we got up to leave.

"Damn, I'm buzzed pretty good," Gregg said.

"Me too," Ken added. "We can go chill at my house. My folks are away until late tonight."

"Sounds good," I said.

I was glad I had remembered my sunglasses because it was damn bright out after being inside the darkened theatre for so long. We made our way to my copper-colored 1973 Monte Carlo. I wrecked the Duster for the last time a few months before. More on that later. Of course, we had Zeppelin (IV) in the eight-track player, and we rocked on over to Ken's house near our school.

Though the split-level brick ranch house was in a neighborhood, Ken's family's home was on the far northwestern side of the development and had a huge back yard with a fenced one-acre field behind it. The property backed up to some heavy woods. It was a great spot. We started to head in for some serious munchies when Gregg noticed something out back.

"Hey Ken, when did you guys get goats?" he asked.

"Beats me," Ken said. "First time I've ever seen'em."

"Let's get'em stoned!" I declared.

Gregg and Ken looked at one another and then at me. We all laughed. It was one of those moments when you know you are about to attempt something incredibly stupid, but undeniably fun. There was no doubt we were going to give it a go and the goats were going to get "shotguns".

We sat on the picnic table behind the house under a stately old oak tree and each rolled a doobie. We fired them up and passed them around a time or two. It was a little competition to see who could roll the best joint. Ken won, he always rolled great joints. Mine was significantly better than Gregg's, but Ken was a true rolling master. Perfect in every way. I never witnessed anyone with such a touch and feel for marijuana. He grew his own plants by a creek bed behind the fenced field.

"Ok," Ken said. "There are four of them and three of us, so let's each get one high and see if they screw with the other one."

Well, the next few minutes looked kinda like a Keystone Cops meet the Three Stooges short. Only thing missing was the cool funny music they played during chase scenes. After chasing, falling, chasing, and falling some more, we finally figured out it was going to take at least one of us (two for one big fella) to hold a goat while someone else got him or her high.

Boy, do I wish there was a film of that action. I don't think I've ever laughed so hard in my life. We managed to give three of the goats pretty substantial shotguns of sweet leaf. After some initial resistance, once we finished with them, they actually appeared to want more, trying to horn in on the next one's turn. One little brown speckled gal fell down a few times, but looked to be smiling and having fun.

The big ol 'male with a jet black coat and a white spot just above his nose ran around like he was a bull hunting for calves. The third stoner goat was pretty mellow and seemed to nod her head as if listening to some cool goat jams. The fourth "straight" goat was quite curious as to what was going on. At one point she tried to take a little nip at Gregg when he was chasing her just for the hell of it. It was so funny. That goat turned the tables on Gregg so quickly, chasing him halfway across the field before abruptly stopping to munch on some tall weeds.

We finally had our fill of the sweet goat action and laughed our way back to the house. We entered through the rear basement door. Ken had the basement decorated in black-light posters and rock art. The room featured red, white, and blue bean bag chairs, and an old brown sectional sofa. Ken had a small dorm fridge we quickly raided for some leftover pizza and drinks. We sat around for a couple of hours listening to Zep and Pink Floyd music and talking. We didn't think to check on the goats.

Our dazed and stuffed selves also failed to keep up with the time. We were jolted from our semi-comatose stoner dreams by the unmistakable sound of Mr. Russ' booming voice.

"Ken! You and Lenny get the hell up here right now," the 6'5" former Marine bellowed from the top of the stairs.

After checking to see if we'd pooped our pants and giving each other death stares, we managed to right ourselves sufficiently enough to head up the stairs. We looked at each other's eyes to make sure they were not too red. We also did a quick 10-second clean-up of the room.

"This is unbelievable," Mr. Russ shouted even louder.

We all looked at each other again as we started up the steps.

"You think we killed the goats?" Gregg asked.

"Oh shit," Ken said.

I wisely brought up the rear.

"What are we going to say?" Gregg said looking back at me.

I shrugged my shoulders. Damn, maybe goats were allergic to dope. Naw, those scavengers can eat anything, can't they?

When we reached the top of the stairs we were in a hallway connecting the living room to the kitchen. Mr. Russ was standing on the back deck, the kitchen door wide open. We slowly made our way out. He had his hands on his hips surveying his back yard and field.

"That damn Walter, he ripped me off," Mr. Russ yelled looking at us as we stood beside him on the deck. "He said it would take two or three weeks for those goats to clear that field. Hell, I just got them two days ago and it's damn clean as a whistle. That bastard!"

That was as hard as I have ever bit my tongue, literally. Gregg quickly excused himself to the bathroom to keep from laughing in Mr. Russ' face, well, shoulder. Poor Ken, he tried to summon his inner DeNiro and act perplexed, putting his hand to his face and lowering his head in his rendition of Rodin's "The Thinker".

"Do you see that? Do you see that?" Mr. Russ continued.

Oh boy did we see…

The stoned-ass goats had the munchies so bad they cleared the entire field in just a few hours. Mr. Black goat was humping away with the goat that had been nodding to the goat jams and the other stoner goat was licking the butt of the straight goat with the power of a pressure washer. Drugs, food, and sex, those goats were giving a masterclass in how to live the goat good life.

"Margaret, Margaret," Mr. Russ yelled some more heading back in the house. "I'm going to go see that no-good, thieving Walter snake."

"Honey, honey," she said grabbing Mr. Russ by the arm. "You wait just one minute. I'll call Juliet first and see what this is all about. I'm sure it was just a misunderstanding or maybe a joke. You know Walter loves practical jokes, he gets you every year on April Fool's Day."

Thank goodness Ms. Russ could get Mr. Russ to do whatever she said. If you ever saw her you would know why. A six-foot Greek goddess who looked like she just stepped down from Mt. Olympus. Though in her 40s she still looked no older than 30. Her perfect olive skin, soft voice, and gentle manner only added to her allure. She was the best-looking mom I ever ran across growing up. The term that just popped in your head wasn't around then, but would definitely apply. Poor Ken, knowing all your friends think your mom is hot.

"Are you boys hungry?" Ms. Russ asked.

"No thank you, Ms. Russ," I managed. "Gregg and I've got to be going."

"Wait one minute," Mr. Russ said.

Oh boy…what else had we screwed up?

Mr. Russ went over to his briefcase, bent over, and looked like he was searching for something inside.

"You boys wouldn't mind a little early graduation present would you?" he asked smiling.

And with that he rose, holding four tickets so high they got hit by the ceiling fan.

"How about tickets to see Led Zeppelin in Greensboro in two weeks!"

Track 3-Boom! Boom! Out Go the Lights!-Pat Travers Band (5:04)

It had to set some kind of record. You know how many times I was called into a principal's office over my infamous march through secondary education? A gazillion, at least. But that's not the record I'm talking about. Not only was this new thing likely a record, it was also probably a first.

"Well, we know you did it," the principal said. "Just admit it."

We just sat there.

"Look, it's just a matter of time," he continued. "Someone else knows how you two pulled this off, there is no way two people could have done all this alone, and we will find them, they'll talk, and it will be much worse for you."

Bullshit.

Like all the cool cop shows of the 1970s taught me, I knew to stay silent or say very little, admit nothing, and make them prove it. I knew B would stay silent or close to it and I was pretty sure they couldn't prove what we, of course, had done. They were right 100 percent. They just had nothing but a hunch and a bunch of cross-town fingers pointing at us.

You see, we weren't in OUR school's principal's office, we were in the office of J. Michael Thornton, the longest serving principal in our county, our state, and likely the nation. He was so old he made ol'man Graham look like a debutante. He had been principal at our cross-town rival since before WWII.

He was standing during this entire exchange with us. He was the most intimidating physical specimen of a man I ever saw. He looked like Dwayne "The Rock" Johnson on steroids after he had just eaten Hulk Hogan for lunch.

"You two won't get away with this," he proclaimed. "If it's the last thing I do, I will prove you two turds ruined our kids' prom! You two will get expelled and go to jail."

He was wrong. The last thing he ever did was poop himself, right after he checked out in that very office two weeks later just before the end of our senior year and on the day we headed off to see Led Zeppelin. He had just finished most of an egg sandwich. Poor clean-up crew.

That crew likely contained several of the people who had to scramble into action the week before to try and restore order at our cross-town rival's gym just after I led a small company of the "Zeroes" in a near-perfect execution of a plan I'd hatched just after our final prom a week or so before theirs was slated to start.

The day I began developing the plan started on our little island with me sitting on my board on a lackluster wave day late in the afternoon the Sunday after our prom. Our cross-town rivals had ruined our baseball field and trashed our fieldhouse the night before our prom driving four-wheel drive vehicles across the field tearing up the turf and running through a fence. They had spray painted their team colors all over the place and generally just wrecked the fieldhouse including broken windows. They were mad, I guess, because we had knocked them out of the baseball state playoffs earlier in the day.

I was thinking of a way to get back at them and also to make up for my behavior the night before. I had gotten pretty sideways from some nice ol' Ron Bacardi before, during, and after our prom and wasn't feeling my best. I felt like all the power had been zapped out of me. I was pretty bummed out. Darlene wasn't returning my calls due to my behavior at our prom and there were freight trains running through my head.

"Yo," B yelled from the shore. "Got something for you!"

B was holding a folded piece of paper and waving his hand for me to come ashore. I drearily paddled in. There wasn't even a wave to help me along. Maybe the ocean had a hangover too.

B handed me the paper. He shook his head. He didn't say anything just plopped down on the sand. His silence told me most of what I needed to know. I just dropped my board and joined him on the sand. The paper was folded twice. I opened it…

"Lenny,

I'm so hurt and confused, I don't know what to write. I've never seen you like that before, it was as if all your negative energy decided to erupt in one night. Dad, Lexi, her parents, your parents, and my aunt worked so hard for prom to happen for us and you did, well you know what you did, I guess. Do you even remember? If not ask B, he might tell you. I'm sure he'll sugarcoat it some. So whatever he says, imagine much worse.

I'm not going to tell my dad, but Lexi's parents might if they hear about it, so you better prepare for that likelihood. I don't know what will be worse for you, his response or your dad's when my dad tells him or even worse, makes you tell him. You might want to run off and join the French Foreign Legion or in your case, the circus. You acted like a stupid, drunken clown, and then became a human wrecking machine. You didn't physically hurt anyone else really, but you destroyed a lot of stuff. You were lucky you weren't caught or arrested. Someone at your school may tell on you though, even if the teachers or Bossy didn't ID you.

Don't call me for a while. Lexi said not to try and talk to her either. B has something for you.

Bye for now,

Darlene"

B reached in his pocket and handed me Darlene's promise ring. I looked at him. He just looked out at the ocean.

"You screwed up man," he started. "Big time, you were lucky we got home without us all going to jail."

I didn't remember being THAT bad...

"You were a one-man demolition crew," he continued. "It was a little funny at first, before you started tearing things up, you were just being an enhanced version of drunken funny Lenny. You remember putting that first pint in right after we got there? Well about an hour later, you poured a second pint into the punch bowl. You stood there and drank about five cups straight down. That was all she wrote."

Ok, ok, I did remember all of that. The first pint got a few people laughing and even a few teachers smiling more. We were all having a good time. Of course, I was already buzzing pretty well from some sweet herb. We burned a few when I picked Darlene up several hours earlier. She looked so pretty. She wore a glittery Duke blue three-quarter length sleeve gown with a nice, high slit up the left side. She had on some sexy new matching strappy high-heel sandals. Her hair was in a swept-up do with ringlets and wisps of hair around her shoulders and neck. She had dangly razor-thin silver earrings and a matching necklace. She took my breath away.

She was staying with Lexi for prom. Lexi was now dating college-boy Felton (Ted went out to Iowa to play college football) and I was the last to arrive at her house. B, Hal, and David went stag. We were all going to meet at a swanky restaurant near Knotty Beach.

Our gang had all rented our tuxes together and had a blast drinking at Munchies and ripping on one another during the process. B and David chose traditional black, I went with gray, and Hal, well, you know ol' Hal always reaching. He went way off rack on this one. Not quite sure how to describe it, kinda like a combo of Prince the singer purple and Barney the dinosaur purple. He definitely stands out in the photos, biggest, best smile too.

The time at the restaurant was one of the high points of the night. We reserved the biggest private room overlooking the Intracoastal Waterway and we had about seven or eight couples there plus the three solo gents. Copious amounts of alcohol were consumed. Lobsters and steaks were ravaged, lots of laughter, and all kinds of plans made for the rest of the night.

I had made a ton of money selling booze for the event, putting my fake ID to good use with several trips to the big ABC store on the mainland. I charged cost plus three dollars for a pint, cost plus five dollars for a fifth, and cost plus eight dollars for a half-gallon. I also set a personal record for weed sales that week. The stuff coming in late that spring was the best since Dalton's party almost three years before. Everyone was feeling outstanding!

Track 4-No More Mr. Nice Guy-Alice Copper (3:00)

My drunken rampage during our prom had given me the impetus to plan "The Night the Lights Went Out on Broadway". Our cross-county rival's prom theme was "A Night on Broadway". As soon as I heard it, I began to plan how I could exact revenge on our rivals and redeem myself with Darlene and my schoolmates.

My late uncle D had sometimes worked as a lineman for an electric co-op and he taught me a few things about how our country came to be "electrified". I knew I could take some of that knowledge and deliver the coup de gras on our rivals as one last great act of high school hijinks.

I kept most of the plan to myself, as the sign above old school New Orleans Mafia boss Carlos Marcello's office door said: "Three people can keep a secret, if two of them are dead". I doled out limited action items to my core group of friends without telling them the whole story, just enough to wet their whistle and get them to buy in.

Having played so many sporting events against our cross-county rival and having been to their school so many times over the years, I knew their school's layout well. The thing that made my plan so near perfect was they only had one main transformer leading into the gym, the site of most prom festivities back in those days. Snipping a line or some other method of cutting the power could be easily restored and would likely not result in the desired impact. I knew it would take many, many hours to replace a transformer, so I focused my energies on how to best destroy one without blowing myself up or electrocuting my ass in the process. My hair was already curly enough.

B and I were the only ones in action on the night in question, except for one outside guest who will remain unidentified, who played a small, but important part. Others had helped with supply acquisition, but now it was time to kick the tires and light the fires. Or in this case, deflate the tires and light the fuse.

Proms back then had minimal levels of security. Outside of the requisite teacher/administration chaperones, there was only one security guard and two uniform officers with one patrol car on the night in question. The security guard was stationed inside the gym so he was zero threat, unless he stepped outside as that was where we would do our damage. The plan could have easily failed if the cops had done much of anything different than they had done at our prom, but they didn't.

"All set?" I asked B.

He nodded.

We figured the vast majority of their prom attendees had arrived or were about to enter. We watched from two blocks away in a borrowed car. The cops eased out of their vehicle and began to make their way toward the gym. B drove us a block closer and parked the car at an old tire store strategically pointing down a one-way street where I would make my getaway. We nodded at one another and exited the vehicle.

The three-pronged plan swung into action, the outside agent did his job perfectly. When he saw B start to approach the start of the school property from the east, our helper set off a large pile of M-80s, super loud and powerful fireworks at the far western end of the school property. The cops immediately began running in that direction. B, clad in his prom attire, calmly walked up behind the police cruiser, acted like he dropped something, and knifed the right rear tire.

Meanwhile, at the far eastern end of the property, I blew the transformer with a simple homemade explosive package I had attached the night before. The gym went dark. I calmly kept walking northeast, circled the block, and leisurely drove away. B just kept walking, crossing the street southbound, wiped, and tossed the knife. He then strolled to another car we had left two blocks from their school earlier that day.

No plan I've ever come up with in my life worked to such perfection. A bunch of things could have gone wrong, but they didn't. In one fell swoop, I had infuriated my rivals, left a hilarious (for my gang), unique memory our foes could never erase, and cemented myself among the ranks of the all-time greatest high school pranksters. Oh, and most importantly, I hoped, earned some points back with Darlene and my school's crowd I had pissed off by tearing up our prom.

Everyone knew not to gather together in one place for a while. Not a bunch of cameras peeping in on life back then, so we were safe that way. It was sweet, so tasty sweet.

And to all those who just "knew" it was me? Well, you were right…Congrats!

Track 5-Running on Empty-Jackson Browne (4:59)

According to legend, and from the reliable bits and pieces my friends and others have shared over the years, this is what went down at OUR prom. There are as many versions of these events as you would expect. This is what is reliable, I think.

We had been at the prom about an hour, maybe 90 minutes or so when I poured another bottle of Bacardi rum into the god-awful swill they were serving as punch. I drank a pretty hefty amount straight from the bottle. I already had several "spiked" cokes at the restaurant. I then proceeded to continue to dance with Darlene and was an enhanced version of my usual charming, witty self for a while, a very short while. Darlene's smile was so radiant and beautiful. We had been through some tough times the last couple years and had been battling hard to maintain some type of relationship regardless of the distance and the setbacks. Despite all the markers against us, tonight was going well, quite well. That was about to change. I can be a real jackass sometimes. Back then, I was quite often.

After a few more dances, more than a few super-hot kisses, and some fun times talking with our friends, I decided to go burn one. Darlene and Lexi headed to the bathroom. I made my way outside. I wandered over to the Zero Tree and took a whiz, doobie dangling from my mouth. People were calling my name, but I blissfully ignored them. I continued watering my close friend, the Zero Tree, and was in the middle of a conversation with the tree when several classmates approached.

"Man, Lenny what you doing out here?" voice number one said.

"They're not going to let you back in dude," voice number two said. "You're toasted. Mossy done sent orders."

I waved them off like they were door-to-door salesmen. I continued my conversation with the Zero Tree.

"Nah, I'm fine," I said.

"Well now Lenny," the Zero Tree said. "I've known you for almost three years now, I have never seen you like this, and I've seen you feeling pretty large."

"I'm good," I continued. "I'm good."

"Umm," the Zero Tree continued. "Your fly is still open. Be careful with that zipper."

Damn, too late, hurt my Gila monster pretty bad. I bent over in pain.

"We don't want to see you get busted man," voice number one said.

I ignored their concerns and went over to the Monte Carlo to get another pint of rum. I stood outside the vehicle for a bit and took a couple more sips of rum.

"Tell Hal to let me in through the weight room back door in 10 minutes," I yelled as they walked away.

I finished the joint as I jammed to some Black Oak Arkansas.

"Jim Dandy to the rescue, Jim Dandy to the rescue," I sang/yelled at the top of my lungs. "Go Jim Dandy!"

I took another couple sips of rum. Well, maybe more than a couple of sips. Fine, fine, I drank a bunch of it and yes, I know "Jim Dandy" is a Laverne Baker song. I was simply doing the harder rock version.

"Lenny," the Zero Tree started on me again. "That might be enough."

I gave the Zero Tree the bird.

"You're a stubborn ass," the Zero Tree said. "Oh well, I tried. I hope you make it through the night my dear friend."

"Damn, where you been?" Hal asked as he opened the metal door that was seldom locked and often left propped open during school hours to let the weightlifters' funk out. "I been standing back here at least thirty minutes."

I shrugged.

"Man, Darlene is pissed," Hal said. "Shit, you're in no condition to go back in there. Hell, Bossy Mossy will probably have you arrested. I'll go tell the gang you're sick. Just go to the car and go to sleep Lenny."

I stood by the back door for a bit as Hal walked away. I hated that room. It stunk so bad and was the scene of so much macho bullshit behavior. I seldom went even though athletes were supposed to go at least three times a week for an hour or more.

I think I decided, "screw this place" and began my unplanned attack. I cleverly re-arranged a bunch of crap in the room, drew wieners on some of the posters showing how to "spot" for a fellow muscle-head, adding porno cartoon bubbles declaring the lifter's love for the other's wang. I erased all the weightlifting propaganda on the blackboard and instead wrote "goat fuckers meet here daily 2 pm" with a giant title saying:

Weight room-"Where the men are men, the women are absent, and the sheep are nervous."

Pleased with my change of the ambiance of the space, I decided to apply my perverted sense of *Feng shui* to the site of the prom itself...the gym.

That year's theme was "Some Enchanted Evening" complete with a giant half-moon and lighted stars hanging from the gym rafters. As the band rocked on the stage below, I took my intimate knowledge of the place and used it to create quite the spectacle.

First, I turned the smoke/fog machines to max output and the stage quickly resembled a scene from a Poe story or a Cheech and

Chong movie. The billowy smoke cascaded out onto the gym floor in waves as I climbed up the girders. I made my way out onto the catwalk, crawling past the band and grabbed ahold of a rope holding the lighted moon in place. I would love to say I planned what happened next but it was just dumb stupid luck. Like I noted in Crazy Beach Disc One, non-gender specific luck has more often than not sided with me in my mischievous exploits. Praise Elvis!

Just as I got a good hold of the rope, a few folks spotted me. I took my right hand off to give them the shhhh sign, but just as I did, I lost my balance and off I went. Much of the floor was obscured by the clouds of smoke now covering about half the dance floor.

I swung wildly in an arc over the snack and punch table, the moon following me. We plunged pretty quickly, slowed a bit by two giant stars I'd accidentally snagged with my legs. Accounts vary, but most suggest I lost a shoe and it fell into the punch bowl splashing Ms. Randall, the biology teacher. Another account has the shoe hitting her, and yet another says a running student who was following my flight path knocked her into the tables, capsizing them.

Whichever occurred, this fact is undisputed, the tables came down, and Ms. Randall got the worst of it, soaked in sticky rum fruit juice. I didn't get to enjoy this sight as my crash landing was imminent. As I descended, I somehow jettisoned one of the stars, much like a NASA space capsule dumping its booster rocket, and former helper into space for a lonely death. The star bonked the tennis coach on the shoulder and he brought down another student or two with his tumble into the stands.

I rapidly complied with gravity's demands, releasing the rope as I crashed into the stupid space-themed photoshoot area. I bounced off of my kinda fluffy former football teammate Aldon. We brought down the whole mess, including his date, a real fox. No, seriously she was hot, but Fox was also her real last name. Other casualties included but were not limited to; the cameraman, all the camera equipment, the lighting umbrella, and the inane backdrop. It was the beginning of the Star Wars era, so yea.

Aldon and the cameraman were locked in a forced embrace covered by equipment and horribly-decorated room dividers. Miss Fox and I did a slight barrel-roll entwined as any two lovers have ever been.

"Sorry," I said, kissing her on the forehead and bolting toward the front gym lobby and its two entrance doors.

I ran into the gym foyer, a loud ruckus following not far behind. I turned over multiple vending machines in an attempt to slow any attempt to catch me. Tons of people spilled out of the gym in search of me or to watch the chase. Incensed administrators, teachers, coaches, security, and eventually, the cops were hot on my trail or so they thought. Angered boyfriends, teammates, and others tried in vain to catch me. Groups of laughing friends, classmates, and others gathered in small groups to discuss the events.

They did everything but call out the bloodhounds to try and find me. At least the power was still on. You might be asking yourself, how did my stoned, drunken ass escape from so many sober or somewhat sober people? Simple, I hid the one place I knew they wouldn't look...they looked and they looked, boy did they look. They searched so hard and for so long I fell asleep, well maybe passed out. So...what's your guess? Where did I hide? Climbed the Zero Tree? Pretty good guess, but nope, I was too sideways for that, besides the tree didn't have any low branches and the chasers were close enough behind they would have seen me. And nope, didn't try to escape by car or hide in an unlocked one. Even I knew I was too wasted to try and operate a vehicle besides, they would have seen me in the parking lot. Ok, ok, I'll end the suspense.

I hid in an elevated brick semi-circle cupola that separates the two main gym entrances and overlooks the promenade where Lexi gave me Darlene's note nearly 2.75 years before.

The thing was never used except by the drama department for lighting purposes once a year when they presented a short play on the promenade each spring. It had a metal hook-on ladder that I pulled up with me. This ladder was inside, between the two gym exit doors. You would never think to look up there as it is so small and the entrance tile is exactly the same as all the others. From the promenade, if you even notice the top of the cupola, the wall only rises a couple feet above the very small floor space up there. How did I know about this unreal hiding place? Yep, you guessed it; I did the lightning for that show the month before. I forcefully pushed open one gym exit door to make everyone think I ran outside when in fact I had scurried up into the cupola. I had quickly climbed the ladder and pulled it up behind me and replaced the tile. The whole search party rushed right below me. Everyone was chasing a ghost outside. To them, I simply vanished.

I could hear the voices shouting below. Mossy giving directions. The cops asking for more coppers, people laughing, people cussing. I could hear my friends being questioned. Then I fell asleep or passed out.

"Lenny, Lenny, wake up," I heard a seemingly far away voice say.

They repeated the mantra several times. I tried opening my eyes, but things were blurry. I was flat on my back. Someone was shaking me.

"Damn man, get up," the voice said. "Someone's gonna see me. Then you're screwed."

I managed to get my eyes to focus. There kneeling above me was my soccer and former football teammate John. He and I were also the sound/light techs for our drama/stagecraft class. He was the only person that could have figured out where I was. If I had tried to escape myself, I would've been caught for sure.

"Let's go man," he said, attempting to drag me to my feet. "No one's around. You been up here a long time. The dance been over for hours."

I managed to get to my knees. John was putting the inside ladder back in place. We struggled to get down ok, carefully making our way down the mini-ladder John had brought to be able to reach my tiny perch from the exterior of the 10-foot or so tall cupola.

John and I had made an ABC store run from that perch just the month before. We had all the stuff set up for a show slated to start on the promenade in 40 minutes. We guessed correctly we would have just enough time to blaze the Monte Carlo to the liquor store, grab a pint, some cokes from the convenience store, and make it back in time to do the show. We made it by three minutes. So we both had experience in entering and exiting the space undetected. Two for two!

Track 6-Someday Never Comes-CCR (3:55)

Things go that way sometimes, you know what I mean, work out in your favor and all. The problem was for me, in one of the most important areas of my life, they seldom did or not as much as I would have liked anyway. Yes, I mean in regards to Darlene. I wish this could be a shiny, happy area with nothing but great memories and don't get me wrong, you have seen there were tons and tons of great moments I will never forget and deeply cherish. Moments helping forge who I am today and a treasure trove of joy which will likely be among my last thoughts when it's time for me to check out. As the English poet Felicia D. B. Hemans (1793-1835) said: "Tho the past haunt me as a spirit I do not ask to forget".

But, always seems to be a but…almost exactly as Ms. Winter predicted, she died a year and little more than a month after they moved to Durham, just as our junior year was moving close to fall break. I remember it was a Thursday in late October when I got called to the principal's office. For this time, I couldn't figure out why. An old misdeed catching up with me, a new one I deemed too trivial to be called on the rug for perhaps attaining higher offender status?

I walked slowly to the office passing from one classroom building to the outside quad. I walked across the tree-lined square. That day was a somewhat mild, colorful autumn afternoon with a slight breeze. A sad looking Oriole sat on the ground just before the steps leading to the office building. I stopped to look closely at the little chirper. The tiny black and orange bird was probably sad because his namesake Orioles (and my favorite team) had just lost to the Oakland Athletics (A's) in the American League (AL) baseball playoffs for the second year in a row while fighting for the AL championship and the right to play in the World Series.

Miss Rhodes was not at her desk when I entered. Mossy was leaning on his door frame. He motioned me into his office without saying a word. I saw the phone receiver off the hook on his desk. No name calling, no dumbass, no shitwad, no "King of the Zeroes". He pointed at the phone. I took the few steps over, knowing it was something awful. I picked up the dingy old cream colored receiver.

"Son," it was my father. "You need to come home, Anika has died."

"Yes sir," I said hanging up quicker than I probably should have.

That was the only time I ever spoke on the phone with my father until after college. I had never heard his voice on the phone. Hell, I had never seen him use one. My mom did all the communicating via Mr. Bell's invention in our house. I was almost as struck hearing his voice on the telephone as I was about the news of Ms. Winter's death. Maybe that's why I hate the telephone so much. The last six weeks had been rugged and she'd been hospitalized a few times. We all knew it was coming, but still…

"Don't worry about your teachers or coaches," Principal Mossy said. "I'll take care of all that, you go home Lenny, we'll see you next week."

It was the only time the ol' jarhead was ever nice to me. It was the only time I would ever miss a game I was supposed to play.

"Your sister is staying with Aunt Monty," my obviously shaken mother said. "Pack yourself a bag."

My dad was just sitting at the table, coffee cup in hand. "I'm so Lonesome I Could Cry" by country icon Hank Williams Sr. was plaintively spilling from the ancient AM-FM clock radio that always occupied the spot under the calendar at the end of the bar. Yep, you guessed it, Mom was messing around in the kitchen cleaning, packing some things for our trip.

I quickly went to my room and tossed a few things in my travel bag. I paused to look at a couple of pictures of me and Darlene through the years. The photos anchored each side of my desk. One was the summer after eighth grade, taken during our families' annual July 4th cook-out, this one taken at our house. It showed the seven of us on the back deck. I think my mom's sister, Monty took it. It was a great picture. Ms. Winter was smiling. Although she would live for 39 more months, it was one of the last times I saw her beautiful, million-watt smile before the disease robbed her of much of her lust for life.

"You drive," my father said. "I just got off graveyard shift."

We took the Duster. Mom sat in the back and Dad went to sleep as soon as we got on US Highway 421 heading northwest to the Piedmont. There was no I-40 to the coast in those days and getting pretty much anywhere was a hassle. I turned the volume on the radio way down. It didn't really matter because my dad could sleep through the sound of a freight train barreling through the house. There's a great shot of him as a young man during the Korean War fast asleep in his Amphibious Tractor as the battle rages around him. I've seen him sleep through raucous family shindigs, game night revelry, me and my friends' yelling during televised ballgames, and through pretty much anything else. I wasn't worried about waking him, but for one of the few times in my life, I just didn't want to hear any music.

Darlene's house was near Duke University. They'd bought a ranch style type home on a hill with a full basement. I drove up the long paved driveway past several cool, old magnolia trees lining the entrance area. There were tons of cars I didn't recognize, but I managed to find a spot behind the house. There was a basketball goal, a large garden, and a huge deck looking out over a nice big yard to a small grove of trees beyond. We entered through the back deck sliding glass door into the kitchen/dining area. The house was packed with folks and the familiar old giant oak table that was way too big for Darlene's house at the beach was just right for this one. As always happens during these type times, the family table was overflowing with a bounty of food.

As we made our way inside, I didn't see anyone I knew right away. Finally, Mr. Winter emerged from a hallway with some of his relatives and a pastor. He walked right past several folks to greet my dad. They shook hands and had the firm, manly exchange of no-emotion men from their era wore like a medal from the war. My mom began talking with some of the ladies. I just stood there.

"Thank you for coming Lenny," Mr. Winter said shaking my hand, just like that first day on the boardwalk 4.25 years before.

Damn time sure slips away. I wanted to ask, I didn't. I waited. Thankfully, I didn't have to wait too long.

"Darlene is in her room," Mr. Winter said. "With her cousins and school friends, she's been waiting for you to get here."

I nodded at folks I didn't know as I headed toward the hallway. It felt so weird but so normal, because at every funeral or visitation I had been to thus far in my young life, people just nodded at one another a lot. An odd, but strangely comforting gesture uniting a communal feeling of grief and barely held in check despair. Hopefully, none of us has to experience it too often. The nodding, it does bring a sense of peace though, doesn't it?

The hallway was crowded, and in chronological order, oldest to youngest. I made my way past a few septuagenarians and those nearing retirement age, then the middle-age folks, then some 25-35-year olds talking in groups. It was elbow-to-elbow. I finally reached my demographic huddled around the entrance to Darlene's room. I continued the nodding as I didn't know any of these people. I guessed they were her school friends or cousins. As I entered her room, I did see some girls, and a couple of guys I had met over the last year on my semi-monthly trips to Durham.

Darlene was sitting on her bed, head down, with two girls on each side of her, and two guys standing nearby. She was holding hands with the girl to her left. Darlene was wearing jeans and one of my faded Duke t-shirts. She was barefoot. She stood when she spotted me and before I could take another step was in my arms. She burrowed her head into my right shoulder. I closed my eyes. We held that embrace for a long time.

"Could you guys give us a minute," she finally said, lifting her head ever so slightly. "Meet us in the basement, please get some food."

The teenage throng emptied pretty quickly.

"Glad you're here," Desiree, her school friend said as she walked by.

She was squeezing my hand I had wrapped around Darlene's waist. She gave me a little downturned-smile and motioned for everyone to hurry on out. Once the room was completely empty Darlene lifted her head. Her eyes were moist. She didn't have on any make-up. She was exquisite. She looked at me the way a puppy in the pound does.

"Early this morning," she said. "Dad and Aunt Tessie were there. I was asleep."

And for only the third time of the four I would ever see, she busted out crying. It appeared she hadn't yet and was just waiting for me to get there to let the floodgates open. She sobbed uncontrollably into my chest for a long time. I just held her.

I'm not sure how much time passed. We stayed locked in that position. One of her friends broke the spell.

"Darlene," Desiree said, peeking her head inside the open door. "Your dad wants you to come on out in a bit and see some people."

"Ok," she said. "I'll be out in a few minutes. I got to get cleaned up."

"I'll step out," I said.

"No," she commanded. "Sit right there."

She pointed to a pink side chair. I just nodded and did as told. Darlene and I had never been alone in her room more than a few moments, at the beach or here. Her dad was really old school. I felt strange, well, I was sitting in a pink chair, and I was in her room. It was a pretty big bedroom painted Duke Blue of course, with its own full bath. She quickly disappeared to take a shower. She had a white vanity beside the pink chair, double windows behind her bed and a huge walk-in closet on the other side of the bed. She had posters of The Rolling Stones, Peter Frampton, Pink Floyd, and the new band

Boston's first album cover plastered on her walls. She was definitely a bad-ass girl, no bubble-gum, or pop crap. Like her favorite band, The Stones sang: "She's my little rock-n-roller".

Mr. Winter popped his head and shoulders through the doorway just as the shower cut off. He looked at me. He looked at her half-open bathroom door. He looked at me again. He nodded. I nodded. He pulled the bedroom door closed.

Track 7-Indian Reservation-Paul Revere and the Raiders (2:52)

Death always seemed like such a demarcation point for me, you too, I bet. I guess it is with almost all who call themselves human. Another one that severely jolted me was my maternal grandmother's death in 1986. Sometimes funerals deliver a surprise or two. Granny's funeral sure delivered one in a big way. We all wondered if he would show up or if he was even still alive. Well, he was alive alright, and damn, he showed up.

So we hadn't seen George for over 15 years when he strolled into her funeral in late summer that year. Just before he arrived, I was talking with Mr. Smith, the owner of The Landmark, who along with his father, the previous owner, had served as Granny's bosses for the 32 years she worked at the restaurant.

"You know Lenny," Mr. Smith began. "All those years Delphia worked for us, it was so amazing, I never saw her write anything down. She could wait on 17 drunken sailors and never messed up one order, not even one time."

What little bit of smarts I have, I think I got a lot of them from my maternal grandmother.

Now when old George, my maternal grandfather walked in, no one would talk to him much. After he silently and reverently walked past the casket alone, he just stood in the corner. He still stood tall, his once jet-black hair was about half white now, but he still looked sharp. He was well-dressed and carried himself like always, like the baddest mother-fucker in town. I walked away from my wife and went over to speak with him.

"Hey Pawpaw," I started.

"Hey Lenny boy," he said. "Looks like you did well."

He was motioning toward my gorgeous 5'11" quite tanned, long-legged new bride who simply fussed with her long curly raven locks and looked away.

"Yep," I said. "We've been together three years now."

"Kids?" he asked.

"Two-year-old girl," I said. "Another kid due in January."

"Good, good for you," he said. "I got to be going, I don't drive anymore, my gal's got to get to work."

"Ok," I said. "I'll walk you out."

I have never seen one person get the evil eye from so many people at one time. No one dared say a word to him about anything or to me for exiting with him. I strolled out to an obviously waiting vehicle parked right at the front entrance of the funeral home. The engine was still running. I could see a pretty blond in a nurse's uniform behind the wheel of a relatively new four-door, blue Buick sedan. She looked to be about 35 or so.

"I'll be seeing you Lenny boy," he said.

The blond never turned my way. That was the last time I saw my grandfather. He died a decade later in a flophouse after being kicked out of two old folk's homes for having consensual sex with the female caregivers. He was 84.

My maternal grandfather Talmidge, (white name George) was born on a former Oklahoma Indian reservation the same day the Titanic sank. Talk about forewarning, oh boy. The reservations in Oklahoma had been dissolved in the lead up to Oklahoma gaining statehood in 1907, but were for all intent and purposes still mostly in place for many years. George's mother was full-blooded Cherokee and his father was a white Army private or so he was told. He never knew his father, just like my mother never knew hers until George waltzed into our life the fall after I returned from Woodstock.

According to the many tales I heard my grandfather spout, life on the reservation was unbearable with little food, and less joy. George's mother died when he was 15. He ran away the next day. George made his way to Chicago where he worked washing dishes for a few years and learned the commercial kitchen trade. Chicago Bears' founder, ex-player, owner, and coach George Halas was a frequent customer at one of Pawpaw's workplaces and eventually noticed the high-cheekbone, 6'3" broad-shoulder young Indian and invited him to training camp in the early 1930s. My grandfather George displayed a knack for the game, especially defense, and quickly became one of the notoriously mean Halas' whipping boys due to George's lack of knowledge about the intricacies of the game.

George had never played organized sports, much less played in college, yet made a professional football team on his first try. My grandfather was otherworldly strong and underworld level mean.

George would play football during the day and work at a restaurant at night. He did this for a couple of years until he got himself into a tangle even Halas couldn't get him extracted from. As you know Chicago was pretty much a mob-owned town in the 1920s and for much of the 1930s. George got into a barroom scrape with some gangsters from the south side during one holiday season crushing one gangster's face with a barstool and nearly killing another with his bare hands.

George went to Halas for help. Halas gave him one word of advice:

"Run".

Run he did, first to Richmond, Virginia for a few months working for restaurants in "the bottom". He tried to make some extra dough playing semi-pro football, but by the late fall, the south-siders found him and he narrowly escaped with his life, dodging gunfire as he stowed-away on a tramp steamer heading down the James River. He managed to secure a job in the galley and made his way to Charleston, SC.

After a season or two in Charleston, he moved again, this time to the Piedmont of NC where he met my 18-year old dark-haired future grandmother Delphia. Delphia had a powerful personality and big, dark eyes. It was lust at first sight for both, and teenage Delphia was quickly pregnant with my mom.

There was one huge problem (besides the pregnancy of course). My grandmother was already supposed to marry another young man, from a family you may have heard of...the Pettys. Yep, you guessed it, the NASCAR legends from little Level Cross, NC lived just minutes from my maternal great-grandfather's store which was basically a front for his moonshine business.

My great-grandfather, John Vickers was a master moonshiner, horse-trader, and hustler (sound familiar yet?). He had been sent to the county farm several times and during one stint in Halifax County, NC was incarcerated with and cellmate of David "Carbine" Williams, the dude that invented the Carbine rifle.

Those years were wild times across the country as the Great Depression kept an icy grip on the vast majority of Americans' finances. People had to really scrape and claw just to stay alive. Moonshining was one of the ways people in the mountains of Appalachia and the Piedmont tried to stay afloat. Huge distrust and anger toward the government ran Grand Canyon deep and Alcohol Revenue Agents ("Revenuers") were seen as the devil. Young men would drive brazenly souped-up cars blazing along dangerous roads to deliver their "shine". Moonshine was basically untaxed booze and the government wanted it eradicated. Many of the young moonshiners would race their juiced-up hot rods against one another on the weekend all over the south with several loosely knit organizations forming to make a dollar on the new "sport". All of these endeavors led to the eventual formal development of NASCAR just after WWII.

My maternal great-grandfather was such a moonshiner. At least two of his sons, Fletcher and Hubert ran moonshine. They were all good friends with the Pettys of that era. One of the Petty cousins was blind, but an expert mechanic. It was said he could take an engine apart and rebuild it with no help. Well, one day the three of them had been drinking and thought it would be a fun thing to let the blind guy drive. They got hit by a train. All perished. I have the newspaper story.

Anyway, my great-grandfather was not happy about the turn of events concerning my grandmother. Delphia broke the news to the Petty she had promised to marry and quickly left town with George. George got a job as a chef in Raleigh and promptly ran off with a teenage waitress. My grandmother didn't hear from him for many years.

George had seven sons with the waitress, settled in Forsyth County near Winston-Salem, worked as a chef for over a decade and eventually came to own his own restaurant. Two of the sons, Trick, and Rich you may remember from Crazy Beach, Disc One. They were the ones that convinced me and Darlene to hitchhike to the campground when we were 14. Good ideas abound on my mom's side.

So things were going well for old George, nice big house, big family, business owner doing something he truly loved. Trouble was he loved women more, lots, and lots more. Yep, you guessed it, on his 42nd birthday he ran off with a teenage waitress. He later said the mob was still after him, but women were the most powerful force in my Pawpaw's life, mob or no mob. They ran and ran, all the way to San Diego. Guess how many children they had? Yep, you got it, seven. Seven more sons, so when my grandfather headed back east at the very tail end of the 1960s, my mom had 14 half-brothers she didn't know about, and a father she had never met.

George came to call the fall of 1969. I was still in the throes of recovering from my Woodstock experience and was on our front deck trying to talk to some twin girls that had moved in next to us, when this tall, obviously part Indian, well dressed, good-looking man approached from the boardwalk side.

"This Delphia's daughter's house?" he demanded to know more than asked, one hand on the rail and his right foot on the first step.

"Yes sir," I said.

"She home?" he asked.

"Yes sir," I said.

He walked up the steps like he owned the place. The twins just looked awed. I felt thunderstruck. Here was this ultra-imposing man coming right up our steps. It appeared he was heading right for the door to let himself in. I moved over toward the door.

"Who should I say is here?" I asked him with my left hand on the screen door.

He smiled at my obvious attempt to protect my mother.

"Her father," he said matter-of-factly.

I would love to have a picture of my face at that moment.

"Oh, ok," I finally managed. "I'm her son, Lenny."

"Nice to meet you, Lenny boy," he said. "I'm your Pawpaw."

I opened the screen door and walked into the kitchen with my grandfather close on my heels. I had left the twins standing still. So, I met my grandfather before my mom met her dad, weird.

For once, Mom was not in the kitchen. The house appeared empty. Dad was at work, I think. The twins, seldom shy, walked right on in a few steps behind us.

"Mom, Mom you here?" I rang out rather loudly.

"I'm out here," her soft, southern voice wafted in from the back deck.

I walked toward the open doorway with my grandfather and the 11-year old twins close behind. I had no idea how to make this introduction. They don't teach you that crap in school and Dear Abby sure never had anything on it.

"Uh…Mom…uh…," I attempted.

"Ginny, I'm Talmidge," the tall Indian said. "I'm your father. Call me George."

My mother almost fainted, catching herself on a high-back deck chair. Just then, as Gordon Lightfoot sang, "...twas the witch of November come stealing..." a bone-chilling, hardy northeastern wind blasted the shore and what had been a pleasant early November Saturday turned immediately dark and gloomy.

The twins, clad only in some little summer terrycloth shorts and tank tops rushed back inside. My mom braced herself with both hands against the same chair.

"Well...hello," my startled mother began.

George waved his huge right hand as if commanding the weather.

"Delphia told me where you lived," he continued. "She said she was going to call from the restaurant."

"Uh, no," Mom continued. "She didn't. Son, check on the girls. Let's all go in."

The twins, Dana and Jana, were playing checkers at the bar. They had moved in just before school started and were a grade ahead of me. Dana, in particular, loved being at our house and she and Mom had already formed a close bond. They were there a lot on weekends and a few nights each week. Both their parents worked, somewhat of a rarity in two-parent households back then. Well, on the island anyway.

"Can I get you some coffee?" Mom asked.

"Sure," George said. "Black is fine."

"I won," Jana said. "Lenny do you want to play?"

I just shook my head no but did move to sit at the bar beside her. Dana was standing on the kitchen side of the bar as my mom headed to the stove.

"Dana, will you get me two coffee cups please?" Mom asked.

"Yes ma'am," Dana said, reaching behind her to retrieve the cups from one of two cabinets on the right side of the stove.

George was standing at the end of the bar. Mom was heating up water. Jana tapped me on the leg. She whispered in my ear.

"Did you know you had a grandfather still alive?" she breathed into my ear. "And that he was an Indian?"

I just looked at her with eyes real big, like no not now!

"Dana, will you girls be staying for supper?" Mom asked, her back to the rest of us.

"That would be great," Dana said.

"Can we go to your room?" Jana whispered again.

I shook my head no. I wanted to hear what was coming next. Well, not much is what came next. After several minutes of extremely awkward silence, George tried to ease the tension.

"I guess I should have waited for Delphia," George said.

Mom poured coffee and didn't say anything. Dana and Jana started another game of checkers. Jana leaned in for another whisper.

"He sure is big," she said lightly. "He sure looks like an Indian. Think he might be a Chief?"

"Jana, honey," Mom smiled. "Let's not whisper with company here."

"Yes ma'am," Jana said.

Well, there are few secrets on an island and news of my grandfather's arrival would not stay secret long. Now both the twins were mighty little gossips and we quickly learned all of us would have to be careful what we said around them. They would only live next door to us for about 18 months, but in that short amount of time, they did a world of damage. Thankfully, none of it was too deep or lasting, but those are tales for other days.

I had only been back from Woodstock for a couple of weeks when a mid-size U-Haul appeared the Saturday before school started at the house two doors south of us on the street side of Carolina Avenue South. Dad was at work. Mom and Lil'sis were helping Granny clean the beauty shop owned by their friends Vera, and her daughter Gail.

I was going to the gym inside the old town hall/police station to shoot some basketball. Someone had abandoned an old panel truck in the dirt parking lot beside the paved one. There was a basketball goal at the edge of the paved lot. We used it when the gym was closed. One of our crew had sprayed the old panel truck with some red graffiti: "Your Momma's Meat House". Some locals still refer to the lot by that name.

There was a similar panel truck parked next door along with a larger moving van. Two almost identical girls about my age with jet black bowl-cut hair were standing beside it. They were lanky, energetic, and plain. They were both dressed in shorts and dark t-shirts helping a man, who I assumed was their father move items from the back of the truck. A lady I assumed was the mom was giving directions from a small front porch almost identical to ours. She was a taller, older version of the girls with a better haircut. She was the skinniest mom I had ever seen.

They looked like they were struggling with a dresser. I reversed direction and dribbled the ball down the street their way.

"Need a hand?" I asked.

"Sure that would be great," the dad said.

I wordlessly took over from the twins and helped carry a pretty heavy dresser up the stairs and into the family's new home. The former owners lived in another state and seldom visited. Introductions were exchanged after we placed the dresser in the master bedroom. The Grants were moving in from Columbia, SC and Mr. Grant was to be our new Postmaster. Ms. Grant worked for the Federal Government as well, doing exactly what I never found out. We never saw her much.

Anyway, you know how long it took you to read that passage about the twins, right? Well, that's about how long the stretches of awkward silence were at our bar area. Finally, praise Elvis Granny appeared, coming in through the front screen door.

"George, I told you to wait," she said sternly.

"I told you to call," George replied in like fashion.

No wonder they never made it as a couple. After some more give and take in that realm, things settled into a little bit more of a somewhat (barely) less uncomfortable zone. And no, there were no grand pronouncements, no back-and-forth question and answer sessions, just stumbles through rough attempts at conversation and connection.

It would eventually come to light George had appeared every decade or so at Granny's to try and re-connect with her. This was the only time she gave him more than a fighting chance. It didn't last long.

Granny had a hell of a time after my mom was born. Being an unwed mother in the 1930s and 40s was a pretty heavy cross to bear. So, it turns out, Mom's grandfather, the moonshiner John Vickers and his wife, did much of the raising of my mom until John Vickers checked out in 1947. Then my great-aunt Nina mostly took over. My mom considered her grandfather and her aunt Nina to be her true nurturers.

That was one of the main reasons Mom never met George until 1969, along of course with George's adventures "running" from the mob and chasing women. He was pretty damned good at both.

We had a really interesting couple of years with George in our life. We had one great extended family Thanksgiving with lots of photos showing genuinely happy people smiling and laughing. George played grandfather a bit, coming to my games, giving sage or perverted advice about life, women, sports, gambling, etc.

He worked as Head Chef for Mr. Smith at another Smith-owned eatery, The Mermaid Restaurant. Mr. Smith said he was damn good at his job. George was just lousy at relationships. He was charming, good-looking, funny, smart, athletic, and a profound drunk. Man, could that dude drink. I thought my dad's oldest brother Uncle C was the champ, but geez, I think my Pawpaw may have belonged in a different way-elevated league altogether.

I saw him drink all the local drinking legends under the table with ease and while all of those fell out, passed out, or threw up, George would only appear slightly intoxicated. It was staggering to behold. One night, near Christmas that year, he lapped my dad, Uncle D, Uncle Ed, and a veritable who's who of drinking pros from that era on the island.

He took no charm from his feat, except when it came to one beach legend. George loved to drink "Chicken" Hicks under the table. Chicken, so called because of his appearance; tall, angular, and prone to wearing white leisure suits, was the island's best shag dancer, one of its best drinkers, and notorious lady hound. He and George were about the same age. Chicken often proclaimed himself the inventor of the shag and the historical data, including photos, shows he was around at many of the early places the shag was known to have been first performed in NC and SC.

I always got the feeling, later borne out by others, Chicken had a thing for my granny and George took great pleasure in whipping Chicken regularly at the gaming and drinking table. Their battles were legendary and Chicken put up a better fight than most, but even he was no match for my grandfather.

With barely concealed derision, George would taunt Chicken when it became apparent, once again that Chicken was about to tap, fall, or pass out.

"What's up Cat Daddy? We're just getting started," George would mercilessly needle. "Thought we were all going dancing later."

More than once the following summer, I woke to several boardwalk drinking icons passed out on our back deck with George calmly sitting there having another cold one. He never smoked or did drugs that I saw, but man could he drink. No one else has ever come close. He was a wonder.

Then one day before school started the next year, he was gone just like he arrived, without warning or conversation.

Track 8-One Mint Julep-The Clovers (2:30)

I was actually dreaming of my grandfather and all his women when I heard "Lenny, Lenny," a disembodied voice seemed to be calling from the darkness. "Lenny, Lenny, why are you asleep on top of my refrigerator? And what is Willie doing sitting naked outside against the fence with a TV in his lap?"

Uh, I don't know…

Well, the day before had started out great. I was hanging with my buddy Marty on a glorious spring day late in my junior year when he suggested we have a little get-together at his house because his parents were away. It was early May and most school spring sports were near wrapping up for the year. Marty and I played soccer together for a couple of years and had a blast partying, girl-watching, and regularly exercising general 17-year old guy misbehavior. In the course of slightly less than 19 months we'd created quite a history of debauchery.

It was at Marty's house on the mainland where I had discovered the ad for my fake ID in the back of his Rolling Stone magazine. We quickly ordered us both one. They were only five dollars each. I had been putting mine to great use making money selling booze out of the trunk of the Duster to my schoolmates and beach friends.

It was with Marty where I was officially "arrested" for the first time. Of course, as you know, I had been in trouble since the day I was born. I had numerous run-ins with the law on the island centered on my adventurous nature. None of those led to an arrest, just washing police cars, and other crap the island coppers made my crew do to make amends for our youthful shenanigans.

We got popped on the mainland back in the fall of our junior year for taking a whiz behind a pizza joint. A narc (undercover narcotics police officer) we knew was dining with his old lady and they happened to be leaving when Marty, Hal, a couple of other friends, and I were relieving ourselves behind a shuttered adjacent building. The copper's car lights cast their beams upon us and he made a big deal out of it, put us in cuffs, and hauled us all of to the local city joint.

The narc grilled me over and over about Dutch, the Rec Hall, and other vices happening on our little island. He was in the Rec Hall often, but fooled no one with his undercover "act". I just laughed in his face. He made several outrageous claims and swore he was going to get me for "something big". Of course, he never did.

Marty's dad came and got us all released on recognizance (ROR). That means no bail, praise Elvis, I wouldn't have to call home. You just promise to appear in court to face the charges. The charges were dropped after Marty's dad, an attorney, told the narc he would put the narc's wife on the stand and ask her if she enjoyed seeing our teenage Johnsons! That narc stayed on us hard for a long time after, trying to bust us for this or that, but nothing ever stuck, and we knew better than to carry any illegal substances around town.

Marty's dad gave us all a strict "talking to" about the possible consequences of our deeds and how a police record would negatively impact our future if we didn't "straighten up and fly right". Well, we promptly got Marty's family car stuck running from the cops two months later and Marty's dad had to be called to rescue us again. That list goes on and on, but we'll get back to our regularly scheduled program instead.

We gathered a few buddies together and hit the ABC store on Castle Street.

"Hey it's Kentucky Derby day," Marty said. "Why don't we make some Mint Juleps and watch the races."

"Damn right," Hal said. "Lenny, can we place some bets with Dutch?"

"Sure," I said. "I already have my bets in, but I can call some in for you guys from Marty's house."

"I'm betting with you Lenny," Marty said. "Spread my 10 bucks around as best you can."

"Give me five dollars on the longest shot," said Willie, our school's cross-country star and my first Jewish friend.

"How about you Ethan?" I asked.

"Sure, bet me a couple of two dollar trifectas," he said. "Pick one that you picked and give me horses one, two, and three."

We made a couple of stops to gather all the needed mixing ingredients and made it back to Marty's house just after lunchtime. Post time for the race wasn't until six or so but we didn't wait to get the festivities started. We followed the recipe from a Playboy Mixology guide I had received as a free gift for subscribing.

"Oh wow, this is strong stuff," Hal said. "Won't take many of these to get plastered."

"Well slow down some dummy," I said. "There's a lot of liquor in there."

"Let's step outside and burn one," Marty suggested.

We had the television volume up so we could hear the early races as we stood around in the garage and burned one down sipping on Mint Juleps the whole time. They were delicious! This is the recipe. Have one…or several.

You'll need bourbon whiskey (you can use other spirits, but this is the traditional southern way), four mint leaves per drink (spearmint is the Kentucky Derby preferred mint); some powdered sugar, and crushed ice.

Mint Juleps belong to the boozer's family of "Smashes" like Brandy Smashes and Mojitos so you have some muddling of ingredients to do. Gently crush up the mint leaves with a teaspoon of powdered sugar and two teaspoons of water in a silver or pewter glass (we used pewter, but a highball glass will work as well). Fill the glass with cracked ice, add bourbon, and stir well until the glass is frosted. Then garnish with a mint sprig. Viola! Mint Julep.

Be careful to only handle the glass at the very top or bottom so you don't screw up the frosting process. Do the same while consuming. Enjoy!

The afternoon became a bit of a blur rather quickly between Mint Juleps, sweet herb, and music. We also listened to a George Carlin album and laughed our asses off. We loved George. He is most certainly one of the funniest dudes ever. John, my rescuer from the prom debacle and I had even performed Carlin's "Hippy-dippy weatherman" bit as our talent that month at the Thespian Club's spring talent show. We came in third, and yes, there were more than three entries. Not many more, but still, we were pretty funny or so we were told. There were a lot of laughs.

We watched the derby, "the most exciting two minutes in all of sports". Hal was amped up, he won $22 and the rest of us mostly lost. As soon as the derby was over and another round of Juleps were consumed, someone came up with the bright idea of challenging Willie to do something bizarre. Willie would do these types of things frequently for small sums, like five bucks or so. Well, what would transpire from this five dollar bet is one of the funniest things I ever witnessed, right behind the stoned goats episode.

Now Willie was about 6'2" and maybe a buck-fifty, dark curly hair, big ears, and a great giant smile. Our school's best cross-country athlete, he was all-conference both his junior and senior years. He would get a track scholarship a few weeks after these events. To say Willie was a bit odd or eccentric may bring true offense to those who are, as Willie was, well, judge for yourself.

"Oh, I could do that easy, no sweat," Willie responded to Hal's challenge. "But it'll cost each of you five bucks."

"I only got three dollars left," Ethan said.

"Good enough," Willie said. "Let's go do it."

We all piled into Marty's dad's old green AMC Ambassador Wagon with real wood side paneling. We drove over near the college.

"We're going to drop you off in front of the store," Marty said. "Meet us over at the record store on Kerr."

"Ok," Willie said, getting out at the front entrance of the Kmart on South College Road.

He proceeded to disrobe and put a ski mask over his mug. We drove off as he walked buck naked past startled shoppers exiting the store.

Now "streaking" had come and gone as a fad a year or two before, but one could still witness runners in the buff here and there.

"Pull over by the Kroger, and we can watch," I said.

It didn't take long before two cop cars pulled up to the entrance, lights flashing.

"Oh crap," Hal said. "He's a goner for sure."

"Damn," Marty said. "I'm not calling his mom."

"Oh ye of little faith," I said. "Look!"

Willie, pieces parts flying in the wind, bolted from the store barely eluding one diving cop. What was that guy lunging for? Willie held a small 13-inch television over his head. That was the bet. Swipe a TV buck naked from Kmart.

Well, keystone cop hilarity ensued as some of the coppers piled in their squad cars and others began a way fruitless chase on foot. Willie left them in the dust, deftly crossing a major roadway in the process, TV gently bouncing up and down above his head, other parts not bouncing as gently. He jetted down South College Road and as he was making his turn behind a store we began driving to the pick-up site.

Marty swerved the big green monstrosity into the record store lot.

"Bluuuu-p,"

Ethan puked in the back floorboard.

"You almost hit me you idiot," Hal yelled.

"Damn," Marty said.

Willie tossed the TV in the back seat hitting Hal in the shoulder.

"Move over, move over," masked naked Willie said, shoving Hal closer to a spew-covered Ethan.

"Holy crap," I laughed from the front passenger seat. "I knew you would do it. You guys all owe me two bucks."

In times like these, we often managed to achieve the joy resulting from the unfettered and exuberant mayhem of youth taken to the extreme. On occasion, we sometimes took it a bit too far, but like the old saying goes "the life of a hedonist is the best preparation for becoming a mystic". Pretty sure none of my crowd made it to the mystic stage though.

The rest of the night got blurrier and blurrier. No one in our company that day had experience drinking bourbon more than a sip here or there, so there was that, plus we'd started so early, and didn't eat much. How or why I got on the fridge remains a mystery and why Willie never put his clothes back on does as well.

Track 9-The Hurricane-Bob Dylan (4:57)

I did my best to look normal heading back to the house after that fun debacle. My mom and my great-aunt Pat were sitting at the table.

"Hey Son, come sit with me and Aunt Pat for a bit," Mom said.

Boy, I just wanted to shower and go sleep some more, but Mom made few requests and I tried to honor most.

"Something happened while you were in town," Mom started.

She and Aunt Pat both had in front of them old-school faded, half-full cream-colored coffee cups resting on our old shop-worn maple table, with little bits of steam still rising into the air like smoke signals from a miniature western museum display. I could hear my lil'sis singing along to her favorite song of all-time, "I Think We're Alone Now" by Tommy James and the Shondells, which was blasting from the giant elongated console piece of furniture stereo in her room.

"Mr. Robert was found dead yesterday," Mom said.

"What?" I asked.

The rest of the conversation was a blur. I showered and slept a long time.

The next day's ride over to Mr. Robert's funeral at the old graveyard, scene of so much "Marguerite" fun was pretty somber. This graveyard is also the burial site of Cappy (1985), my granny

(1986), and my mom (2012), along with a few other family members, a host of friends, classmates, and other islanders. B's 1944 Willy's Jeep rumbled down the pock-marked trail leading to the heavily wooded area on the island's western "buffer zone".

"Do you think somebody hurt him?" Hal asked from the back storage area.

"I don't want to think about that right now," I dejectedly responded. "If somebody did, they're going to pay."

The WWII surplus Jeep ground to a halt near the spot where we always parked to play our pranks on unsuspecting soldier boys.

"Hey, wasn't it about this time of year when we went over to Bald Head with Mr. Robert?" B asked.

"Yea, I think you're right," I said.

"Damn, that was a fun trip," Hal started. "A little scary, but fun."

B and I nodded our agreement as we walked over to the gravesite. Mr. Robert's gravestone epitaph would read: "He made people think".

"Did I ever tell you boys about Captain Thompson, the Blockade Runner?" Mr. Robert asked us one late spring Saturday a few years before.

The three of us, me, B, and Hal shook our heads no as we all sat around a little fire Mr. Robert had stoked from the prior night's embers.

"Let me look back in the bunker, I think I got an old newspaper story on him," Mr. Robert said as he was moving toward the bunker he had called home for the past 15 years.

He returned a minute later empty-handed. We thought maybe it was just a ruse to get us to believe what he was about to tell us. Mr. Robert was a great storyteller, but we could never be certain how much was fact, how much was fiction, and how much or what degree of an artistic license of the truth Mr. Robert embellished. We didn't care, they were great stories and we just loved hanging out with the old guy.

"I know you boys know all about the Civil War around here and the Blockade Runners," he continued. "But did you know that one of, if not the most successful captain of the blockade runners was from right over there?"

Mr. Robert was pointing west across the Cape Fear River in the direction of Southport, a tiny seaside hamlet just a short ferry ride away. Mr. Robert then went on to enthrall us with one of his classic tales, weaving an adventure story upon a century old history lesson.

"You see, the ol'man, Captain Thompson by name, was the craftiest, most knowledgeable sea dog this side of the Atlantic those days," Mr. Robert said gesturing wildly.

Mr. Robert was laid back most of the time, except when he was getting all involved with one of his tales. He would alternate between sitting, standing, leaning, and pacing around. Pausing for emphasis, he would contort his face to relay the desired emotion, using his hands and feet to help bring the story to life.

In Mr. Robert's version of events, the good captain ran the most blockades, made the most money, was paid in gold, and lived in the most ornate, fancy seaside house around.

In the ensuing years, we found out all of the above proved to be true. Captain Thompson was indeed the most successful of the Blockade Runners. The captains, working for themselves, in the hire of the Confederacy, piloted their sleek ships past the Union blockade of southern ports, bringing in goods from Europe and the Caribbean Islands to provide provisions for the southern army, along with some fancy stuff for the ladies and gents of the era.

"Thompson's ships were the fastest and hardest to detect," Mr. Robert continued. "He made 34 successful trips around the ol' Union blockade. At three grand a pop, paid in gold mind you, he was also the richest…"

"Hey look, we found him, it's the Hermit!" exclaimed a rotund 40ish looking guy with a wife and two little kids in tow. "Well hey there."

"Well, hello friend," Mr. Robert said. "How y'all doing?"

"We're great, just great, now that we found you," the visitor continued. "We walked quite a ways in from the road, got turned around a bit, but here we are."

"Well, glad you found me," Mr. Robert said. "These are some of my friends here, young Lenny boy, Hal, and B."

The visitor introduced his family and Mr. Robert gave them the grand tour of his bunker, his fishing apparatus, and the surrounding sand. It was his usual tour guide persona in play. Mr. Robert had thousands of visitors over the years and at one point was one of the top draws for bringing tourists to the Old North State.

"Thank you for stopping by," Mr. Robert said. "Me and the boys are going on a little trip."

Mr. Robert pointed down toward his ever-present frying pan, perched on some stones near the fire pit. There was always a few dollars in the pan. The most recent visitors dropped in a few singles and Mr. Robert ushered them back toward the path leading to the main road, right near a hairpin turn just above the ferry entrance.

"Well come on boys," Mr. Robert continued. "Don't want to make a liar out of me, do you?"

We all looked at each other. We had no idea what Mr. Robert meant about going on a little trip. Usually, he would just walk around the bunker area some talking to us, but today was to be different. Much different, in fact, it would become our greatest adventure with Mr. Robert. He'd never invited us or anyone else that we had ever heard along for one of his famous "walkabouts". It was at that moment we found out where we were headed. Mr. Robert scooped the cash up from the frying pan as he continued his tale.

"My research indicates the good captain likely hid most of his gold over on ol' Baldy," Mr. Robert said looking back at us with a big smile on his face. "Bout time somebody found it, might as well be us."

Holy crap! We were going hunting for treasure with the man almost everybody else called the Fort Fisher Hermit. We followed the sandy path out to the road, walking our bikes along the way.

"Now boys, this isn't no wild goose chase," Mr. Robert said. "I've done my research on this, years and years' worth, lots of it, even before I came down here in 1955. But the last few pieces of information I needed always eluded me to just recently."

Then Mr. Robert clammed up a bit and shifted gears. A fire that had been simmering in his eyes burst into full bonfire fury.

"But, I knew I would need some help," he continued. "And you boys I trust, just you and Deputy Pickler."

We walked south for a bit in silence down an almost empty US Highway 421 the couple hundred yards to the Ft. Fisher-Southport Ferry entrance. The ferry began operations just a few years before in 1966 and offered locals and tourists a quick way to connect to the quaint village of Southport from our little island. The highway, which begins in Minnesota, ends just a few hundred yards past the ferry entrance. Battery Buchannan, Fort Fisher's southernmost point still stands guard over the mouth of the Cape Fear River just as it had on a cold January morning in 1865 when the last few Confederates defending the "Gibraltar of the South" surrendered at the battery to Union forces.

We rolled our bikes onto the crowded ferry, populated by a few dozen cars, crew, and mostly tourists for the short ride across the river.

"This should be a lot of fun," Hal said. "This is the first time I've been on the ferry."

No sooner than Hal put the period at the end of that sentence a super fluffy lady in a purple dress leaning over the rail right next to him puked over the starboard side. Hal jumped back. We all couldn't help but snicker a bit. No matter where or when over the course of our growing up years, Hal always seemed to be the one next to or the one doing the vomiting.

Gulls swooped down, thinking the lady was feeding them, then upset no food was coming their way, squawked their displeasure from just overhead, but they still followed us about halfway across. We could see lots of cool sights, small islands, other boats, a lighthouse, and finally the landing for the ferry at Southport. Mr. Robert didn't say much on the journey over. He appeared to be taking mental notes or something similar. As we exited, he stopped to check the large sign displaying the ferry schedule.

"Ok boys, we have about six hours to get our job done," he said.

We hitched a ride into town with an old guy wearing a black fedora in a brown GMC truck. Mr. Robert sat up front and we loaded our bikes and ourselves in the back. There was quite a refreshing breeze. We laughed and talked during the less than five-minute bumpy cruise into town. We pulled up next to a pier with a bunch of boats, mostly fishing vessels on each side. We unloaded our bikes and looked out over the water.

"Alright fellas," Mr. Robert said. "Jackson that gave us the ride said we could get his cousin Winston to give us a boat ride from here to old Baldy."

Winston ambled up the pier. He looked like a piece of human leather from decades making a living on the water. Short and squat, wearing an old blue button-up shirt, and some ragged jeans, he had a big cigar stub in his mouth and a bottle of beer in his hand. He had a messy head of white hair and a bunch coming out of his ears as well.

"Jackson said you could take us over to ol' Baldy," Mr. Robert said.

"Yup, yup, I can do that," Winston said nodding his head. "Big storm coming though, how long you staying over?"

"Just the afternoon," Mr. Robert replied, removing his straw hat and wiping his brow. "We need to catch the last ferry back across and we'll need a few supplies."

"Yup, yup, ok, sure," Winston said. "It'll be five bucks for the trips and you boys can leave those bikes in the boathouse there. I'll show you what I got up here you can buy or borrow. I'll be back over there at five, pick you folks up, and we'll get you back to the ferry.

We hurriedly pushed our bikes into the old worn boathouse housing an ancient barnacle-covered 32-foot trawler on a hoist inside. "Just looking" was painted on the side.

"This is too cool," Hal said. "You think there is really any gold over there?"

B and I looked at one another. We both shrugged our shoulders.

"Doubt anyone alive knows," I said. "We can take a look and see what Mr. Robert is talking about. Should be fun wither way."

"We need to keep a lookout too," B said. "Sky looking pretty rough over there."

Track 10-Mexico-James Taylor (2:57)/Carefree Highway-Gordon Lightfoot (3:45)

B would utter almost exactly the same thing many years later as we stood on a footbridge between Brownsville, Texas and Matamoros, Mexico. We were pursuing our childhood dream of hitchhiking across the United States once we graduated high school. We had only made it to Texas. We were almost out of money, and college started in 18 days.

"Man, I don't know, looks kinda rough over there," B said.

"Don't see we have much choice," I said. "No work here, nobody will give us a job. We need a few dollars more to start heading home with."

"Ok," B said. "Let's go to Mexico."

We crossed over on foot and wandered into old Mexico. Matamoros at that time was a laid-back port city. We hit a few cantinas offering to wash dishes or whatever. I spoke a little Spanish, but we found no takers the first few hours. Frustrated, we retreated back toward the United States.

"Hey, might be a place down there," I said, pointing at a small side street just before the footbridge.

B shrugged his shoulders and followed me down the dirt street. About 30 yards down at the road's end was a small porch overhang with four tables underneath. A Mexican and US flag anchored opposite ends of the overhang. We strolled through the arched entranceway. Two average size men appeared to be having an animated conversation in Spanish at the kitchen entrance to the right. B and I made our way past a few tables and sat at the bar. We spent some of our last few precious dollars on beer.

"Tequila," one of the arguing men told the barkeep.

In Spanish, the bartender reminded the man he had to perform that night but served him anyway. He took the shot quickly, slammed the glass down and asked for another. The barkeep obliged. The drinker looked our way. I was two barstools away from him. B was at the jukebox against the back wall on the far side of the little cantina.

"Hola American boys," he started. "One of you wouldn't happen to be a drummer, would you?"

His English was ok. B turned from the jukebox to look our way. I glanced at him and raised my eyebrows. He shrugged his shoulders. I took a big chug of my draft beer.

"Uh, yea," I said. "I play the drums."

The guy's eyes lit up.

"Blessed Mary!" he exclaimed. "Are you any good?"

"Sure, I can hang," I said.

"Hang?" he quizzed.

His questioning look made me realize I needed to use straightforward words.

"I can play Marty Robbins, Freddy Fender, Santana," I said, tossing out some names whose music had a strong Tex-Mex or Latino feel.

"Praise Mary again," he uttered. "Cousin, another tequila and two for the gringos."

Our new friend led us over to a table as some of the music B played began blaring from the jukebox. "Jesus Just Left Chicago" by ZZ Top rocked hard to start the afternoon off right.

"My name is Rigo, Rigo Tovar," he said. "The guy I was fighting with was my drummer and cousin. I had to fire him. He is very lazy and not much good on the drums anyway."

I just nodded. B did his shot and chased it with the rest of his beer. I did the same. I looked over at a tiny, cramped stage behind Rigo that had a chair, a shopworn four-piece drum set, and one missing board. I figured he was going to ask me to play with him and I guess one other guy because that stage couldn't possibly hold more than three people.

"Does your friend want to work tonight too?" Rigo asked.

"No, no, I don't play," B said.

Rigo laughed a hearty laugh as he saw I was staring down at the poor old drum kit.

"No, not here gentlemen," he smirked. "In the town square, it's a big celebration tonight, this is my homecoming concert!"

We had no idea the guy buying us drinks and offering us a badly needed job would go on to be Matamoras' most famous son and the man who is credited with melding traditional Mexican music with American rock and pop. At this point, he had released a couple of albums and was already considered a big star in eastern Mexico. We had never heard of him and of course, he had never heard of us, yet.

"So what do you say young gringos?" Rigo asked. "We begin setting up in an hour, your big friend here, I will hire him to help move equipment and for security. We will have sound check at six and the opening band will play at seven, we will go on at 8-8:30."

We looked at each other; we sure needed the money, but really had no idea what we were getting into.

"Sure," I said. "We're game."

"Well, ok!" Rigo said excitedly. "My songs are on the jukebox, listen to those. We will play all of those and some others you should have no problem with if you can play the music of the people you said."

He yelled at his other cousin behind the bar to feed us and give us beer, but no more Tequila.

"I will have someone pick you up in about a couple of hours or so," he said. "I take it you want to be paid in US dollars?"

We nodded yes.

"Excellent," he continued. "Greenbacks for the gringos. Emil tell Frida to prepare these boys a place to sleep tonight next door. Give them five dollars for the jukebox."

Emil grunted an acknowledgment and forked over five dollars in US quarters.

So for the next hour we listened to the most famous musician from where we were seated. Rigo's tunes were simple, mostly love related ballads and more poppy than rock, but super solid song structure, and rhythm. He fused elements of traditional Mexican music with light American rock, some Tex-Mex blues, and a hint of Nashville country. I didn't have a problem catching on and even played along on the crappy drum set to several songs just to get the rhythm.

Emil fed us some great Mexican food and several beers. He showed us were we would bunk down for the night. We had really scored. A job for us both, free food, lodging, beer, and a cool meeting with a Mexican music legend to be.

"Time to go gringos," a tiny, well dressed Mexican man in his 50s said from the doorway.

Wow, the time had passed fast. B and I had a little beer buzz. Timing was certainly on our side that day. Wouldn't it be great if there was an instrument of some kind to help us all with our timing regarding life events?

Track 11-Wonderful Tonight-Eric Clapton (3:43)/Stone in Love-Journey (4:27)

You know how I mentioned early on in Crazy Beach Disc One my timing always seemed to be off a bit with Darlene? Well, this is the one that probably best epitomizes my line of thinking on the matter. It happened right after the events of the first book conclude. Darlene and her family had moved to Durham due to her mom needing to be near Duke for regular treatments of the disease that would kill her anyway before our junior year reached Christmas. These events take place in the late fall of our 10th-grade year. My family, sans Lil'sis who was staying with my aunt, headed to visit our relatives in the Piedmont during my dad's monthly "long weekend" which ran Friday through Monday. My folks included a night in Durham to visit the Winters on this, our first trip to their new house.

"Those steaks were delicious," my mom said. "This deck is so nice and the weather is so great for this close to Thanksgiving."

"Thank you," Mr. Winter said. "I stained it right after we moved in."

"May we be excused?" Darlene spoke up for the both of us, once again always a step ahead of me.

"Sure," Ms. Winter said. "Just clear the table first."

"Grab me and G.R. another beer too," Mr. Winter said.

We quickly cleared the table and I began washing the dishes while Darlene took our pops a fresh cold one. I looked out at the scene. It all seemed so normal, just like the dozens of cookouts we had enjoyed over four summers, except Ms. Winter was now in a wheelchair. I saw Darlene talking with her folks. She was already different, even more assertive, more focused. Our phone conversations and her letters provided me with lots of clues as to what was happening in the Winter household. Darlene had always been quite private about her family matters but had been more forthcoming in the two months since they had moved to Durham.

"Finish those dishes boy!" she said excitedly as she entered through the sliding glass door. "I finally get to ride in your car! I'm going to go change."

I just smiled. This was going to be fun. I didn't think she needed to change. She looked really great in some blue denim shorts and a Led Zeppelin t-shirt. I worked hard to get the dishes done as quickly as possible. Then it started to rain. Mr. Winter quickly wheeled his wife into the house, my folks right behind.

"Well looks like we'll be playing cards inside," Mr. Winter said. "Lenny, you guys might want to wait till it lets up a bit."

My dad nodded in agreement as they all gathered around the Winter's big old oak table. I very reluctantly offered no disagreement. I didn't want to wait. Darlene and I detested the fact we had exactly zero alone time in over two months, almost 10 weeks. Then Darlene re-appeared.

"Oh my sweetie," Ms. Winter said. "You look so lovely."

"You sure do!" my mom said.

I had a huge lump in my throat. I was stunned. Darlene always looked pretty, oftentimes downright smoking hot, but this was different. She looked like she just stepped out of the pages of Vogue or Seventeen. She had on a red short-sleeve silk top tucked into a form-fighting black leather mini-skirt accented by black Roman sandals with straps wrapping around up to her knees. Her golden hair curled in waves in front and back with an Indian braid around her crown and a quarter-way down her back. She smiled her million-watt smile and nodded at our folks.

"You ready?" she asked looking at me.

I stood there dumbfounded. I was wiping my hands on an orange dishcloth. I just kept wiping. She tilted her head.

"Lenny?" she said giving me our little wave and a concerned smile.

That snapped me back to reality.

"Yeah," I managed.

"You two have a good time," her mom said.

"Back by 11:30," her dad said. "Keep an eye out if it gets worse."

"Have fun, be careful," my mom said.

My dad just gave me a sideways glance. Our conversation the day I got my license a few weeks earlier replayed in my head.

"Will do," I said.

We bolted out the sliding glass door. I opened the passenger side door for Darlene and she very ladylike seated herself despite the tight, tiny skirt. Her legs, as always, were one of the big stars of the show, and were simply unbelievable. Darlene could have easily been a leg model or any kind of teen model as far as that goes. I just wanted to stand there and stare.

"Thank you," she said tilting her head again in a manner that I took as "get a move on dumbass".

I hustled around the back and opened the Duster's driver side door. I was soooo glad I picked this car over the Chevelle. You see this car had a black front bench seat, the Chevelle had blue bucket seats. Darlene immediately scooted over about as close to me as possible. She gave me a quick kiss on the lips and smiled her famous naughty-girl smile. Seatbelts, are you nuts?

"Finally," she said. "I love your car, it fits you. I thought today would never come. Turn left to go to the theater, turn right if you want to go somewhere else."

Oh boy...

Did that mean what I thought it meant? I was pretty sure it did. Do I just ask? Do I just turn right?

"We can do both if you want," she said, placing her left hand on my bare right knee and kissing my cheek as we reached the end of her long driveway. "I love you, you pick"

Do what? Pick what? Damn my mind was blown. She smelled so good. Oh crap, she's wearing Love's Baby Soft, the same scent Melissa always wore. What the hell am I doing thinking about Melissa?

"Well?" she said, staring deeply right into my eyes as I turned my head to face her.

She kissed me intensely, repeatedly. I slid my left hand between her thighs.

"You little devil," she said fake sheepishly pulling away slightly. "We can't even make it out of my driveway! Pick, movies or the party I wrote you about, or both?"

In that moment I think we both felt the best kind of freedom in the world.

Track 12-Bald Head-Professor Longhair (3:11)

The ride over to Bald Head, also called Smith Island back then, was going to be no party for sure. The seas were already pretty choppy and Captain Winston had to turn the boat into the waves a couple of times as we made our way over. Mr. Robert stood near the bow with the wind in his face. He resembled some of those old sea dog pictures you used to see in every water town bar.

"Where's Hal?" I asked B who was returning from inside.

"Puking over the stern," B replied.

I just shook my head. The 28-foot boat, usually a fishing charter, was rocking pretty violently, but we made it over without additional issues, despite a somewhat ornery bilge pump that seemed to work just every now and then.

"See you fellas bout five," Winston said. "I'll get ya back to the ferry."

Mr. Robert gave him a sweeping hand motion, like a great English stage actor lauding his co-stars at the end of a play.

"Well boys let's get to work," Mr. Robert said. "We're heading over past the lighthouse."

So the second phase of our treasure hunt began. Hal had recovered enough to tote his share of our equipment we had borrowed from Winston. Mr. Robert led the way with his knotty walking stick and old leather satchel draped across his shoulder. B and I carried each end of an old metal cooler filled with drinks and snacks. Hal carried several tools, both long and short handled. The rain began just as we crested the far southeastern dunes of the island. This spot has sometimes been called North Carolina's chin and it's been bopped squarely dozens of times by hurricanes or tropical storms.

We dropped a lot of our crap at the foot of Old Baldy. The lighthouse is the oldest in North Carolina and one of the oldest period. It was built in 1817 on the almost six-square-mile island to help guide ships through the treacherous shoals and sandbars that gave rise to the local river being tagged with the moniker Cape Fear.

Bald Head Island, despite its ultra-small size, was active in two major wars. During the American Revolutionary War, it featured Fort George, a British fort. During the Civil War, the earthen fortifications known as redoubts served as Fort Holmes, a strategic Confederate stronghold for shipping and smuggling. Basically, it's a big sandbar, with its natural highest elevation point not much over five feet.

"Lenny boy, you and B dig just to the west of the lighthouse about 10 yards out," Mr. Robert started. "Three or four feet at a time then slide over three feet and do the same. Dig down about three feet each time. We are looking for gold dollars or gold coins. But be sure and pick up anything you find."

Mr. Robert took Hal over to the east side and did the same. The wind was much stronger now and some heavier rain was beginning to fall. I glanced out at the ocean. The waves were getting bigger and bigger. I felt the salt-laced wind in my face. Remembering my history, I wondered if the soldiers here ever experienced any wicked storms or saw the same certain color of water that only a severe storm brings and I was witnessing. The side B and I were working once saw action in the Revolutionary War.

You see Mr. Robert, an avid historian, told us in 1776, Bald Head Island played a minor role in securing the south for Great Britain after British Major General Henry Clinton and Lieutenant General Charles Cornwallis used the island as a staging area preceding a voyage to Charleston, South Carolina. The British stationed a small band of soldiers where we stood. They anchored some ships just off the coast attempting to help keep our port closed to Continental shipping. The first blockade of our coast if you will.

The garrison of about 30 troops, under the command of Captain John Linzee, built Fort George, named for King George III on the southwestern corner of the island. I tried to imagine what it might have looked like and the lives of the Redcoats stationed on this tiny speck of land, what was then a desolate place.

"Time for a break boys," Mr. Robert said as we met at the base of the lighthouse. "You see ol' Patriot Brigadier General Robert Howe was stationed across the river in Fort Johnson. After watching the British carefully, he had Captain Polk and the Continentals launch a raid with about 150 men."

Mr. Robert said it was early September when Polk's raiding party captured five British sailors but then had to retreat when the other 25 Redcoats took cover and the British vessels moored just off-shore opened fire and the ground troops then initiated a pursuit. Polk used his knowledge of the local area, fleeing through a maze of shallow creeks, and escaped losing only one soldier. By October, the British troops abandoned the place and Bald Head went back into hibernation.

"I didn't find anything," Hal said guzzling down a Dr. Pepper.

"Nothing so far on that side," Mr. Robert said. "You boys have any luck?"

"A couple of things," I said. "Show'em B."

B reached in his pocket and pulled out a couple of pottery shards and more importantly, a coin. He handed it to Mr. Robert who analyzed it carefully.

"Well, I'll be," Mr. Robert said, using a well-worn southern euphemism for surprise. "Not one of Captain Thompson's, but I believe you found yourself something even older, a Continental dollar."

Just then some strong waves came crashing inland and the rain and wind picked up even more. We all scurried inside the old abandoned lighthouse. It smelled dank and funky. We crammed into the small landing just by the stairs.

Our shelter from the storm, Mr. Robert said, was a lighthouse at the mouth of the Cape Fear River authorized by the Commissioners of the Cape Fear in 1789. The commission specified that the light be built "at the extreme point on Bald-head or some other convenient place near the bar of the river," according to Mr. Robert. He said it was so ships could avoid the greatest shoal in the area which was called Frying Pan.

I double checked Mr. Robert's recollections a few years later using various source materials printed in the ensuing decades and then much later, various websites all concurring that Mr. Robert was spot on.

He told us money was raised for the implementation of navigation aids by taxing vessels entering the Port of Brunswick at sixpence per ton. Additional funds were provided by the newly formed United States Congress, who in August 1789 assumed responsibility for construction, maintenance, and operation of all "lighthouses, beacons, buoys and public piers" in the United States. Land for the light was donated by Benjamin Smith in exchange for increased hunting regulation on the island.

Mr. Robert told us the building of the original light was completed in December 1794 at a final cost of about $12,000. The light was placed under the care of light keeper Henry Long, who operated the light until 1806 when he was killed in a hunting accident on the island. After Long's death, Sedgewick Springs was appointed as keeper of the light at Bald Head after twelve local residents signed a petition to President Thomas Jefferson recommending him for the position.

Less than twenty years after it was built, the original light succumbed to erosion as it had been built way too close to the water. By July 1813 the light was officially declared inoperable

Mr. Robert continued the history lesson by sharing that in 1813 Congress allocated $15,000 to build a new lighthouse on Bald Head. This time they planned to build a sturdy lighthouse on higher ground, away from eroding shores. Revenue Commissioner Samuel Smith wrote a detailed blueprint outlining how the light was to be built to ensure its longevity. Daniel Way was awarded the contract to build the light and keepers quarters.

Using bricks from the original light, Way completed the project in 1817 at a cost of about $16,000. Mr. Robert could reel off names, dates, and figures unlike anyone else I've ever encountered. I did some more research in later years and compared my findings to notes I made when I was a kid and in college about the experience. Mr. Robert's figures were not just close, they were exact. He missed one by a few hundred dollars, that was it for his errors of memory or perhaps he wasn't wrong at all, the source material he was checking back then may have been mistaken. He was something else believe you me.

Immediately after the initial lighting it was discovered that the new light was not tall enough or bright enough to help vessels navigate around Frying Pan Shoals. Its purpose was limited to helping vessels enter the southern entrance to the Cape Fear River. To avoid Frying Pan Shoals, many vessels decided to enter the Cape Fear through New Inlet at Fort Fisher about seven miles north of Bald Head Island. As a result, Mr. Robert said, little emphasis was placed on maintaining "Old Baldy" and by the mid-1830s the lighthouse began to fall into disrepair as the longtime keeper, Mr. Springs, an elderly veteran of the Revolutionary War could no longer handle the job.

Old Baldy was effectively decommissioned for the first time at the outset of the Civil War when the Confederacy turned off all their lighthouses in order to hinder navigation of Union vessels. After the end of the war Old Baldy remained dark. The light was in disrepair and of little use with most vessels at that time entering New Inlet, which had its own lighthouse at Federal Point.

Circumstances changed by 1879 when a hurricane closed New Inlet. The Federal Point light became useless. This brought life to Old Baldy once again. Improvements were made to Old Baldy including a new light, keeper's quarters, and a stone jetty to stabilize the shoreline which had begun eroding quickly due to the closure of New Inlet. According to Mr. Robert, the jetty was built just in time to prevent Old Baldy from falling into the sea during a hurricane in September 1883.

Old Baldy was downgraded from a lighthouse to a navigational radio beacon in 1935. It was completely decommissioned in 1959 when the Oak Island Light was built. The lighthouse is on the National Register of Historic Places and is open to the public.

Go find yourself some treasure.

Track 13-One of These Nights-The Eagles (3:52)

"Hello," Ms. Winter answered the phone.

"Hi, Ms. Winter, it's Lenny," I said. "Is today a good day?"

"Actually Lenny it is," she said. "Charlie and I sat outside and watched Darlene and a few of her friends play basketball. Charlie got her a goal."

"That's cool, I'll check it out when I come up," I said. "May I speak to Darlene please?"

"Of course," Ms. Winter replied. "Are you coming up this weekend?"

"Yes ma'am," I continued. "If that is still ok?"

"Oh yes, yes," Ms. Winter said. "I so look forward to seeing you. Darlene is so excited to be coming down to the beach for a few weeks. Darlene, honey, Lenny is on the phone for you."

"Hey," Darlene said. "I got it Mom."

Her mom hung up the phone.

"Hey, what time you leaving?" Darlene asked. "Is everything ok?"

"Yea, yea," I said. "I just got out of the shower. Was just letting you know I'm about to roll that way."

"Great," she said. "I'm sooo glad school is out and freaking 10th grade is over! And I'm happy you got out of that trouble. You gotta be more careful or you won't have a license then we'll be screwed."

"I know, I know," I said. "I'll try. I'll try harder. I hope I'll try harder anyway."

"You are a funny dumbass," she said. "Now get your fine butt up here so we can go to that concert."

"Leaving now," I said. "Be there about four or five. Love you."

"Be careful," she said. "Love you more, bye!"

She hung up before I could say anything else. I grabbed my gym bag off the bed and gave Mom a kiss before I headed out the door. I tossed the bag in the back seat and fired the Duster up. The 340-cubic inch (C.I.) turbojet engine sounded so mean. I had McCartney and Wings "Band on the Run" album in the eight-track player. This was my fifth trip to Durham since the Winters had moved the prior September. You've heard some about the first one (don't worry there is more on that one coming in a bit). I also visited for Christmas (with family), Valentine's weekend (by myself), and during Easter break in April (with family). This would be Darlene's first time coming back to the beach since she moved 8.5 months before.

We were going to an Eagles (original lineup!) concert in Greensboro, about an hour or so west of her house. We planned to leave the next morning to head back to our little island. Darlene was going to spend the rest of June with Lexi's family and Darlene's folks were supposed to come down for our annual July 4th cookout.

We were full of hope. But I have already warned you that our story doesn't have a very happy ending. We did have a bunch of fun with tons of laughter. Those 30 days or so…man, they were sure something.

Track 14-Ain't No Sunshine-Bill Withers (2:09)

Well, it was just too much. Crushed by distance, death, the weight of growing up, and finally, the inevitable despair that comes with knowing there isn't a damn thing you can do about it, mine and Darlene's journey together reached a fork in the road neither of us could navigate. She was going to be moving, again. This time much farther away. To Virginia, way out in western Virginia, almost out near freaking by God West Virginia.

Mr. Winter had accepted a position as an instructor at the famed Virginia Military Institute (VMI) in Lexington, Virginia at the southern tip of the legendary Shenandoah Valley ("Clear Daughter of the Stars"). It was and still is, I guess, 350 miles or so from our little island to VMI. With today's interstate upgrades it is still a six or seven-hour drive each way. Back then it was nine plus if you didn't stop. Of course, you're going to stop. We tried, Elvis knows we tried, but damn talk about horrible timing and bad breaks in a relationship, jeez.

The news came just before graduation via a phone call, the first time she'd spoken to me (not counting a couple of short letters) since all of the prom debacles. It was a quiet, eerily still early June evening when Lil'sis picked up the ringing old phone from its spot on the wall above the AM-FM clock radio on the bar and beside the calendar.

"Hey Dar-Dar," she said. "When are you coming back to the beach?"

Lil'sis listened intently as Darlene spoke. My sister's smile faded a bit as she looked at me.

"Here," she said. "It's Darlene."

Lil'sis went out the front screen door to join Mom on the deck with Mom's aunts Pat and Nina. All of them smoking up a storm so big it looked like fog. Dad was at work.

"Hey," I said. "I'm glad you called. It's so great to hear your voice."

"Lenny," she began. "Sorry, I haven't called. I started to a couple of times, but, but, I just didn't. I was so mad and hurt."

"It's ok," I said. "I was an ass, like I said in my letters I am sooo sorry. I'm trying to stop doing all that crazy stuff. Can I come see you?"

"I'd like that," she said. "But something has happened and you're not going to like it."

Suddenly I felt like I was back in the tent after Dalton's party almost three years earlier. Was she calling me to tell me she had sex with someone else? Or that she had a guy she wanted to be close to? We'd both tried to walk the line, but after her mom died the fall of our junior year and the ensuing holidays were so tough, we both felt something kinda falter a little in our relationship as well. What? Why exactly? Hell if I know. Neither of us could ever figure it out. A loss of innocence maybe? Maybe we were both just so starry-eyed with one another for so long. We were struggling to figure out how a mature relationship might work. Plus, we were both barely 17 when her mom died, so there was that.

We together decided that come the New Year, just before our junior year's spring semester would start, that we should hang out with who we wanted of the opposite sex. Not really date-per-se, but if you were at a party and wanted to do more than talk to someone, we felt we should have that option. Go to the movies, stuff like that. We didn't end our relationship, we still loved one another deeply, but we were both realists who were at that time four hours apart and decided we might be fighting a losing battle. We were not surrendering to what became inevitable, but perhaps trying to call a truce and hoping for a miracle. The miracle never came.

"We're moving again," she said. "Dad got a job in Lexington, Virginia, way out there near West Virginia."

Gut-punch number one. Now she was going to be nine hours away.

"We're moving this week," she continued.

Gut punch number two. I'm leaning on the bar now for support. My head is spinning. A million memories flood my mind, a gazillion possible tomorrows vanish into thin air.

"And Dad is sending me to a finishing school in Alexandria (Virginia)," she said. "Episcopal High School, it's an old upper-crust boarding school."

And yes you remembered correctly, Alexandria is Darlene's middle name.

Uppercut, knockout. I was so stunned, I was just silent.

"Lenny," she said. "You still there?"

"A, yea," I said. "So when did all this happen?"

"Just the last few days," she told me. "I've been kinda in a shock zone really."

"I bet," I said. "Damn, this is too unreal. It just seems like you are slipping both farther and further away all the time."

"I told him I didn't want to go," she said. "We had a big fight. It was really the first time I ever really stood up to him. I told him I was 18 and all, but he we just so matter-of-fact, like this is what's best, and telling me not to let my emotions run my life. I said I wasn't. That I didn't know exactly what I wanted, but I knew damn sure I didn't want to move again."

"Damn, that was ballsy," I said.

"It's kinda been a mess since then," she continued. "I know you were hoping for better news when I called."

"Yea, yea, I was," I said. "But I'm glad to hear your voice. I missed you."

"I've missed you too," she said. "I don't know what to do."

"Did you ask your dad if you could live with your aunt?" I asked.

"Yea," she said. "I tried that, but he said they were moving as well, to some retirement place in Florida. I even asked if I could live with Lexi. He didn't even respond to that."

"Damn, I thought my old man was tough," I chipped in.

"Lenny," she said. "I'm sad. I've just started fitting in around here and I've made some good new friends around here the last couple of years, most you've met. I was finally settling into stuff and I'd even told Dad last week I was going to pick where I wanted to go to college. I said I'd listen to his advice, but I was going to apply where I wanted."

"What did he say to that?" I queried.

"Surprisingly," she continued. "He was somewhat ok with it, suggesting we each narrow a list down to five schools and we would discuss each one. So I was happy at that point. Then this, but in his defense, they sought him out, as you know he'd been teaching here in Durham and his boss knows the Chancellor at VMI, so presto-wham-o-fuck-o off we go to the mountains of Virginia."

Track 15-Sister Golden Hair-America (3:14)/Almost Cut My Hair-CSN&Y (4:22)

So it was a new calendar year and in a few weeks a new semester, the spring semester of my junior year. Life just inched along slowly, mine and Darlene's "New Deal" went nowhere fast. She and I talked on the phone each week in January and neither mentioned anybody or much of anything else. She said our pops were discussing possibly watching the Super Bowl together, so that gave both of us something to look forward to at the end of the month.

Fate took a turn away from us at this point, as January was a really rugged month weather wise and the planned Super Bowl get together never materialized. Also, Darlene's aunt had been spending a lot of time at the Winter's home. She was helping them with household stuff and handling Ms. Winter's things and making sure they ended up where Ms. Winter would have wanted. During this period Darlene's aunt stressed to Darlene that while she appreciated all we meant to one another, she felt we were way too young and way too far apart distance-wise to put so much stress on ourselves trying to maintain something that is difficult for mature people in the same household or even the same zip code to achieve.

Darlene called me the last Saturday of January and I could tell something was up right away. I had an idea and I was right. After some general chit-chat and the requisite discussion of us both being bummed about the weather preventing our Super Bowl shindig, she shifted gears.

"Lenny," she continued. "Our new classes started this week."

"Yea," I said interrupting. "Ours start Monday."

"Well," she said. "I got asked out to go to a Super Bowl party here tomorrow."

Damn, poop, damn. You know those moments your life changes? Sometimes you catch them, sometimes you don't. Well, I damn sure caught that one.

"Lenny, Lenny," she continued. "You there?"

"Yea, yea," I said, once again leaning on the trust-worthy bar for support.

I've been leaning on one ever since.

"It was a new guy at our school," she said. "The other guys around here never hassled me because of us, and I hadn't told anyone about what we'd agreed on about that kinda stuff, but this new kid, Jason, he sat down beside me at lunch yesterday and just asked."

"Oh," I said, unable to offer much commentary.

"My girlfriends were kinda stunned," she said. "I just said ok without thinking much."

"Uh-uh," my eloquence continued.

"I mean it's a daytime deal, a kinda welcome to the neighborhood thing for his family just a few streets from here," she said. "I guess this is kinda what we were talking about, right?"

Damn, what had I agreed to? Definitely not going to lose my place in the Dumbass Hall of Fame. Talking about shooting yourself in the foot, err, scratch that, how about shooting yourself in the crotch and heart?

"Lenny, Lenny?" she asked.

"I'm here," I said. "Just thinking."

"If you don't want me to go, I won't," she said.

Hell no, I didn't want her to go. But crap, I couldn't say that, could I? I damn sure wanted to say it. But I didn't. In another one of those, "how would my life have turned out differently if" moments, I simply went with the better angels of my nature. They do exist, they don't show up much but they powered through right then. Bastards…

"No, go," I said. "It should be a good game and I want you to have fun."

See what a smart, mature person I can be? Problem is, I seldom choose to be those things. But I did then and while Darlene and I still had several hands left to play, I always felt like that moment was the beginning of the end. Scratch that again, her mom dying probably was, or her moving to start with, or hell, who knows?

The next day was the least fun I've ever had watching the Super Bowl, well scratch that as well, the second least, no third least. The two worst were Super Bowl III when my 15-1 Colts, the biggest favorites in Super Bowl history (17-21 points) lost 16-7 to the upstart New York Jets led by playboy Joe Namath. It was an earth-shattering day for me and outside of the deaths of loved ones, one of the darkest days of my life. The second was the Colts' other Super Bowl loss, to the Saints that time. We've won a couple Super Bowls and those have been great days. But Darlene's first official Super Bowl party without me is third and likely altered the course of both of our lives.

Well, you can probably figure out how I spent the day. I got sailor-on-leave drunk and Cheech and Chong level stoned. I even got to go to a college Super Bowl party and had a few opportunities to do more than talk to a couple college girls there, but I was more interested in trying to not think about what Darlene might be doing than what I could be doing. I got so blistered, I just passed out in the apartment of people I barely knew on the mainland and missed school the next day.

When I managed to pull myself together, I drove back to our little island. I pulled into the carport in the spot formally occupied by the pool table. We sold it at the end of summer as we didn't use it much anymore and it was beginning to show its age from almost a decade of being pounded by the ocean breezes and sea mist despite being covered by a tarp most of the time. Dad's car was gone, so he was either at work, the VFW, or the golf course. I knew Mom would be helping her best friend Gail at the beauty shop, Lil'sis would still be at school. I wearily climbed the stairs and went straight to the shower. I then went to my room. There was a note on the bed from my mom.

"Darlene called 8pm Love, Mom".

I felt a bunch of different emotions. I was glad she called, sad I had missed her. Had she had a crappy time and wanted to tell me about it? Did she have a great time and wanted to tell me about it? Something else? Well, there would be no way to know till tonight. I just went and crashed on my bed.

"Don't you have a game tonight?" the unmistakable sound of my father's mighty voice woke me from some fragmented dreams about stock car racing.

"Yes sir," I said.

"Supper is on the table," he said from just outside my doorway.

"Yes sir," I said.

"Get a haircut," he said walking away.

My father and I had started to grow distant from one another the last couple of years for a myriad of reasons. I had reached the point I still wanted to watch games with him, but really would rather be hanging with my friends or talking to girls. Most parents and children reach this point eventually. I had been there for a while. Now of all the forces pulling us apart, I think the increasingly contentious debates about the length of my hair were probably number one. Always curly and unruly, my hair was the wishbone that we both pulled on that would lead to a severe fracture in our relationship. Dad always insisted on me getting it cut before it got too long.

When I was a little kid, before I had a say in the matter he would buzz cut it like his. Once we moved to the island, he would take me to Mr. Cheek's barbershop near the boardwalk on the main boulevard and have portly old Mr. Cheek make me look like a mini-Marine. Mr. Cheek was a cool guy. I heard many pearls of wisdom from him as he traded banter about politics, sports, and women. One of the best was his squashing of some misogynistic banter about the University of Southern California (USC) cheerleaders during a fall Saturday football game when I was about nine.

Now the USC cheerleaders are about as beautiful a set of women as you will ever see in one place, any of their cheer squads from any era. Well, Mr. Misogynist commenter guy said something very suggestive about some activities he wished to pursue with one of the young ladies yelling for the Trojans in the Los Angeles Coliseum that beautiful early autumn day.

"That young lady is somebody's daughter," Mr. Cheek said.

Mr. Misogynist shut right up. Well done Mr. Cheek.

My mom put a stop to the buzz cuts along about third or fourth grade in elementary school and I had been pushing the boundaries ever since. I would've loved to have heard the first conversation that led to a cessation of the buzz cuts, as my mom seldom bucked my dad's wishes, but she damn sure did on that one. Thanks Mom.

Anyway, B now wore his in a long, long ponytail and many of my other friends were aligned with the styles of the time. Once mine got much over my collar or close to my shoulders, I was commanded to cut it. Not asked, told. This night would be the first time I mounted more than a few words counter attack. Another dark day in my life. Back-to-back no less. It took my father and I almost a decade to recover from what was about to transpire. Our relationship became solid again post-college, but it took quite a few years, some distance, and the birth of my first child to make us whole again.

I changed into my basketball uniform. I played in the church league on the island. The coaches at school wanted me to play, but it was just too much after our soccer team advanced deep into the playoffs in the fall and baseball practice was starting February first. I needed a little breather. Church League games were twice a week but close to home at the old gym in the town hall building by the marina.

While very competitive, Church League basketball wasn't as intense as school ball with no traveling or everyday practices required. You just had to go to church a couple times a week. Over the years I played for several different churches on the island and enjoyed it a bunch. I came in second one year to my good friend Edwin Lem (one of the best players I've seen) in scoring average, third another time, and made some All-Star teams. I had great teammates and the old gym was a trip.

The gym was so old. It was built back in the "set-shot" days before jumpers became the standard outside shot. The gym had low rafters. If you were more than a few feet beyond the foul line to take a shot that had any chance of going in you had to calculate for an arc to split the rafters, over the first beam, below the highest beam, and down to the rim. Several of us became skilled at making that type shot and it was cool to see. It was also funny to see shots clang off the rafters, as long as they weren't yours. Anyway, if you're ever down that way stop by the Federal Point Historical Society building by the "new" municipal building (the old Blockade Runner Museum). The old one, gym, jailhouse, and all had to be demolished after severe damage from a hurricane. The new building houses a great many artifacts from the island's history, including tons of photos from the old church basketball league. Lots of good times.

Well, I was about to have far from a good time. I sat down at my usual spot at the table. The chair closest to my room, the same one Darlene and I had sat in all those years ago...the night the storms knocked the power out and we played family Monopoly and listened to "Exile on Main Street" in my room.

"Who are y'all playing tonight?" my mother asked in her sweet southern accent.

"I'm not sure Mom," I truthfully replied.

"Man should know his opponent," my father said.

I let that one ride. Thankfully, Lil'sis was studying at a friend's house.

"Well, have fun," Mom said. "Are you coming right home after?"

"I don't know Mom," I said.

My dad popped a top on another ice cold Pabst Blue Ribbon.

"Well, what do you know Son?" he asked.

Now, I should have thought before I spoke. I didn't. In true Hall of Fame dumbass fashion I blurted out:

"I know I'm not cutting my hair."

Oh, boy…Darlene had chosen her education as the place to make her stand against her rigid, military-minded father. I chose to make mine against the same type of mind, at the very heart of what he considered a man should look like. My father immediately went to his go-to move to show he was pissed. The rolling of his tongue under his front teeth, very ominous.

"Yes you are!" my dad said raising his voice.

"Not this time Dad," I countered, my blood beginning to boil. "I'm old enough to decide for myself how I want to wear my hair."

I stood up to leave the table. My father stood as well.

"You're getting a haircut," he said.

"No, I'm not!" I said raising my voice.

I stepped toward my room, my father moved to block my path.

"Tomorrow," he demanded.

I shook my head no. The next few minutes are blurred by the intensity of the moment, time, and my family's way of dealing with stuff like this, as you know, eternal silence. My recollection is that at this point my father grabbed me by the shoulders and I attempted to push his hands away. Whatever transpired at that moment the next few were no fun. A wrestling match ensued with both of us tumbling over the couch, crushing the coffee table into splinters, and basically beating the crap out of one another for a minute or two. While mostly a stalemate between two stubborn, bullheaded people, the ramifications were long-lasting. The whole thing is simply a memory time can't extinguish. I would trade everything short of my soul or my loved ones for an erasure. I damn sure wish I could. During a brief separation, my mother stepped between us and facing my father said "no more". It was the only time I ever saw my mother give my father a direct order. He obeyed and walked away

"Go to your game," she commanded me.

Track 16- Riders on the Storm-The Doors (7:09)

The storm grew more intense as we sought refuge in the lighthouse. It was pretty rough for several hours. Mr. Robert tried to keep things light with some stories from his youth.

He then told us about first coming to our little island in 1955 and some of his run-ins with the law and some area teenagers who were less than kind. He emphasized most people treated him just fine or shunned him altogether, which was ok with him. Many people, including some in law enforcement, think those less than kind teenagers may have had something to do with his death. No one has ever been charged. Those that shunned him have no idea what they missed.

"Their loss," he chuckled as the wind and rain pounded against the ancient lighthouse.

Mr. Robert regaled us with more tales of Captain Thompson, the fearless Blockade Runner.

"He built that beautiful sea-side house we passed in Southport. The one with the widow's walk," he said. "But didn't spend a lot of other money. My research indicates it has got to be around here somewhere. That's a lot of gold."

Well, B had found the one old weather-worn Continental dollar, but there was no proof that it was part of Captain Thompson's supposed treasure trove. We passed the time with more stories, punctuated by what we would come to find out later was a damn tropical storm churning outside. It was way early in hurricane season for one, but that's damn sure what it was. We were never really too afraid, we figured we were safe in the Ol' Baldy lighthouse, after all it was almost 160 years old at that point and had survived Hurricane Hazel in 1954.

We did begin to get a little concerned when water started coming in through the old door and from above us. The wind and rain had found a passage in from the top of the lighthouse. The deluge poured in splashing all around us. The water level rose several inches and then slowed, but still climbed steadily for quite a while.

"Now boys, be on the lookout for snakes and such," Mr. Robert said, as he made his way up the rickety old stairs. "Come on up a few steps."

It became apparent our return vessel would not be coming as the storm grew more intense and the late afternoon gave way to the early evening. Thankfully, we had a few packs of crackers and some other munchies, along with a small cooler of drinks. We made sure to ration stuff out.

"Boy, my mom is going to be pissed," Hal said. "I was supposed to be home by supper."

Mr. Robert rubbed his scruffy, grey-white beard with one hand and wiped his brow with the other just after removing his near ever-present straw hat.

"Yeah boys," he said. "I didn't feel this one coming. Usually can tell when a bad storm is about. Dang sure missed this one though."

"Don't matter," B said. "We'll get back soon enough."

Mr. Robert had given B back the Continental Dollar. B was looking at the cool old coin.

"Bet that dollar could tell some tales," I said.

"Man, I'd like to hear those," Hal said.

"Me too," Mr. Robert said. "Let's imagine a few of them. I'll go first."

So for the next few hours or so we took turns spinning yarns about the history of the dollar. It was too worn out to make out the exact year it was produced so we were all over the place timewise with our tales.

Mr. Robert of course had the most intricate, suspenseful tale including French Privateers, the British garrison once stationed on Bald Head Island, and some local boys serving as spies for the Patriot cause.

B and Hal had pretty good tales focused on shipwrecks, women, and the men who went down with both. I managed a decent story that seemed to hold their attention, borrowing bits from "The Old Man and the Sea", "Treasure Island", and a funky, "Twilight Zone"-like twist ending that elicited a couple of wows and oohs from my captive audience. If I ever do a book of short stories, I'll include that one.

"Lenny boy," Mr. Robert said. "You might make a good storyteller one day, if you were to write some of that stuff running round your head down."

I took Mr. Robert to heart and for the first time since the Woodstock trip a couple of years before, I started jotting down ideas, events, pieces of songs that would pop into my head inspired by the day's events, people, and places. Over the years some of the things I put pen to paper on led to some decent newspaper stories (I won a North Carolina Press Association Award in 1993), a few decent songs, and some ideas I was able to receive a patent on. Of course, some of my favorites are the things you read in Crazy Beach Disc One and the stuff you are reading now. I hope you're having as much fun reading about my misadventures as I am telling you about them.

Anyway, I was a little concerned I hadn't let my mom know I would be away for the evening. I hoped she figured I was staying at one of my friend's houses. Our little island was a cool place to grow up. There were no real worries back then about weirdos trying to snag a kid or some other modern malice creeping into our lives. You were assumed to be safe, of course, if you had any sense. Some didn't and paid the price.

The storm continued to rage for a few more hours and Mr. Robert started having us take turns at the top of the lighthouse to make sure the ocean wasn't going to threaten us too bad. I had third watch after my buddies and I have to tell you the view from Ol' Baldy during a bad storm is some awesome sight.

A couple of times I had to remind myself of Twilight Zone creator Rod Serling's quote: "There's nothing in the dark that isn't there when the light is on".

It appeared much of the island had disappeared beneath the sea with water lapping at the lighthouse base, almost like we had become just a tiny speck of mortar in the middle of the ocean. I looked back toward town, but the power was out, so it was pretty eerie. The might and majesty of the forces of nature when witnessed up close and personal help you realize how powerless mankind can become.

I saw incredible sights upon the water and sky. Though nearly pitch black save for Mr. Robert's flashlight, which we were told to use as little as possible to conserve battery life, I was still able to discern the wave action, the lighthouse's fight against the tide, and the constant howl of the wind as it carried debris to certain destruction. I even witnessed a poor old trawler, torn from its moorings by the storm, adrift not 100 yards from the lighthouse. It gave up the fight and sank beneath the waves just as Mr. Robert came to relieve me of my watchman chores.

So there, that is the tale, of how for a few hours, while not the formal "keeper of the light", I did serve in nearly the same capacity as the great lighthouse keepers of old. And while I didn't save the one ship I encountered during my watch, I imagined that if she had a crew, Mr. Robert's trusty flashlight and I would have made Ol' Baldy and the past "keepers of the light" proud.

Track 17-Young Girl-Gary Puckett and the Union Gap (3:12)

Speaking of making people proud, my 18.75-year-old self certainly made 11-year-old Lenny proud with that hitchhiking adventure I was telling you about earlier. I'll let you know what happened the night of the concert, but thought you might like to hear about how all those things came about, and how we ended up at the Mexican border.

B and I had known one other a couple of years when *Easy Rider* was released. The seminal film burned quite the indelible pathos into my heart and soul about adventure, thrill seeking, and living life on your own terms. B and I of course hit the Wave Theater on the boardwalk to check it out and came out forever changed. Well, me anyway.

For one, as I noted in Disc One, Peter Fonda's character, Wyatt, riding his motorcycle dubbed Captain America, sheds his watch very early in the film, signifying a rejection of contemporary society's need to always be tied to a timeframe or schedule. So, I've never worn a watch. Also, the film planted a seed concerning going cross country. B and I promised one another we would save our money and one day, when we graduated high school, go on such an adventure.

Well, we managed to keep that promise. We talked about it only a couple of times a year, but whenever the other was about to waste too much money we would bring it up. When we pulled a cool scam on some of the tourists we always tried to put a portion of the proceeds towards our, as yet sketchily detailed, future cross-country adventure.

The realization we were probably going to really do it came after I got my first car. You may remember my dad gave me the option of paying for the car or the insurance and I chose insurance. Well, after paying for my first six months insurance in one swipe, I put half of the rest (about $500) into the trip jar. B was working a lot in the summertime at various restaurants and he always put some in each week. When it was all said and done and we reached into the jar (hidden in the carport closet behind the pool table) we had a little over $3,400. We were rich!

Of course we rolled a lot of change to get to that point. Every year or two we would take an hour or so and spend it rolling up countless pennies, nickels, dimes, quarters, and placing half-dollars back in our pocket in exchange for currency. It was tedious work but we passed the time working on our still mostly empty itinerary.

Finally, after 11th grade, we started doing some serious (for us anyway) planning. We decided we wanted to visit New Orleans, just like Wyatt and Billy, take a paddle-wheel steamer, and head up the Mississippi some, then head west from Kansas City. That was as far as our planning went, besides looking at some maps. We figured we would just wing it in the Duster. Well, my notorious driving misadventures put an end to that portion of the dream, with the

Duster totaled well before graduation. I got another car, but for reasons neither of us remembers (to save money on gas?) we decided it would be best and far more fun to hitchhike.

My dad, my future college coach, and my American Legion baseball coach weren't too happy I decided to pass up a summer of American Legion baseball, but my mind was set. I still loved sports. I just loved adventure, girls, music, and beer more. So much more.

Back then hitching was way more common, and while still potentially dangerous, we figured with two guys we were less likely to encounter trouble on the road. In that detail, we guessed correctly. In fact, we encountered very little trouble at all, except after the concert in Matamoros and our time in Mexico came to end. One of our first rides back in the United States was an idiot who about killed us in a car accident. We were smart enough to only carry a minimal amount of drugs with us, just a bit of marijuana. We correctly figured we could score pretty easily anytime we needed to catch a buzz and honestly we didn't smoke that much anymore. We drank a lot of rum. We would start early with a pint, usually finishing it off by one or two. We would then buy a fifth of good ol' Ron Bacardi for an afternoon on the beach with our friends when we weren't working. For the nighttime festivities, a half-gallon to share with our friends for evening adventures. We were already pretty serious drunks.

The few people that knew of our plan thought we were crazy. Of course, we were! But you've seen a peek at where this craziness led and wait till you hear the rest. Oh boy, are you going to love it.

"Are you two still serious?" Lexi said one night as the four of us played pool at the Rec Hall during the summer after 10th grade during Darlene's stay at Lexi's.

"Yep," I said as I broke on our second game of the night with me and Darlene as teammates.

"You guys should eat the state animal every place you go to," Hal declared as he missed an easy straight-in shot.

"Eww!" Lexi shouted. "Some of those hillbilly states they will be going through have a possum or some other nasty ass creature they worship. I worry about this crowd sometimes."

We all laughed as did the couple playing on the next table and a few of our friends hanging close to us.

"I'm not worried about B and Lenny," Darlene said. "It's the poor people they run into I'm concerned for."

Everyone laughed even harder.

"Yep," I said. "They are in for a time!"

Of course, that's the line Gene Hackman, as Buck Barrow says to his brother Clyde (Warren Beatty) in the epic 1968 Robert Penn masterpiece *Bonnie and Clyde*. Buck, just sprung from the Big House, and his wife Blanche (Estelle Parsons won the Oscar for Best

Supporting Actress for the role, you may know her better as Roseanne's mom on the show of the same name) help form the foundation for the Barrow Gang. You know the rest of that story; it doesn't end well for the Barrow brothers or their women. Hopefully our "time" would be almost as adventurous, but hopefully no one would get hurt, or go to jail, or get their eye shot out like poor Blanche, who wasn't much of a gangster

Two summers later, we set off the week after graduation. We didn't want to miss all the cool graduation beach house parties and we didn't. The tradition back then was different school clubs, mostly those run by the girls, would rent a house(s) at Knotty Beach sometime during summer with the week after graduation being the high water mark. Several houses were rented by various groups and there were parties most every night. After getting our fill, and there were some wild nights indeed (more possible future short stories). We decided to head out on Monday.

We packed as light as we could with just clothes, a small tent, a flashlight, a first aid kit, money, and our ID's. As luck would have it, one of our buddies was going to Atlanta for college. He was heading that way early getting a head start to live with his aunt and uncle. He wanted to try and land a summer job, so we tagged along.

We said our goodbyes to our crowd at the Rec Hall around 11 in the morning.

"Lenny," Dutch called me over. "You boys have fun and we'll see you in a few months."

Dutch pressed some money into my hand. It was a bunch of 20s.

"Dutch, we're good, really," I said. "We both been saving up for years."

"I know, I know," he said as slapped me on the shoulder. "I've had to hear about this trip since you were a little kid, but a bit more never hurts."

"Oh," I said. "I'm sorry about the window."

I had got tossed through one of the big plate glass windows on each side of the front entrance the week before during an infamous street brawl with some tourists we had whipped at pool. The window was still boarded up.

"Not a problem," he said. "Insurance, now get outta here."

"Let's roll," I said tapping B on the shoulder as he collected hugs from some of our gal pals that had come to see us off.

We crammed into Scotty's brown Gremlin, which was loaded down with his stuff for college. B sat up front as he needed way more legroom than I did.

"See you late August," I yelled as we pulled away from the old Rec Hall.

And just like that we were off on our next Crazy Beach road trip adventure. We got to I-95 in about an hour and a half and shortly thereafter rolled south past the famous "South of the Border" amusement park that welcomes southbound folks to the Palmetto State.

The park is well known to I-95 travelers due to the large number of billboards it utilizes to advertise. With corny, funny sayings such as "You Never Saw Sausage a Place" with a giant wiener and the park's stereotype mascot Pedro urging you to visit. Another great billboard has Pedro pointing to some rotating sheep saying "Your Sheep Are All Counted at South of the Border". Each billboard also tantalizes kids and antagonizes parents with a countdown of how many miles till you reach the park. Parents have been sickened since Pedro's inception in 1949 with cries of "how much longer till we get to South of the Border?"

We, of course, made it our first stop. We grabbed some ice cream and flirted with some New York girls who followed us over to the fireworks store (fireworks were illegal in our state). The four Yankee chicks had a good time telling Scotty how funny he talked.

"Well, y'all sound funny to us," he said laughing.

"Except you blondie," Yankee chick number one said. "Where are you from?"

"Same place as these guys," I said.

"You don't really have much of an accent," she said.

I just shrugged my shoulders and paid for some M-80s and cherry bombs.

"Want to play a game of putt-putt?" New Yorker number two asked.

Well, take a guess what happened next? Do you think you got it? O.K. no cheating.

"Sure," B said.

"Man, we probably should get back on the road," Scotty said. "I told my aunt we would be there by nine."

"So we'll just call and tell her we'll be a little late," I countered.

"Lenny, I don't know," Scotty said. "Every time I listen to you I get into big trouble. You know, like last summer when we had to wash police cars for a week"

"I know," I said, grabbing him by the shoulder. "That's because little trouble is no fun, besides you love every minute of it."

We never made it to his aunt and uncle's. Well, I guess Scotty did, eventually.

During the putt-putt game, it became apparent that there were some mutual attractions going on with the tallest and one of the cutest of the Yankee girls gravitating to the ponytailed 6'2" B. The quiet one, if there is such a thing among teen New York girls and Scotty seemed to hit it off. That left me double duty to try and keep the other two girls "entertained" so my buddies could have a shot of lov'n they both desperately wanted and likely, needed. I didn't mind, it was fun. I made a game of the proceedings.

We had a blast playing putt-putt with tons of fun goof-ups, balls clanking off the windmill, bouncing over to the wrong hole, even Scotty somehow losing his ball. He had to pay to get another and we charged him an extra penalty stroke for being such a dumbass. How do you lose your ball at putt-putt? We wrapped up the game with B and I tied for first, Scotty a distant last, and the girls bunched together in third through sixth. I don't remember their exact order of finish. We then started walking toward one of the restaurants.

"When are you girls leaving?" Scotty asked. "Where are your folks?"

"Tomorrow," number two, the tall one said. "This is our halfway point. We're heading to Florida to spend the summer with our grandma."

"Oh, wow," I said. "That sounds like fun. Are you all sisters?"

"Us two," number two said pointing at the quiet one sitting next to Scotty at the big circular table we snagged in the middle of the kitschy eatery. "I just graduated, she's a year behind. They (pointing at the other two who were seated one on each side of me) are our cousins, our three moms are sisters. This is our first big, road-trip adventure without the parental units."

After a few more minutes of conversation and revelations from both sides, I laid out a bit of a game plan in my head. Turns out, they had a room for the four of them. After our meal, everyone headed to the restrooms.

"OK, here's the deal guys," I said. "Looks like you two are in with the Amazon and shy girl. I'll go and get us a room as close to theirs as I can. I saw the room key earlier (back in those days of old metal keys, you often got a key fob with the room number on it). Ok?"

They both nodded. The girls, of course, had been doing their own plotting as well.

"You guys want to go for a swim?" Cousin number one asked grabbing my arm.

"It'll be fun," cousin number two said looping her arm around mine on the other side.

Damn, girls sure are smart. I thought I was slick, but as usual, the ladies are always way ahead of us fellas.

"That sounds great," I said. "I'll go snag us a room."

"Try to get one near us," tall girl, the obvious leader of this female wolf pack said playfully yanking on B's ponytail. "We're in 119."

I did as requested and planned (by both sides). I was able to snag 117 right next door to the girls' room which was on the first floor far corner away from the office which was great, not so many neighbors to piss off and far away from management and those that would thwart our good time. I got Scotty to pull the car around and everyone changed and headed for the pool.

Well now, I hadn't been around many Yankee girls since Woodstock and they are tough to beat. Fun, fun, fun! We played and goofed off in the pool. Some playful romance started to take place and it wasn't too long before it was obvious everyone wanted to head back to the rooms. Now came the somewhat tricky part. How to split this up. I had an idea how it could work, but I decided to let the Amazon drive the train. Well maybe I didn't "let her" she just did.

"Why don't you guys mix us some drinks and we'll be over after we shower up," she said kissing B on the lips.

Nods all around and we broke and went into our separate corners.

"Oh shit," Scotty said. "This is…this is…oh shit, I got to call my aunt, what should I tell her?"

"Just tell her, you were a little tired and decided to stop for the night and grab a bite," I said. "Be sure and sound nonchalant, just assure her everything is fine, and ask her to buzz your mom because I know you were supposed to call her when you got to your aunt's."

Some people can handle such situations, others can't. Scotty was definitely burdened with a checkmark in the "other" category.

"I don't know," he said. "Maybe, I should just go."

"Are you insane?" I asked. "You have a hot little New Yorker ready to have some serious fun with you and you're thinking of bailing because you're scared to call your aunt?"

"Man, Lenny," he continued. "I can't just pull stuff off like you do. It's second, hell maybe first nature to you."

Thankfully, B was in the shower while this conversation took place. He would have simply killed Scotty and that would have been it for messing with his chance to roll around with a girl almost as tall as B himself.

"OK, OK," I said. "How about if I call your aunt, she always liked me on her annual summer visits. I'll tell her you have laryngitis or some shit."

"Will you?" Scotty asked. "Will that work?"

"Sure," I offered. "Write down the number and hit the shower next."

Of course, I pulled off the subterfuge without a hitch. Scotty's old aunt was a sweet gal who loved playing bingo with my granny when they ran into one another on the boardwalk during Scotty's aunt's annual summer visits to our little island. She wasn't worried about Scotty too much. She just told me to feed him some soup and hot tea. I told her a bit about our hitchhiking plans begging us to reconsider and come spend some time in Atlanta.

"We might pop by for a bit," I said on the old payphone outside the fireworks shop. "I'll watch after Scotty, he'll be there tomorrow."

By the time I made it back to the room, B had us some Bacardi and cokes poured, and I filled him in on the latest developments.

"He better not screw this up," B said. "So what's the plan?"

I pretty much said we should just let his gal run the whole show for a bit and see if it was heading in the direction we wanted. We both felt sure it would, unless Scotty managed to sabotage the proceedings.

We clinked our glasses together offering a united "cheers" to what we hoped we would be an epic evening. I managed to get cleaned up, rolled us a couple of doobies, and checked on my baseball bets on the nightly local news sports broadcast all before the girls came over.

They didn't disappoint. The Amazon knocked hard on the door and B answered. The four of them entered looking like they were going to a swanky teen nightclub.

"Fire that up!" B's date for the evening demanded upon seeing the two rolled doobs on the nightstand.

Scotty complied as his girl sat down beside him on the bed. B's gal immediately and passionately kissed him guiding him to sit on the other queen bed. The festivities were underway. I worked on getting the girls some drinks whipped up.

"Here you go ladies," I said placing two drinks down in front of the cousins, Sasha and Emmy.

They were sitting on two worn wooden side chairs by the room's little press-wood table near the window. The old motel air conditioner's rugged attempts at cooling the room required an elevated decibel level for conversation. Both the cousins were cute with silky dark hair below their shoulders, bit of an Italian look and vibe overall. The joint made its way to our side of the room.

"Why don't you give us a double shotgun," Sasha, who was 17, said.

Well now, that was the first time I had heard that expression and hell, she may have even made it up. But, that was fine by me. I joyfully granted the request to the two cousins who placed their faces right next to my lips to receive the blast of smoke.

Both smiled and gave me a kiss on the cheek. It was interesting, very interesting, to steal a line from the old Hogan's Heroes television show. We all laughed and hung out a bit talking about music and movies, the summer, and our trips. Time flowed freely and quickly with lots of laughter. We smoked the other joint. We were all buzzing pretty good.

"I want to go ride the Ferris Wheel," Scotty's shy girl, Laney (from Elaine) said.

It was the first time I had heard her say anything besides her name. She had talked to Scotty some, but in quiet, measured tones I couldn't make out. Not that I was trying. Her line seemed to come clear out of the blue. B and I looked at one another suspiciously. Was this a good sign, a bad sign, a scripted cue, or none of the above?

"You guys go ahead," B's gal for the evening, Jema said. "I think me and B are going to head over to our room and watch some TV."

TV? Yeah, right.

Sasha rolled her eyes, but took my hand and motioned for Emmy to follow. The five of us headed out into the damp night air. For a very brief moment the place reminded me of our little island vacation destination. It was like our city center without an ocean, but with many of the same rides, games, food stops, and even a putt-putt.

We had some fun riding the Ferris Wheel with me wedged in the middle between the two cousins. I could see Scotty and Laney making out in the bucket ahead of us. I wasn't quite sure how to proceed with the two cousins, so I just enjoyed the ride with an arm draped over the shoulders of the girls. After a couple of revolutions, I turned to say something to Sasha and she kissed me pretty hard. I could feel little Emmy running her hand through the back of my hair. Oh boy…Was this going the way I thought it was going?

What if it was? Do Scotty and I share a room? That would be weird, kinda, I thought. Sasha kept kissing me and I participated, lightly at first, and then I became more engaged.

We broke for a moment and I turned to give Emmy some attention. She was other-worldly pretty, delicate features, and soft, almost oval chestnut brown eyes with her eye make-up curved up and out situated to give off an Egyptian, Cleopatra-like vibe. I looked intently at her; she was really the prettiest of the four girls, by far. The rest were cute, but Emmy had an almost Natalie Wood-like appeal about her I've not encountered since. She seemed so innocent and oh…shit! Now I got it…so young! Just before I leaned in to kiss her something grabbed hold of me deep inside and said don't. Too late. She came more than halfway and kissed me very passionately and kept kissing me. Damn it was good; sweet, tender, not too hard, but fluid like a good kiss should be.

Just then the ride stopped and we broke our lip-lock. Scotty and Laney were being released from their chair by the carney. The ride lurched forward a few feet and he released us as well. We all played a pretty haphazard game of putt-putt and as we were leaving, Sasha glanced at her watch and speaking directly to Laney said:

"I think it would be cool if you two headed back to our room, B and Jem are probably ready to get out for a while."

Laney just smiled, took Scotty's hand and I swear, almost appeared to be skipping back to the girls' room.

"Lenny, will you make us another rum and coke?" Sasha asked.

Boy did they have a script or what? Of course, I didn't mind. We strolled back to my room and I made us all another round. The girls plopped down on the bed nearest the bathroom. I handed the girls their drinks and sat on the edge nearest the door, Sasha was closest to me. I leaned over to kiss her with a different agenda really.

"How old is Emmy?" I whispered in her ear with a kissing motion so as not to arouse Emmy's suspicions.

She pulled back slightly and mouthed the word 16. I wasn't buying it. Emmy was looking at the TV and I stared at her for a second. Sixteen my ass, I wasn't going to jail, I didn't care how pretty and different she was. Since I'd turned 18 that past fall, I'd been extra careful not to mess with any girls under 16.

I took a sip of my drink and leaned back in with more neck nuzzling and whispering.

"I don't think so," I whispered. "Maybe soon, but not yet."

Thankfully, Emmy got up to use the bathroom.

"Come on, tell me the truth," I said softly. "It's cool, you and I can still have fun. I just want to know for sure."

Sasha hesitated for just a moment.

"Ok," she said. "But this better not mess us up. I want me and you to have a lot of fun, but you can't ignore her. Just don't try and have full-on sex with her. She's almost 16."

"So 15?" I asked, a bit too loud.

"She'll be 16 in a few months, on Halloween," Sasha said.

Oh boy...no wonder I felt something so strong about her, we were both Scorpios with near identical birthdays, month and day-wise anyway. Yep, you guessed it, almost the same age difference as Melissa and I were, with the gender reversed.

She came back in the room and plopped down on our side of the bed, laying on her right side behind us...She rubbed my left bicep.

"You must play a lot sports," she said.

"Yea," I said sitting more upright and letting my legs hit the floor with Emmy inching closer and closer and wedging her head and shoulders between Sasha and I. "I surf a bunch and I'm going to play soccer and baseball when I go to college later this year."

Emmy kept rubbing my arm. Damn, she was fine. Have you ever seen Franco Zefferilli's film adaption of Romeo and Juliet? Fifteen-year-old Olivia Hussey plays Juliet. That is who Emmy looked like, exactly. Enough to be eerie, very eerie, and yep, you guessed it, Olivia Hussey was one of the biggest crushes I've ever had in my life. Darlene and I'd gone to see the film at the Wave. We held hands throughout. It was a great night. I snapped back from my quick trip down memory lane.

"How about I fix us all another drink?" I asked.

Emmy was already a little tipsy, so I was hoping another drink or two might send her to bed early, help prevent her from trying to go too far with me, and give me an easy out, because you know those two little devils I have on my shoulders seldom rest.

"That sounds good," Sasha said. "I'll help."

I made Emmy's a little strong. We watched TV and drank our drinks, with me sandwiched between the two girls. Sasha put her drink down and started nuzzling my neck while Emmy began rubbing her right hand along my left thigh. I instinctively reached down and held Emmy's hand and caressed her fingertips, plus it kept her from inching her hand up my leg. Sasha gently pulled my face towards her and we began making out.

Well now I do get myself in some predicaments, don't I? Was I having fun? Hell yes! Was I concerned? Hell yes! What was I going to do? Emmy was now kissing my left shoulder and upper arm. I held tight to her hand, but she did have two, so I knew the other was about to come into play. I felt her turn toward me, her left hand came across my chest and quickly sank to my belly button, oh boy…

I quickly broke my lip lock with Sasha and hurriedly excused myself to the bathroom. Damn, what a dilemma. I damn sure knew Sasha was ready, willing, and able. I damn sure wanted to do business with her as well. But crap, Emmy was so beautiful, and the second drink hadn't got hold of her yet. I wasn't sure I could trust myself to not take her too far, but I couldn't afford to piss her off, and cause a scene which might sink us all. She definitely struck me as the kind that would make a scene if she didn't get what she wanted and it was pretty obvious she wanted some Lenny.

I had never had a ménage a trois, not yet. Of course, almost every guy dreams of finding themselves in such a circumstance, but I figured it would be college time at least before I had to deal with this kinda stuff. I told myself I would just make-out with Emmy and if she wanted to fool around with me I wouldn't make a fuss, but I was hopeful I could focus on Sasha for the serious playtime.

I flushed the toilet and came back into the main room to the sight of two beautiful teenage girls nearly naked as the day they were born. There was only one problem, they were both passed out. Talk about a sigh of relief and a wave of disappointment at the same time.

I just stood there, and stood there, and stood there. How long? Who knows? I damn sure don't. Finally, I walked over and sat at Sasha's feet. Mission accomplished knocking Emmy out, but damn, I had also knocked out a sure thing, and boy, those don't come around every day. I debated what to do. Who suddenly showed up? Yep, you guessed it, the devils on both my shoulders appeared as sure as Hitler's nuts burn in hell.

"Uh, what ya waiting for dumbass?" devil number one on my right shoulder said. "Two for the taking."

I sure could use an angel on my shoulder, any shoulder for once, just once. No such luck, of course.

"Ok choirboy," devil number two on my left shoulder said. "I'll let you off easy. Cover up the one you want least and wake up the one you want most."

Well, they aren't called the devil for nothing. I would love to say I ignored them both and just crawled in between the girls and went to sleep, but Hemingway said the only thing that's important is to live an authentic life and believe you me, I have. So, I rationalized myself into an understanding with myself.

"Lenny," I said to myself. "You know you want Emmy the most and you know you could make what is likely her first time really great, but...she's not quite 16 yet and more than a little buzzed."

I stopped talking to myself and covered Emmy up. Yeah for Lenny.

"Pussy," devil number one said…and poof!

He disappeared. The Bible says resist the devil and he will flee from you. It doesn't say anything about the second devil though.

"Ok, ok, Mr. Chivalrous," devil number two continued. "Do you know what you are giving up? Look at her? You might not ever have a shot with a girl that fine and pure the rest of your life. And she looks just like Olivia Hussey, same age, and all. Plus, if you're number one, she'll never forget you."

I would be lying if I said I didn't consider his opinion. I thought about waking Emmy up. I probably considered it longer than I should have. That long pause I just took before writing this sentence was a bit of penance for my lingering consideration. But I finally did the right thing, for Emmy at least. I woke Sasha up and we got in the next bed.

"Idiot," devil number two said wrapping his cape around his face.

Poof! He was gone.

Track 18-I'm Your Captain-Grand Funk Railroad (10:13)

I awoke to find Mr. Robert already out and about. I nudged B and Hal to wake them up. We stumbled out into the early morning sun. The storm had passed, but the island was a mess. Downed trees were everywhere, along with ocean debris churned ashore by the waves, and sand piled in odd configurations here and there. Mr. Robert was beachcombing, looking along the waterline for anything interesting or of value the sea might have given up.

"Man, my mom is going to be pissed," Hal said. "I know I'm going to be grounded for a month, at least!"

I knew my mom would be concerned as well. B's mom wasn't as tight on keeping up with him. She had enough of a job trying to keep his sister Dylan from blowing up the world.

Mr. Robert walked back toward the lighthouse.

"You boys spread out and look for anything you think might be interesting," Mr. Robert said. "Look close now, take your time, might be something small."

Well, there was always stuff washing up after a storm. You see we live in a part of the world called the "Graveyard of the Atlantic". In one of many informal history lessons Mr. Robert gave us over the years, he had related that more than 5,000 ships sank along the coast of North Carolina dating back to 1526. Among the better-known shipwrecks was the ironclad USS Monitor, a participant in the famous **Battle of Hampton Roads** during the Civil War. The Monitor foundered and sank on December 31, 1862, off of **Cape Hatteras** while being towed back north.

The Graveyard extends along the whole of the North Carolina coast, northward past Chicamacomico, **Bodie Island,** and **Nags Head** to **Sandbridge Beach,** and southward in gently curving arcs to the points at **Cape Lookout** and **Cape Fear,** right where we were at the moment.

The first recorded shipwreck off the coast of North Carolina was in the early 16th century. This wreck was reported off the mouth of the Cape Fear River very near to where we were standing. The large numbers of explorers who came to the area in subsequent years had to travel through the rough waters to get to the coast of North Carolina. In June 1718, **Edward Teach,** better known as **Blackbeard** the pirate ran his flagship, the *Queen Anne's Revenge*e, aground near present-day Beaufort Inlet, NC. Thirty-two years later, in August 1750, at least three Spanish merchantmen ran aground off North Carolina during a hurricane. The *El Salvador* sank near Cape Lookout, the *Nuestra Señora de Soledad* floundered near present-day Core Banks, and the *Nuestra Señora de Guadalupe* crashed ashore near present-day **Ocracoke Island.**

During **World War II,** German **U-boats** would sit offshore and silhouette passing freighters and tankers against the lights on shore. Dozens of ships along the North Carolina coast were torpedoed by submarines in this fashion in what became known as **Torpedo Alley.**

A German U-boat actually bombarded one location on our little island during World War II, striking at the Ethyl-Dow Plant that was seaside just north of where the museum is today. The most recent ship lost was on October 29, 2012 (my birthday you may remember). The *Bounty* sank off Cape Hatteras when Hurricane Sandy passed through. Two people died as a result.

So there's a lot of history along our coast and we were trying to discover some. Of course, we dreamed of finding treasure. Doesn't everybody? We had a better shot than most, but despite several hours of searching over two days, we had little to show for our endeavors.

"There's our ride," Hal yelled at the approach of our rescue ship.

"Sorry to be so late fellas," the captain yelled. "No way could I make it back till now. Town is flooded too."

Mr. Robert and the captain seemed to be in an intense discussion the whole way back. I'm not sure the content and I dared not approach. We were busy drinking some water the captain had brought for us along with some sandwiches.

All of us made it back safely, and yes, Hal did get grounded for a month. This was later reduced to two weeks for good behavior and for painting the garage and fence. Of course, B and I helped with the painting as did David.

"What was it like over there during the storm?" David asked for the 13th time as we were finishing up the day-long paint job.

Hal shrugged his shoulders, B paid him no attention.

"Man it was just some weather," I said. "It passed."

"Yea David, but I had to take a dump outside during that mini-hurricane," Hal said. "I hope the next group of dummies looking for treasure finds my turds and takes'em home thinking they've found something great. So there's that."

Track 19-Your Love Keeps Lifting Me Higher-Jackie Wilson (2:59)

I decided to turn right and go to the party.

"I was hoping you'd pick the party," Darlene said. "You'll get to meet some of my new friends. It's a birthday thing for one of my girlfriends, but her parents will be there."

Well damn, I was hoping for some unsupervised time with Darlene. I was starting to wish I had picked the movies. The storm grew more intense. Darlene kept giving me directions until I was thoroughly lost, but she seemed sure of the location.

We ended up in a neat little old neighborhood near Wallace Wade Stadium. There were tons of old oaks and other trees lining the roadways and filling the yards. Plenty of Duke banners, flags, and university insignia on almost every home and/or driveway.

"Up there where all those cars are," Darlene said, pointing to the end of a cul-de-sac.

It had been raining more steadily for the last few minutes. Complete darkness had fallen. I pulled in behind a newish brown Mercury Marquis.

"Want to wait a minute till it lets up?" Darlene asked squeezing my leg and raising her eyebrows.

"Ok," I said. "What do you want to do after and tomorrow?"

"Damn Lenny," she said giving me a provocative look. "I don't want to talk about after, forever, or even tomorrow for that matter."

That was all it took. The rain came down in torrents as we rocketed into a make-out session that escalated to DefCon Four faster than a dragster burns up an asphalt track. The windows almost instantly glazed over with our steam. It was so intense, it's hard for me to describe. It was as if all of our years together, the stuff we had been through together, and the bond linking our souls just all exploded at once. Talk about power and glory, fireworks, and noise! Well, I hope you get the picture.

We hadn't been alone together 15 minutes and we were already tearing at one another like ravenous wolves that hadn't eaten in weeks. We rocked the preliminaries really hard. We did this and that, and some of this and a lot of that, pretty much everything I could think of and remember I had read *Everything You Want to Know About Sex* (**but were afraid to ask*) several years earlier. I remembered my lessons well. I made sure Darlene got all the attention she deserved. And Darlene, yep you guessed it, she gave as good as she got, and she loved giving. She always loved giving.

The big moment was upon us; she looked at me and laughed her tantalizing, mischievous, naughty girl laugh that echoes throughout my being even unto this day.

"You better have..?" she quizzed.

I nodded vigorously in the affirmative. I reached into the glove box. All the dreaming of this somewhat forbidden moment, the hoping, all the almost, all the times we were on the verge only to have some stupid or tragic thing keep us from rounding third and heading for home seemed to float away in an instant as I tore into the condom package. Trouble was, like most other dumbasses in my circumstance, I had never bothered trying to put a condom on. Usually, I can figure most things out pretty quickly. Well, the one time in my life when it mattered most, I couldn't. I fumbled with it for a minute, maybe two to no avail. Finally, as always, Darlene took charge. She pushed at my chest.

"Sit up," she said.

She reached into the glovebox and ripped open another condom package. She glided it on in one silky motion and straddled me right there in the center of the front seat of the Duster in the middle of a nondescript cul-de-sac far from our little island.

"Me and Lexi practiced on fruit and vegetables," she laughed.

I had always imagined it would take place on our little island, in one of our beds, a motel, on the beach, a tent…but like many things we dream of, the reality is often quite different. But this one time the dream got surpassed, check that, the dream got lapped by the reality.

PRAISE ELVIS!

I don't know about you or how your first time went, but holy crap, mine was mind-blowing. Darlene's hair was flying everywhere, the car rocking, and my eight-track blasting Led Zeppelin IV. Zep's "Battle of Evermore" reached crescendo after crescendo as we did as well.

"Lenny," I thought to myself. "Isn't it super cool that as this momentous life-shaking event is happening the one song that gave Darlene her nickname (The Queen of Light) is playing and there is utter darkness and rain all around?"

Of all people, Dylan (the only person that didn't know she was from Crazy Beach was her) had given Darlene the nickname almost four years prior at a birthday party the fall after Darlene had moved to the beach. You may remember Dalton at his big birthday bash in Disc One calling her by the nickname. Well, she got it during a different party all right. It was Dylan and B's younger brother Max's 11th birthday and my mom was throwing him a party at our house. That was just the kinda mom my mom was, which I take you've gathered by now. She always made sure all my friends had great holidays and special days to celebrate if their parents didn't or were unable.

Trouble was, little 11-year old Max wasn't feeling super good and was pretty bummed out a girl he had a crush on from school didn't accept his invite to the party. The rest of us were gathered around our table getting ready to sing him "Happy Birthday". Led Zeppelin IV was playing on the stereo in my room. The third track, "The Battle of Evermore" began:

"Queen of Light took her bow
And then she turned to go,
The Prince of Peace embraced the gloom

And walked the night alone.

Oh, dance in the dark of night,

Sing to the morning light..."

Max was a bit glum and just sat in the chair with a kinda fake smile on his face. B was supposed to bring in the birthday boy's present, a new bike my folks had gotten him. B was going to bring it in when we started the Happy Birthday song.

"Uh, hang on a minute," B said from the front deck.

We all turned from the lit birthday cake, decorated with police cars and firetrucks. I know why you're laughing there-hush! We all gazed at the screen door. Well, can you guess what happened next...?

Yep, you got it. In walks Darlene hand-in-hand with Max's super cute, little 12-year old crush. Max bolted from his seat, a supernova smile exploded upon his face, the biggest I would ever see from him. We all began to sing. Darlene came over and grabbed my hand. Max's crush stood beaming right beside her and elbow-to-elbow with Max.

"Wow," 14-year old Dylan said from the head of the table. "She really is like the Queen of Light."

The nickname forever stuck.

B wheeled the bike in. Max just stared at his crush, I have never seen any kid give less of a shit about a new bike.

Track 20-For Those About to Rock-AC/DC (5:19)

We got to the city center park where a large crowd had already assembled. A band was playing, people were dancing, and dusk was falling. We got out of the car at the back of the park and our driver motioned for B to go with him and pointed at me to go toward the stage area. B turned and lifted his shoulders as in "what's going on?" I did the same back at him.

"Meet me here after the show," I yelled over the din of the Mexican warm-up band and crowd noise.

B just nodded. I felt an arm around my shoulder. It was Rigo.

"Come on Blondie," he said. "You missed the sound check, but all is well, I want you to meet the rest of the band and we'll go over the set list."

I followed Rigo to a large tan tent behind the stage, a temporary "Green Room" if you will. There were plenty of people milling about inside, at least a couple dozen. I was the only Caucasian in the bunch. I could feel the eyes of about half the crowd turn my way as Rigo led me to the food and beverage table at the back of the tent.

"Grab you some food and a beer Blondie," he said. "No tequila though. I'm going to get the guys together."

Rigo strolled over to a group of a half-dozen men and women at the far back right of the tent. They were all dressed in traditional Mexican performance clothing featuring shiny bedazzled pants and jackets. Two ladies had on tan linen dresses with a bright red fringe along the bottom with the hem about halfway between their ankles and knees. Rigo was wearing a brown suit and tie. Yep, you guessed it, I had on a black AC/DC shirt and black shorts. I did remember to put my black tennis shoes on to help me kick the bass pedal a bit harder.

At that point in my life, my hair was in one of its grand epic eras. I know you've seen the pictures of hair metal bands from the 1980s and the rockers from the 1970s, during that period mine was kinda a mix of those two, with a dash of Jim Morrison and a pinch of Roger Daltrey, but with more of a surfer look. Have you seen Stevie Nicks' *Bella Donna* album cover? Kinda that, except a bit shorter, much blonder. Darlene always thought I could be Morrison and Nick's love child. I wish. Anyway, you get the picture, I certainly stood out in most crowds. In this crowd, it was like I was a damn unicorn or something.

Rigo motioned me over. He introduced me to the band and the ladies, who served as dancers and back-up vocalists. The bass player was married to one of the dancers and one of the guitarists was brother to the other dancer. Oh, there couldn't possibly be any potential trouble in that situation now could there?

Rigo went through the set list and asked if we had any questions. Hell, I had never played with these people. Hell, I had never played any of their music. From what I had heard on the jukebox though it didn't appear to be rocket science drumming, more like drumming 101, so I figured I would be alright.

"Ok, we go on in 15," Rigo said in Spanish.

I nodded. I drank one more cold one real quick and grabbed another to take up on stage with me. A few moments later, the stage manager motioned for us from the front of the tent to head that way. Rigo led the way with me bringing up the rear. He stopped just outside the tent entrance and let the others pass.

"Ok Blondie," he said. "All good?"

I finished chugging that first beer and held up the second.

"Let's rock!" I exclaimed.

Rigo smiled and pushed me forward. I climbed the temporary steps up to the stage. The bass player and two guitarists were already playing some intro music, a bouncy Mexican folk tune. I slid onto the small black stool behind the drum kit. It was a decent older Yamaha set-up that appeared to have been played regularly. They had left me several sets of sticks, so I just grabbed a pair and jumped right in following the bass player to help create a nice rhythm. The bass man smiled pretty big after a few moments as he figured out I wasn't going to embarrass them and kinda knew what I was doing.

Rigo stayed off stage. I glanced over and he gave me the thumbs up. He held up five fingers and began counting down slowly. With his other hand, he kept raising it higher and higher as he counted down, which I took as he wanted me to play a bit louder and faster as he entered. The bass man fell in right with me and we rocked a good intro for Rigo's first appearance.

When he hit the stage the crowd went nuts, almost to the point of drowning out the lead guitarist. The rhythm guitarist stepped closer to me as did the bass man to make sure we could all hear one another and keep a smooth, Latin-flavored Santana meets salsa-like beat.

Rigo raised both of his hands to the appreciative crowd and he clapped back at them. He once again used the five finger countdown to give me the signal to launch into the first number on the set list, a fast-paced sing-along tune that was Rigo's biggest hit thus far. I nailed it.

We rocked through that tune and two other Rigo originals from his first album. On the last of those, the dancers took center stage and put on quite a show, spinning wildly on each side of Rigo, their dresses flying high, exposing very lovely legs, almost showing it all, but not quite.

The crowd knew all these songs and sang along hardily. The dancers, Sofia and Camila, entertained the crowd during our fourth song, an instrumental. Rigo exited the stage, giving me the thumbs up as he did. The ladies glided across the stage and ended up back by my kit as the number was drawing to a close. As the song reached its climax, the ladies whirled like tops a few feet away and stopped on a dime side-by-side directly in front of me, their backs to the crowd, arms stretched skyward for maximum effect their wrists crossing at the apex. They both smiled at me. I nodded back as I struck the last cymbal blast. Sofia winked at me. I grinned. Oh boy…

The stage went dark for a second and I knew that was my cue to do a slow, little drum fill. Soft yellow and white lighting rose slowly, revealing the three guitarists standing center stage having added the traditional Mariachi Band Sombreros to their attire.

They began "México Lindo y Querido" ("Beautiful, Beloved Mexico"), a folk standard that the crowd sang with leads from Sofia and Camila. As the song was drawing to a close, I saw Rigo appear stage left. He had changed into a traditional matador's outfit complete with red cape. He smiled and bowed at me as if he was saying, "You like?" I nodded yes, yes. The girls exited stage right at the conclusion of the song as Rigo made his grand entrance to some pre-recorded standard bullfighters' encore instrumental.

The next song made much more sense now; we broke into a cover of Johnny Cash's 1963 hit "The Matador" as Rigo returned to the center stage area bathed in bright red lighting welcomed by thunderous applause. Rigo's appearance, the song, and performance lifted the crowd to another level. A projector flashed scenes from the old, circa 1938 Tyrone Power bullfighting epic *Blood and Sand* on a hastily assembled screen behind me. The crowd went insane!

We segued into another Mexican standard "El Rey" (The King), a sad tale of a lonely monarch. A few people in the front had tears in their eyes. Rigo was really a great performer and had the crowd flowing in whichever direction he wanted. I had to catch myself a few times just watching him. Thankfully, none of my parts required too much concentration.

Finally, a bit of a break as Rigo talked to the crowd some. I took the opportunity to quickly guzzle the other beer I had brought to the stage. Rigo invited two young ladies from the crowd up and serenaded them to some acoustic flamenco guitar work. While all this was going on, I could see Sofia and Camila stage right preparing to return. They had changed into more contemporary clothing with a pure Mexican flare, tan dress shorts with heels and white billowy tops with red ribbons tying their long, jet black hair into ponytails.

Rigo kept talking to the crowd and asked if they were ready to see Sofia and Camila again. Of course, the crowd went nuts. The bass player motioned for me to leave the stage with them. As I rose to exit I looked over at Sofia and Camila. Sofia blew me a kiss. Oh boy…

All the fellas left the stage and the guitarists hurried back to the tent for a wardrobe change. The ladies took the stage to some soft yellow and blue lighting and began dancing slowly to some pre-recorded music. They were mesmerizing.

"Blondie," Rigo said wrapping his arm around my shoulder. "Bien, bien! You hit the bathroom if you need or grab a drink. No tequila!"

He laughed, patted me on the head, and strolled back for another outfit change, lighting a joint along the way. I thought I probably should hit the head and grab a brew or two, but I couldn't take my eyes off the ladies. They were so professional, stylish, and alluring. I could definitely feel my temperature rise as the music got faster and faster and the dance more seductive and sensual. I finally had to go, so I ran, yep ran to the bathroom. I made a quick pit stop and hustled out snatching two beers from the large aluminum tub full of drinks without really checking to see what I was snagging. When I got near the stage, I realized I had taken a couple of bottles. Damn, I hoped I could find something to open them with. I quickly made it back up to the stage just as Sofia and Camila were exiting. Camila smiled as she rushed past, Sofia paused, perspiring, and breathing heavily. She stopped right in front of me, grabbed a handful of the back of my hair and gave me a kiss on the cheek. Oh boy…

I slid back onto the stool just as the rest of the band was re-entering the stage form the other side. I looked around for something to open my beer with, nothing. I looked over at one of the stagehands while holding up my beer, which was a traditional Mexican brand, SOL, pointing to the top using an opening motion. He quickly looked around and ran out on stage and pointed down. There attached to the side of the snare was a damn bottle opener. Praise Elvis! That family member Rigo fired wasn't all bad after all. I took a big first gulp of what, to this day, is my favorite beer. Damn it's so delicious! Think I'll take a break from telling you this part of the story and go have one. I'm going to a concert too, Chris Robinson (ex-Black Crowes) Brotherhood, back with you in a bit.

Track 21-On the Road Again-Willie Nelson (2:34)

"Sasha, Emmy," Jema yelled knocking on our door. "Time to go."

We managed to collect ourselves and as I opened the door, the whole crowd rolled in. Sasha and Emmy were in the bathroom. There goes that bit I said in in Disc One about girls always hitting the head together again. Everyone was smiling pretty big and B motioned for me to step outside with him and Scotty.

"Uh," B started. "The girls want us to go to Destin with them."

"Do what?" I queried. "Where the hell is Destin? Isn't that a baby ointment or something?"

"I got to get on the road man," Scotty said. "You guys coming with me on to Atlanta or what?"

"Hold on, hold on," I said glancing back and forth at the two. "What the hell is up?"

"Man, I gotta go," Scotty said. "Laney knows that and is cool, but Jema wants you and B to go with them to their grandma's."

"Holy shit," I said, looking at B. "Damn boy, that stuff cripple you that bad?"

"Why not?" he asked. "Destin is in way western Florida on the panhandle. Jema showed me on a map. We won't be that far off our plan. We can stay a few days and roll on west to New Orleans after. We're going mostly that way anyway."

Well now, I was as shocked as you are now. Yep, you thought correctly, that was the most B talked about something at one time that I could remember. I guess for you it's the most he has talked ever. I was just trying to digest it all. Ok, ok it did sound intriguing, instead of going directly southwest with Scotty to Atlanta we would go mostly south through Charleston, Savannah, and then westward towards Pensacola and Mobile. Destin is just east of Pensacola. Of course, I didn't know that back then.

"Ok, ok," I said. "Let me check the map."

I should've picked up on something like this earlier as B had been holding our map the entire time. Scotty's gal Laney came out and the two of them walked over to Scotty's car.

"Ok bro," I said. "If that's what you want, that's what we will do."

I handed him back the map.

"You mind grabbing our stuff from Scotty's car?" I asked. "Let me go in here and take the temperature of the room."

I strolled back into the room. The three girls still inside were chatting up a storm. They stopped when I came in and all looked at me as if waiting for an answer.

"Sure," I said. "Why the hell not!"

Sasha and Emmy ran over to me and gave me a big hug and a kiss on the cheek.

"Ok ladies, let's go make some space," Jema said.

The girls excitedly hurried out of the room. I followed behind to say good-bye to Scotty. He and Laney were having a nice lip-lock session by his car, so I just went back inside and got mine and B's stuff together. By the time I got back outside, Scotty was walking past me to grab his things.

"Lenny," he began. "Thanks man, this has been unreal. You're probably the craziest mofo I'll ever meet, but damn, you sure know how to have fun. So tell me, did you sleep with both those girls?"

"Gentleman never tells," I laughed. "But since I'm no gentleman, just Sasha. Emmy's too young, she passed out anyway."

He slapped me on the shoulder.

"I'll probably see you when I come home for Christmas," he said. "I hope our paths cross again real soon."

They never did.

Track 22-Walk on the Wild Side-Lou Reed (4:15)

The rain was relentless. So was Darlene. I've played a ton of sports in my life, but I think the most I ever perspired was in the Duster the evening we lost our virginity. We had the most fun, like F. Scott Fitzgerald wrote: "I don't want my innocence to return, I just want the joy of losing it again." Man would I like to relive that day, especially our time in the Duster, and later that night at her house, and the next morning, and the next afternoon before we left to visit relatives. Well, you get the idea, once we broke the seal it was whenever, wherever. We were often insatiable in our desire for one another and made some risky choices, but they always paid off. Praise Elvis!

Just like the morning after Dalton's beach party birthday bash in Disc One, we were brought back to the rest of the world by the sound of car and truck engines firing up. Thankfully, the Duster was so steamed up no one could tell there was a small riot going on inside. Also, quite thankfully none of Darlene's friends had ever seen my car, so there was no way anyone could predict or guess she was inside. The rain was still rocking pretty hard. Darlene was laughing between takes.

That was another thing I always found super cool about our relationship, we would burst out laughing during some otherwise serious stuff; weddings, funerals, doing the "happy dance". Of course, we were never too loud at the two formers, but really loud during the latter. We were laughing pretty hard while we were trying to shift positions when we heard a knock on the window.

"Oh shit," Darlene said.

The windows were so fogged up we couldn't make out who was outside. But, thankfully they couldn't make out who was inside.

"Don't dare roll down your window," she whispered.

I acted like I was going to so she joke slapped at my shoulder. Then she started laughing again.

"They can hear you," I laughed with her. "I got to do something."

I've always been pretty quick on my feet in sticky situations. A skill usually enabling me to escape without a scratch or at worst, a scratch with a cool scar, but not all the time. This one was going to be tricky. I didn't have a lot of wiggle room as Darlene managed to wiggle away from me enough so I could slide back over under the steering wheel. I started to crack the driver's side window ever so slightly, rolling it down just an inch.

"Hello," an adult female voice said from underneath an umbrella.

"Hi," I managed. "My car messed up because of the rain. I think it's alright now."

I fired up the engine. Boomboomboom, the Duster rumbled.

"Thank you for checking," I said.

Darlene busted out laughing again. I gave her the "shh" sign as I waited for the defroster to clear the windows enough to be able to navigate around the circle. I had the wipers going full speed. Darlene turned Zep down. I had lost track of how many times the album had played through on the Duster's built-in eight-track player. I couldn't see crap behind me, no rear defrost. The front window was about half defrosted. I turned the lights on. I could make out that there were no cars in front of me. The feminine figure with her bright green umbrella made her way back to the house, peeking back a couple of times to try and get a glimpse of who was inside the car.

Oh boy…It was almost 11 o'clock!

"We better go on the double-quick," Darlene said, using some of her dad's military lingo, meaning twice as fast as the normal marching pace.

Finally, the window cleared enough for me to safely move forward. Darlene put in a new eight-track, "Wings at the Speed of Sound". There were no other vehicles in the cul-de-sac.

"Oh shit," Darlene said. "Desiree is going to be pissed I missed her party. I told a bunch of folks we were probably coming. They were all excited to meet you. Damn, what if she called my house looking for me?"

Well, maybe all we would ever have is the one car date. Darlene was working furiously to get all of her clothes back in their original and upright positions. Once again, I came up with a plan.

"We'll just say we went to the movies instead," I said.

"Ok, ok," she said. "Which one?"

Oh crap, I drew a blank. She busted out laughing again.

"I can't find my damn panties," she said, scrambling hard to search for them bumbling over the seat into the back.

I told you the Duster had a black interior right? Black mats and carpet too. Yep, you guessed it, Darlene's tiny panties were black, to match her black leather mini skirt which was also giving her fits.

"I can't get the damn zipper to work," she yelled from the middle of the back seat. "Where the hell could my panties have gone to? We didn't open the door."

I was having a hard time finding our way back and Darlene wasn't much help as she had several wardrobe malfunctions going on at once. The clock kept ticking closer to her 11:30 curfew. We knew everyone would likely be waiting for us by the big old oak table.

Despite an epic backseat search, and we weren't ever even in the backseat, I don't think, not this time anyway, Darlene returned to the front empty handed or should I say "commando". She plunged back over the front seat like she was diving into a fox hole all her business on full display. It was the first of about a half-dozen times I almost wrecked us.

"Pull over in that parking lot," she demanded. "We're not far from the house. I got to get better situated."

I pulled over into a grocery store lot. Everything was closed. It was just a few minutes till the witching hour, not really, just our witching hour. Still, we were going to be late, just how late? We hoped only a few, maybe five or 10 minutes. That hope was about to be dealt a serious blow.

The rain had stopped so Darlene opened the passenger side door and got out, dropping to her knees to look under the front seat better. Her skirt was still askew and mostly unzipped. Her strappy sandals were all helter-skelter and her blouse was buttoned up wrong. I had never seen Darlene this discombobulated. She was a mess. Damn was I going to be in trouble! Damn was she going to be in trouble! Damn, I might be dead. I wondered who would kill me quickest, my dad or Mr. Winter? I thought briefly and oh so wrongly, "this can't get much worse".

"Whooooop" a short burst of a siren sounded from the rear. A combo of blue and red lights flashed a couple times. Wish I had a dollar for each time I've experienced that, we could all go party for a weekend.

The cops, you've got to be kidding me, right? Like I said earlier, the timing thing with Darlene man, we got dealt some bad hands a few times.

"Miss, you ok?" a Durham cop, right hand on his holster, sternly asked from just behind my left rear wheel.

"Yes officer," she responded. "I'm fine. I'm ok."

Darlene was standing by the open passenger door now. I was watching the copper in my side view mirror. I rolled my window down a bit.

"Driver, exit the car slowly," he said. "Hands raised."

Oh boy...

I did as I was told. This was not my first time responding to that request and it damn sure wasn't the last.

"That's my boyfriend, sir," she said. "We're just looking for something I dropped."

That was the first time I ever heard Darlene call me her boyfriend to another person. How romantic, huh? Anybody top that one? To a cop? Nah, didn't think so.

"Let me see your license and registration young man," the officer demanded. "You haven't been drinking have you?"

"Since I was 11 sir," I smiled. "But not tonight."

Thankfully, he chuckled and made a gimme motion with his hand, asking for the paperwork again. I reached in and opened the glovebox, more condoms fell out. Torn wrappers were everywhere. I managed to find the needed items real quick and was still hopeful we wouldn't be too late. I handed the cop the papers. I didn't notice but a tiny piece of an opened condom wrapper was between my license and registration. He glanced at me, then Darlene, and shaking his head gently lifted the piece of wrapper from the registration card and shaking it between his thumb and index finger let it fall to the ground. He looked me up and down pretty good shining the light in my eyes briefly, then reviewed my license and registration.

"Long way from home," he said. "Me and the wife vacationed down there last couple years, real nice."

"Yes sir," I replied. "My folks are visiting her folks, just up the street. This is our first real car date, although we've known each other forever."

"I see," the officer said lowering his light and looking me over again. "Those look a bit small for you Son."

He pointed his light at my baggies. Yep, you guessed it. Darlene's tiny black panties were sticking out of my black board shorts. I just looked at the sky.

"Miss," he continued, shining the light back and forth rapidly between me and Darlene. "Your boyfriend here, he might be one of those transvestite fellas, likes to wear girls' clothes and such."

Just great, why is it every copper I get is a comedian? Well, I'm 82 shades of red, brighter than the officer's flashlight. Darlene just lowered her head onto the top of the passenger side door.

"You kids get on home," he continued. "Good luck explaining this to your folks. But hey, look on the bright side; if you two work out, you won't have to buy as many clothes as most couples do. Y'all have a good evening."

He handed me back my license and registration and headed back to his squad car. Darlene finally got her zipper to work and the skirt about back to its original position. She re-buttoned her blouse as she sat back down in the front seat. She took her sandals off. She looked at me as I handed her the ripped black panties. She handed them back.

"Souvenir, besides that, how does my face look?" She asked as I stuffed the remnants of her panties under my seat.

"You're just as beautiful as always," I said. "But you may want to take a look in the mirror."

The rain began coming down in torrents, again. Darlene twisted the rearview mirror her way as I headed out of the parking lot.

"Oh damn," she said, looking at her reflection. "We're fucked."

Track 23-Ave Maria-Artist-you'll find out during the track...

Rigo led the crowd through a few more sing-a-longs and we closed with a cover of ZZ Top's "La Grange". The crowd roared their approval and yelled long and strong enough Rigo took us back out for an encore. We hadn't really prepared any set list for this, so I was a bit concerned what songs he would choose. We had played all the ones I listened to on the jukebox at the cantina.

"Can you do Ave Maria, Blondie?" Rigo asked as we were the last ones back on the stage.

Hell, I was already drinking another SOL cerveza in the tent when the stage manager called us back. Did he mean the Franz Schubert composition from the 19th century? Uh, the answer would be hell no. My face must have said as much.

"The one from Mr. Disney," Rigo said, slapping me on the back. "You know, from the movie *Fantasia*."

"Oh," I said. "Yea, yea, I can handle that one."

"The girls will start acapella," he said. "When the light shines on me, you are the lead stroke. Got it."

"Sure," I assured him. "I got it."

Well, "Ave Maria" has about a gazillion different interpretations and I really wasn't quite sure how the *Fantasia* one was arranged. I remembered the tune from one of the Bing Crosby/Bob Hope "road pictures". *In Going My Way* Bing sings the song with some opera dude. My mother loved Bing and all his movies, so I had heard it plenty of times, but damn I couldn't remember the tune. Then it hit me where I knew it better from...the President's funeral.

My first cognizant memories, not just stuff I have been told or seen on TV, are of late November 1963 when President John F. Kennedy was assassinated. I had just turned five. I remember sitting at my mother's feet when the television newsbreak showed the President's accused assassin, Lee Harvey Oswald being shot by Jack Ruby as the accused was being moved from the Dallas jail.

The President's funeral was heart-wrenching and my mom just cried and cried. I remembered my mother telling me Luigi Vena sang a beautiful version at the funeral. We had watched it together and quite regularly over the years when the anniversary of the assassination was still big news.

"Rigo," I yelled, grabbing hold of the back of the black and white coat and tails he was now wearing. "I know the timing better of the one from the President's funeral."

Rigo stopped in his tracks. He turned slowly and put his right hand on my left shoulder. Showing the kind of man he was, he took the time to look me squarely in the eyes.

"A sad day indeed," he said. "I'm sorry for the world's loss. Yes, that is an excellent version. We will do that one."

Rigo then went to each of the band members situated around the darkened stage and informed them of the change.

The lights rose slowly on Sasha and Camila who beautifully carried the first verse. Rigo then stepped from the darkness, a lone white spotlight shone upon him. He was carrying a single white rose. He nailed an excellent rendition that had all the folks up front crying. I played along slowly, wistfully. I have played the drums since I was six. Our rendition of this song was my favorite time doing so. I was blessed to be a part of its performance.

Track 24-Old Days-Chicago (3:31)

So we rolled south, stopping in Charleston for lunch. I hope you've visited and if you haven't please put it near the top of your bucket list. It's probably one of the prettiest cities in the world, and I've seen a bunch of 'em. We had pizza down by the battery and strolled along the waterfront simply gawking at a ton of gorgeous homes pulsating with a real aura of southern charm and hospitality.

"I wish we could stay," Emmy said.

"Me too," Sasha echoed.

"We can't," Jema replied. "We promised Gran we would be there by tomorrow. If we stay here, that's a helluva lot of driving tomorrow. I say we make it to at least Savannah, since we all want to see it so much, stay there, then drive the rest tomorrow."

We loaded back up into their old panel station wagon, me in the back with Emmy and Sasha with the rest of the crowd up front with Jema driving. We heard lots of great music; Frampton's "Show Me the Way", Nazareth's "Love Hurts", and Thin Lizzy's "The Boys Are Back in Town".

"Man, that was a great show," I said. "We saw Boston, Aerosmith, and Thin Lizzy this spring. Boston was cool, but Thin Lizzy kicked all their asses!"

I was hoping to be able to tell y'all a lot more about the gazillions of concerts I have seen, but the flow of the story isn't allowing for as much as I had hoped. I also wanted to tell you about Woodstock 1994, the 25th anniversary one, but I don't think we're going to get to that either. Maybe in my trilogy's finale, "Crazy Beach-Disc III- Craziest Beach. Anyway...

"Look how beautiful," Emmy said as we crossed over the old Talmidge Bridge into Savannah. "It's as lovely as Charleston."

We pulled into a motel on the far eastern end of Bay Street. We all stumbled out of the wagon with Jema, me, and B heading towards the office.

"How many rooms should we get?" I asked, looking at B and Jema just outside the office door.

B shrugged his shoulders.

"Let's just get two to start," Jema said. "We'll let the chips fall where they may."

I wasn't sure that was the best idea, but I didn't want to tick her off, which in turn would tick B off, so I kept my mouth shut.

It started out ok, with me and B dumping our stuff in one room and the girls putting their crap in an adjoining room. We unlatched the lock between the two and flowed back and forth for about an hour, talking and having fun. I mixed us all a drink in some plastic cups we brought, much larger than the room cups. We decided to hit the pool before going downtown. Laney pulled the connecting door closed so they could get their suits on, but Sasha slipped by her, and into our room.

She grabbed me by the hand and took me into the bathroom. She took her clothes off slowly and stood there for a second holding her purple bikini. She was well put together. The night before was mostly a wrestle-fest between two drunks in the dark, but standing in front of me now, I saw how lucky I was. She wrapped her arms around my neck.

"Ok, you two," Jema said knocking on the door. "Pool time first!"

Too late.

We joined them at the pool a little later. We all lounged around drinking, splashing one another, and having a blast. We took turns attempting to do artful or funny jumps from the diving board. We rated each other's dives. B had the best cannonball, Jema was easily the most accomplished diver, and little Emmy hit a couple of nice backflips. I had the funniest dives, Sasha, and Emmy pushed me in more than once. Laney returned to the room a couple of times and made us more drinks. We stayed at the pool much longer than we expected. We finally got back to the rooms to hit the showers and prepare to go downtown.

"Laney hit our shower, Emmy use theirs," Jema commanded.

This gave Jema some mostly alone time with B in the girls' room. It also allowed Sasha and me a few minutes in mine and B's room. Sasha closed the passageway door. We made good use of the time and by the sounds coming from the other room B and Jema did as well.

Emmy came out of our bathroom wearing only a towel and carrying her white bikini. Sasha was under our covers and I was covered up to my shoulders. We were in the bed nearest the bathroom. Emmy paused at the foot of our bed. She slowly opened up her towel and quickly closed it.

Damn! Must run in the family.

She smiled a quirky little smile and after knocking loudly, opened the passageway door. Sasha and I scrambled into the shower. We had some more fun. Boy, do I like fun.

We eventually made it out onto Bay Street and all the cool places along the river. The thing I love about Bay Street is you can have alcohol in public, as long as it is in plastic cups. That should be the deal in every tourist town. It makes it so much more fun. We found a great restaurant and had a blast. We hit a city park facing the river on one side and Bay Street on the other as we made our way back. I fired up the one joint I had brought along.

We sat on a picnic table under a giant, stately old magnolia tree and burned the doob.

"Man, this stuff tastes great," Laney said.

The other girls echoed her sentiment.

"How do you get stuff like this?" Jema asked. "We almost always only get homegrown or damn skunk-weed back home."

"I been working it a long time," I laughed.

By this time, I had risen to Dutch's second in command and was now in charge of almost all financial matters for several of his businesses, including the Rec Hall and gambling. As you know from Disc One, Dutch was our little island's main purveyor of fine, ah hem, tobacco, ladies, gambling, and other assorted vices. He never involved me with the escort side of the business, but I pretty much acquired a doctorate level of education in dealing drugs and gambling in the eight years I worked with Dutch. While ours was only a small island, it was a pretty big business. I guess vice is in most places.

One of the reasons I chose to stay near home and accept a scholarship to play baseball at one of our local colleges was due to my depth of involvement in Dutch's illegal enterprises. I had great offers from some big-time schools from our part of the south, but due to the girls in my life, and my involvement in the business, I turned them down.

Dutch passed in 1989, but before he went to the great casino in the sky, I got a call from his daughter.

"Lenny, its Mirna," a familiar voice said. "Don't hang up, it's about Dutch. Daddy wants to see you. He hasn't much time left the doctors say. I know you and I've had our problems, but he won't stop asking for you. Please don't be mad. I heard you were in Virginia. I got your number from B."

"Ok," I said. "I'll be there quick as I can."

After driving through the night, I slept in my old bed. I opened the three windows to my daily childhood view, an awesome ocean panorama, the breeze was even better. I hadn't seen Dutch in almost 10 years. We had parted on good terms. I felt guilty for not calling him much over the years, after all, he was like a second father to me.

Dad was at work, Mom, as usual...yep, you guessed it, by the stove. She had fixed me a great lunch and I woofed it down.

"Please give Mirna our condolences," Mom said.

"I will," I said kissing her on the cheek.

I headed down the 12 steps off the small front deck. I looked around for a second. No pool table, long gone. Mom had some ferns hanging from hooks around the carport. They looked super healthy. I looked at the small side yard. The old persimmon tree, where Mr. Robert used to help gather the fruit with Mom each November had died the previous winter. Nothing along that side of the house anymore but a small strip of mostly dead grass.

I fired my black 1983 Camaro up. I was parked where the pool table used to be and no lie Chicago's "Old Days" came on the radio. I smiled. I thought of all the fun my friends and I had shooting pool in this spot. I thought of the night of Dalton's party when I used the fishing ruse in this very spot to explain to Darlene and Lexi our plans for the evening.

The old closet door, directly in front of me, after 22 years of wind and weather was in need of replacement. It was warped a bit and no longer closed very well. I stared at a couple of objects inside. I got out of the car to take a closer look.

"Well, I'll be damned," I said as I opened the door a bit more.

I reached down and retrieved an old trophy from a box on the floor. It's once shiny athlete had weathered a bunch, but was well known to me. It was our team trophy for the first year youth soccer was played in our county back in 1971. We had been sponsored by the local drugstore, the only one on our little island. We won the initial championship. I was the goalkeeper, B and Hal were defenders. David played midfield. We only allowed one goal all season and finished undefeated. Back then there were no participation trophies. Hell, there were very few individual trophies. Just a team trophy given to the champs, nothing else. The trophy sat for years and years on the lunch counter at the drugstore. A real source of pride for our team and our little island beating all the mainland teams. Nothing like being the champs!

When the drugstore closed, the owner, who remembered I had been Captain of our team offered me the trophy. I proudly displayed it front and center for many years any place I called home, but it's funny in life, some things so precious to us at one point in our lives lose their luster eventually, both figuratively, and literally. I couldn't remember when this one got relegated to a box in a cramped old carport closet, but there it was. I decided to take it with me. The trophy returned to a place of honor in my home for many years and then somehow got lost in the shuffle of life once again. When my mom, dear sweet Mom, passed in 2012, I found the old trophy in a box of her things labeled "Lenny".

Mom had a box for Lil'sis as well and several for my cousins. Things that were special to her and to the person they were designated for, maybe just a photo, but precious nonetheless. Mom was thoughtful about such things. I wish you could have met her in more than story form. You would have had fun and most certainly a full belly.

How the trophy made it back to Mom, I can't remember. It was pretty beat up and I decided to take it apart. I reluctantly recycled the wood base and metal plate that read simply "Champions". I kept the trophy-topper. He lives on my desk now and has for the past many years. Thanks Mom.

I asked the ladies at the hospital help desk for Dutch's room number.

"Immediate family only, doctor's orders," said a kind, elderly volunteer who resembled Granny from the old television show "The Beverly Hillbillies".

"I'm his son," I boldly and confidently fibbed. "Room number please?"

No lie, Dutch's room number was 420. If it was present day I would have definitely taken a picture. The room held what was left of Dutch's family, his daughter Mirna, and her fourteen year-old son. All the rest of Dutch's family had passed long ago.

He looked pretty rugged, a shadow of his former self. His once jet black, slicked-back hair was mostly gone now with the remnants a dry, brittle mix of gray and white. His eyes lit up when he saw me.

"Lenny," he said, struggling to turn on his right side to face me. "You got here."

He extended his left hand. I reached down and shook it while pulling up a chair to his bedside. I nodded at Mirna and her son. They nodded back from the other side of the bed and Mirna mouthed the words "Thank you". I nodded again.

Dutch shifted painfully back towards his daughter and grandson.

"You two go get a sandwich or something," Dutch said. "Take $20 from my wallet if you haven't already."

Mirna rummaged through her dad's belongings and retrieved some cash.

"You want anything Lenny?" she asked.

I just shook my head no. I had no use for her sorry ass. I had caught her stealing from her father on multiple occasions back in the day and she was always jealous of our relationship. There was no doubt in either of our minds that her father cared more for me than her. She was a loser, a drug addict, and a thief.

Once we were alone, Dutch and I had a great heart-to-heart talk, reminiscing, discussing his beloved Cubbies, how they had come so close a few times earlier in the 80s. We talked about the business. He had long since turned over 80 percent of the business to an organized crime outfit on the mainland who had been running the day-to-day for several years now. Dutch basically just collected a check. In the ensuing years, the racketeers had whittled Dutch's share down to just 10 percent. He wanted to know if I wanted his 10 percent stake. I would have to deal with the mainland folks regularly if I chose to accept, but it was a bunch of money.

"I hate to ask," he said. "But otherwise they're just going to keep it all and as much as she doesn't deserve it, I need to make sure Mirna has some money, for the boy anyway. He's not too bright."

Oh boy...I didn't want any piece of any of that. Sure 10% of the business was a lot, if I told ya how much, you would poop yourself, and I'm pretty sure I would get a visit from the Revenuers. I wouldn't have to do much; collect, meet with them on occasion, get money to Mirna and the boy. I knew the mainland gang, the early 1980s version. They had started to horn-in on Dutch's business just as I was leaving our little island for other life adventures at the dawn of that decade. I had negotiated the first agreement between the two back in the old days.

"Thank you Dutch, that's very generous," I said. "Let me think on it."

"Think on it?" Dutch painfully chuckled. "Lenny boy, in the baseball game of life, I'm in the bottom of the ninth, hopelessly behind with two outs and two strikes. You better hope the pitcher upstairs is a really slow worker."

We talked about more business stuff that I can't really reveal or I would be taking the fifth before you finished reading this track. I got up to leave just as Mirna and the boy came back in the room.

"You know they tore the Rec Hall down this week," Dutch said as I was turning to go. "Guess me and her both heading for the out of town game in the sky the same week."

I didn't know they had torn the Rec Hall down. Talk about adding insult to injury. I turned back around and gave Dutch a big old hug, first time ever. A small tear fell down his cheek, mine too.

"One last thing Lenny boy," he said.

I was afraid he was going to press me for an answer right in front of Mirna and the boy. Then I would be tied to them for life. Damn, had my sentimental ass got me a life sentence of regular dealings with my least favorite person on the planet?

He glanced at his daughter and grandson, then at me again.

"Y'all know them two big ol 'plate glass windows the Rec Hall had on each side of the front door?" he asked.

We all nodded.

"Well five fellas been tossed through them windows over the last 21 years," he continued. "But ol'Lenny boy here is the only one got chunked through'em twice."

I smiled and Dutch laughed.

The last time I would hear him do so.

Track-25-All Right Now-Free (5:35)

We finished our joint and walked back to the motel. As we approached the parking lot Jema told Emmy and Laney to take the girls' room because she and B were going to hang out along the river for a bit. Jema turned to me and Sasha and winked.

Sasha smiled and nodded. What at first appeared to be a sweet deal for us went another direction pretty quickly. We weren't in our room five minutes when Emmy banged on the passageway door.

"Can we get a drink?" she yelled.

Jealous much? Sasha and I had just begun to get the late night festivities underway.

"Damn," she said. "She'll cause a scene if I don't let her in."

I plopped my head back on the pillow.

"Go ahead," I sighed.

The other two girls came busting in. Laney mixed them both a drink while Emmy plopped down on the foot of the bed where I was resting partially covered.

"You guys want one too?" she asked.

I shook my head no. Sasha came back over and sat down beside me. Laney sat in a chair by the TV. Emmy turned it on. She had cock-blocking 101 executed to perfection. Sasha rolled her eyes at me. The girls all began talking. I fell asleep.

I had some pretty powerful sex-fueled dreams that caused me to awaken early the next morning. I could see out of the corner of my eye Laney asleep on the bed to my left. I knew I was in bed with the other two, I figured Emmy just wanted to sleep next to me and was on my right because Sasha was under the covers doing pretty work that probably roused me from my dreams. I just laid back and enjoyed it. I let my head drift right and opened my eyes a bit.

Oh boy…

Yep, you guessed it…Sasha was fast asleep right next to me. That meant you know who was under the covers. No Emmy, please don't tell me that's you under there. I started to peek, afraid of what I was going to find, but just then I saw someone rise from the other side of the bed behind Laney and cross the foot of mine. I had to be seeing things or just dreaming because Emmy passed in front of me just wearing some bright pink panties on her way to the bathroom. I looked under the covers, it was Jema!

She stopped what she was doing, which she was ultra-skilled at, smiled, and gave me the shh motion pressing her right index finger to her lips. She returned to her work. Damn, I do find myself in some predicaments, don't I?

Emmy came out of the bathroom and walked topless between the two beds. She sleepy-eyed looked over at Sasha, then over at the other bed at Laney. She looked at the moving covers. I shrugged my shoulders. She leaned over, kissed me on the forehead, and whispered.

"When we get to Gran's you and I are doing big-time stuff," She began confidently. "Or I'm going to tell everybody everything."

Oh boy…

Track 26-Take it to the Limit-The Eagles (3:43)

Our last great summer of fun as a gang was that 10th grade summer before our junior year of high school got underway. I had picked Darlene up in Durham then hit the Eagles show in Greensboro. They rocked! Or country rocked, or however you view their music. We drove back to Durham and crashed out.

I slept on the couch, what little I slept. Darlene and I tried to hook up a couple times during the night, but we never got very far. Noises or fear of being heard kept us from going much farther than second base. I was restless on the couch. My mind was crazy with planning how to spend as much time with Darlene as possible. I wanted to have a perfect month. I was a bit tired the next morning.

"Oh, Lenny," Mr. Winter said. "Glad you're up. You mind giving me a hand with a few things in the basement."

He walked outside, not waiting for a response. I think after all these years Mr. Winter looked at me like a son. Darlene being an only child and Mr. Winter having no nephews or brothers, he kinda sorta adopted me and my dad as his masculine family. As you know from Disc One, he and Dad spent many hours together at the VFW, golf course, and attending my sporting events. Our families got together at least once a month for almost four years to share a meal and have a family game night. I think Mr. Winter was the best friend my dad ever had and I believe my dad was the best friend Mr. Winter ever had.

I followed him out and saw he was already descending the steps beneath the back deck leading to a fully finished basement serving as a workshop, storage space, and early version of a man cave.

"I want to take this old furniture out and chop it up," he said. "We'll use it mixed in with that firewood I bought. This fall we'll make a bonfire when you and your family come up for the Duke-UNC football game."

We hauled an old couch I had never seen before, two chairs, a bunch of pallets, and other assorted wooden junk out to a clearing 20 yards or so from the deck. It was a good little workout. Mr. Winter was a big strong guy and busted up a bunch of it with his bare hands and combat boots while I used an ax to splinter the thicker pieces.

"Here, I brought you some tea," Darlene yelled from the deck smiling.

She was always so pretty first thing in the morning. She had already dressed for our trip to the beach wearing some cut-off jean shorts and an Eagles t-shirt I had bought her at the show. I immediately headed her way. Mr. Winter strolled that way a moment later after breaking up another pallet.

"How much longer you think you'll be?" she asked.

I shrugged my shoulders.

"I'm ready to get to the beach and see Lexi," she continued. "We can stop along the way as much as you want."

She said the last part with her notorious naughty girl smile.

"If you hurry up," she teased, flipping her long curly blond hair in my face as she turned to go.

"Lenny," Mr. Winter said as he approached. "Let's sit for a minute."

Oh boy…

This couldn't be good. Was I going to get a sex talk, a warning, or something worse? Although I'm not sure what I could've thought of that would've been worse at that moment. I just wanted to get on the road with Darlene. I wanted to get back to our little island and all our friends, for things to be like they used to be before Darlene's mom got real sick. Of course in my heart of hearts, I knew that would never be.

We sat on opposite sides of the picnic table which was a few feet in front of the deck. The tea was ice cold and delicious. Mr. Winter leaned forward placing his forearms, which were almost Popeye-level substantial, on the table. I just knew I was going to get Mr. Winter's version of what my dad had said to me the day I got my license eight months earlier.

"Lenny," he began. "I wasn't going to let Darlene go to the beach for such a long amount of time this summer, maybe a week or two would be ok, but her mother wouldn't hear of it. It wasn't that I was against her being with you, your family, Lexi's family, or your friends. It was just, it was just…I don't think Anika has very much time left, not very much at all. Maybe only weeks, I'm not sure."

I just sat silently and nodded.

"I just want you to promise me one thing that if something happens," he continued. "You'll get my daughter up here right then."

"Yes sir," I said. "I promise."

"Now wait a minute Son," he said. "Do you know what you are promising?"

"Yes sir," I said.

I, of course, did not.

Yep, you folks are much smarter than 16.66-year-old Lenny and I'm sure have guessed what I was promising…sobriety…oh boy...

Mr. Winter proceeded to lay down the groundwork of my promise. That I would be ready, at a moment's notice to return Darlene to Durham, day or night, regardless of ballgame, work, fun time, or other. He stood and extended his hand. I fully understood, told you I'm a quick study.

"Yes sir," I said shaking his hand. "I promise."

It was the first time I felt like a man.

Track 27-Cocaine-Eric Clapton/JJ Cale (3:36)

We all hung out in the back of the tent for about a half hour after the show. It was a loud, boisterous party with the tent filling to capacity pretty quickly and dozens of other invitees hanging out on the outside edges.

"Muy bien Blondie," Rigo said slapping me on the shoulder once again. "You want a full-time job?"

Well now, that was a surprise. I had been playing drums almost my whole life, had been in tons of dreadful bands, a few decent ones, and on this night, for once, an excellent one. It was quite tempting, and I did consider it, for about three seconds.

"Thank you, Rigo," I said. "That would be a dream come true, but I'm chasing some other dreams right now, and one girl, so I gotta say no."

He popped us a top on a couple more Sols.

"A girl eh," Rigo commented. "Well looks like there's a girl right here chasing you."

He nodded over to the two back-up dancers. They were looking our way.

"Just stay for a day or two longer and think about it," he continued. "You can stay by the cantina and if you need more money you and your friend can work there some the next few days and play with the small band there tomorrow night."

He didn't wait for an answer, turning to talk with some other well-wishers who were obviously old friends. I spotted B by the tent entrance still doing security. I grabbed him a beer.

"Here you go Senor Policia," I laughed handing him the cold cerveza.

"Oh boy, I need that," he said grabbing it and taking a big old gulp. "You guys did a great show, but the crowd, talk about some rowdy folks."

B told me he had to manhandle a couple of drunk partiers, break up a fight between two senoritas, and had a drink tossed on him by an old drunk, all the while getting cussed out in Spanish for telling the old coot he couldn't have any more booze.

"You bout done?" I asked. "The after party is at the cantina."

"Yea," he said. "The dude in charge just told me to keep an eye on things for about 15 more minutes a while ago, so I think I'm good."

We hung around the tent for a few more free beers and had a couple of attempted conversations in very poor Spanish with some girls and ate some great Mexican food.

"Hola Blondie," Sofia said grabbing my hand.

B looked down at the gesture and rolled his eyes.

"Hola Sofia," I replied.

Sofia then spoke for about 30 seconds in lightning fast Spanish of which I picked up about four words. I could tell by her gestures and squeezing of my hand she wanted to hang out. Thankfully, sensing we couldn't speak much or understand a bunch of her language, Camila interrupted, and interpreted.

"She wants to know if you two are going back to the cantina and says, obviously, that you are very handsome and that she does not have a boyfriend," Camila said just as rapidly.

Oh boy…

I nodded yes at Sofia and then looked at Camila.

"Tell her I think she is very beautiful," I started. "And I don't have a boyfriend either and that yes, we are going back to the cantina."

Everyone laughed at the boyfriend bit. Timing, sweet timing…

The head of security then approached Rigo, whispered something in his ear, and hurriedly left the tent. Rigo sent one of his flunkies over to inform us a caravan for his people would be heading back to cantina in five minutes and to meet behind the tent.

We spent those five minutes listening to Sofia spout the most Spanish I would ever hear from one person. Camila would translate. I would mostly nod and drink. B mostly drank, catching up quickly to my level of buzz. We couldn't get a word in edgewise, in English or Spanish. Damn this girl was super cute, but crap I didn't want to hear her talk all night. I figured Camila would get as bored playing interpreter as her husband already was, constantly shaking his head. He had been standing faithfully by the whole time, occasionally looking at Sofia and grimacing. Sofia's brother kept a wary eye out a few feet away while he talked up some female admirers.

Our troupe of band and concert personnel began loading into Jeeps, station wagons, and a small bus. Sofia, still going a mile-a-minute got pulled away by Camila so they could get into a Ford Bronco (no not a white one, I forgot what color it was, but it wasn't white). Camila's final translation was: "She'll see you there and she wants to dance".

B and I started to head to the small bus when a big broad hand grabbed my shoulder. It was the head security guy. He was a powerfully built dude, like a weightlifter or boxer.

"Rigo says go there," he said in broken English pointing to a black stretch limo five or so vehicles back.

I just nodded and we headed that way.

"Come in, come inside Blondie," Rigo said sticking his head out of the far back window. "You too Blondie's friend."

B and I looked at one another. It was our first time riding in a limo that wasn't going to a funeral. We clamored inside. Loud salsa music was playing in the crowded vehicle. B and I got the last two available spots, matching jump seats on each side of a well-stocked bar right behind the plexiglass separating the party from the driver's compartment.

If I recall correctly there were about 13 of us in the car, not counting ever how many were up front. There were four people on each side (three ladies and one guy each), me and B, and two model-level attractive ladies in tiny skirts on each side of Rigo in the far back. Their Clevelands were in plain view for most of our trip back to the cantina. Brown Cleveland is beautiful, as are most Clevelands.

"Ah Blondie," Rigo said. "I'm glad I caught you. Now it is Tequila time!"

Two bottles of tequila began making their way around the vehicle. I also saw one of the guys pouring something onto a small mirror.

Oh boy…

I guessed pretty quick it was cocaine. I ascertained right away this guy was "the connection". I remembered seeing him in the tent before and after the show near some of my temporary bandmates. Each of the eight ladies in the vehicle took turns, with those seated on his side staying seated and him holding the mirror in front of their faces. The other five came and knelt before him like they were performing a ritual. Each smiled after doing their "line".

This was the first time I had ever seen cocaine in person. It had not made its way to our little island (that I knew of, I'm sure it was there) yet, but was beginning to explode all over the country in the burgeoning disco scene. Rigo did not partake. We were offered but declined. We drank our fair share of tequila. The music played. Rigo's two ladies kissed on him. Two of the girls on the left kissed on one another. Well, now it was a party.

My first cocaine cowboy continued dolling out his goodies. The ride became wilder and we just seemed to blend in. The former kissing girls came over and sat on mine and B's laps for a bit. B made out with his girl. Mine just played with my hair and said a bunch of crap in Spanish that I took as things she wanted to do to me. Mostly Mexican music was played, but some songs from the "Saturday Night Fever" soundtrack played as well.

B became instantly hooked. My almost life-long rocker friend quickly became a disco devil. It's still his favorite music to this day. I really hated disco. The next couple of years I would regularly decline his invite for a night of hitting the clubs.

"That's where the girls are," he would always say.

So I reluctantly would go with him. Of course, he was right, and of course, we almost always had a great time. And yes, that's where the girls were. That stretch-limo was where his disco addiction began in earnest, better than becoming a coke-head I guess, not by much, but anyway…

Our ride came to a smooth stop in front of the cantina. The ladies all adjusted themselves and piled out followed by the cocaine cowboy and the other gentleman who I took to be his business associate and/or security. They each stood by one of the double doors that opened up on the cantina side of the vehicle. They were serving as ominous bodyguards. Rigo nodded to us.

"Let's go play!" he exclaimed and out we stumbled right into the middle of a raucous street party.

Now, this was a Mexican fiesta! Loud music filled the night air and alleyway around the cantina. People were everywhere drinking, dancing, and partying. Outside of the three official Woodstock festivals I've been privileged to attend, this was one of the best parties I would ever be slam damned in the belly of the beast of. Did it top Dalton's beach birthday bash from Disc One? Nah, but it was close.

We stood with Rigo as he received the adulation of the crowd, which I estimated at around a couple hundred, maybe more. The cocaine cowboy's assistant whispered something to B. My best friend immediately snapped to attention, directed to go back to work. We spotted the head of security head our way. He started to steer us towards the cantina, but I heard Rigo say he wanted to stay outside for a bit.

We all hung out by the limo for a while till it pulled away. They blocked off the street after the car left. The space was immediately filled by more revelers. Rigo talked with friends, fans, and supporters for quite some time. People brought us beer and many joints were passed around. I caught a glimpse of Sofia and Camila near the cantina entrance. Sofia waved. I raised my Sol bottle to her and smiled. B drank, but was working as well and stayed near Rigo along with the other security folks. I danced with an older senorita for a couple of songs and had a good time.

The night roared along and the party lasted till the wee hours of the morning. I steered clear of Sofia for most of the evening because I didn't want to deal with the language barrier, her incessant chatter, or her brother.

At one point Rigo and Camila sang a little duet on the tiny cantina stage backed by just an acoustic guitar. I was right. The tiny stage was crowded to the max with just three people. Sofia cozied up to me and via body language urged me to join her on the dance floor. A ton of couples were slow dancing to Rigo and Camila's emotive, plaintive ballad. Sofia took my hand and I let her pull me into the sea of brown flesh.

Track-28-Rock n' Roll Heaven-The Righteous Brothers (3:33)

I know a lot of you've been waiting for some of your favorite people from Disc One to show up and several that haven't popped up yet or haven't been in many of the stories on this Disc will be here in a bit. But I always hate it when I'm left dangling about the fate or future of people in stories, so I promise not to subject you to that result, for the most part. So, I've decided to take a little sidebar adventure and let you in on what happened to certain folks from Disc One after their time having their story mixed with mine came to a close.

The Zero Tree-The tree has survived many hurricanes and a few more generations of idiots. Checked on it the other day, looking good. Said it was a bit surprised I was still alive, but happy to see me. I shared some of my story with my friend who seemed pleased. The tree just celebrated its 200th birthday and oaks can live to be a thousand or more, so rock on Zero Tree.

Principal Mossy-The old Marine was principal at our school for a long time. I ran into him a couple times over the years and he seemed genuinely pleased I had turned out somewhat ok. After getting my MBA and Doctorate I ran into him at the mall. "I knew you had it in you," he said. "Take care, King of the Zeroes." He smiled and walked away.

Danny and Donny-from the Marguerite fun and for Donny, also Ike's party on Knotty Beach. Danny stayed around the island for years, finished community college and became a recreation director for another nearby county. He married well and they have several grown children. The Marguerite we pulled in Disc One was the last in which he played a part. Donny went on to play junior college football as a linebacker, and a few universities wanted him to play at the Division II level, but he didn't have the grades. He moved to Raleigh and worked construction for years. I lost track of him in the late 1980s.

B's family-His mom passed in 1986. I was living in Virginia Beach and drove down the day before the funeral. B and I got blitzed that night, my first time drinking Long Island Ice Tea. Boy what a mistake. The phone woke us the next morning. B had bought his first house (on the mainland). Dylan screamed "Where are you guys? The funeral starts in 30 minutes!" We were 20 minutes away. We made it, barely. I was so hungover, I had to wear my sunglasses into the church and throughout the service. After, outside, as we waited to ride to the gravesite, Dylan came up to me, punched me on the shoulder and said: "Mom wouldn't have expected any less from you shithead."

Dylan remained a true beautiful butthole, using her looks to have a decent life in various service industry jobs. She traveled some. I saw her recently on the mainland at a restaurant. She said she works at a cosmetic counter. Currently, she said no dude, one kid. Of course, she may have acquired another dude between the time I saw her and publication. She always had a knack for landing'em.

Max-their little brother has had a tough road, but he's a survivor. His wife, after sending the kids off to school 15 years ago, romancing Max, and an overall good morning together, shot herself while Max was in the shower, leaving him to raise their kids alone. He is now as well.

Dylan's friends from Dalton's party and the Rec Hall-Candace, Sabrina, Julie, Jade-Sabrina was a bit of an enigma and always seemed real distant as if she was looking into or searching for another world. She and I had one great night together on the beach during the "house parties" after graduation. She was fascinating and said she was going to become a photographer. I don't know if she did, as I never heard from her again, but some of my favorite photos of my senior spring she was the photographer.

Julie-The first girl to play Little League baseball in our area and perhaps the best pure athlete the island ever produced. She became a pro surfer, later an instructor, and last I heard, lives in Florida running a surf shop with a focus on helping people with challenges learn to surf for therapy and fun.

Jade-Married another one of our childhood friends and they were together till his death around 2010. They have two kids and Jade lives with one of them and her family now.

Candace-Over the years Candace made it clear that she wanted to have some fun with me, but it never happened. One winter's night during my senior year we played a great prank on Candace, Dylan, and another girl, from out of town, whose name I have forgotten. The boardwalk was closed for the season with just the Rec Hall and a couple other bars open on the south end and two bars open on the north end. In between, there was nothing but utter darkness, kinda creepy. Well, we knew those three were tripping on acid from spending time with them in the Rec Hall. They said they were going to a north end bar in a bit. Candace wanted me to join them. Hal had a great idea. We (about eight guys) went and hid in the old "Haunted House" ride just down from the big arcade on the far north end of the inner boardwalk, just before the shuttered "Ring the Bell" game. We knew the girls would pass right by on their way to their next whiskey bar. Just as the three girls, chatting up a storm, walked by in the pitch black, we all leaped out like mad demons or banshees, wailing, screaming, and yelling. Candace collapsed from fright, Dylan slapped Hal, and the other girl ran for her life, never to be heard from again. Candace never spoke to me again. I got into a fight with one of her brothers over the incident. I knocked two of his teeth out and he gave me my second concussion. We laugh about it now and have a drink on the boardwalk most holiday seasons.

Dalton and Salem-Dalton remains on the beach to this day and is generally regarded as a local legend. If you hit the boardwalk bars you might run into him, I have several times over the years, always a good time. His brother Salem died in 2007 as one of the first opioid casualties of the current epidemic.

My great aunts, my aunt, and my cousin Danielle-My great-aunts passed in the late 1980s and early 1990s. My great-aunt Nina's three grandchildren and I have at various intervals been close and then not. I gave one away at her first wedding and I regularly attended sporting events of another's son and daughter. The daughter is playing college soccer now.

My aunt Monty died of breast cancer in 2000 at age 53, her daughter, Danielle in 2014 from liver failure at age 47, despite never drinking more than a glass of wine here or there.

Trick and Rich-my mom's half-brothers from the hitchhiking story after eighth grade. They came down the couple summers my grandfather was around and we visited them and a couple more of their brothers one time in Winston-Salem, NC. That was it. My mom never heard from them again. The seven half-brothers she had in California never entered our lives. We don't know if they ever knew about any of the rest of Pawpaw's children or families.

Bluto-Bluto died from a snake bite age seven in human years out at Boy Scout Lake near Sugarloaf where we always camped on our little island. Bluto got the snake bite while trying to protect Hal. The good news is Bluto sired some pups, as has each succeeding Bluto. Hal now has B5 as his constant companion. And yep, you guessed it, B5 slobbers just as much and barks when he poops. There will be much more on Hal later, just wanted you to not be confused when I refer to Bluto as a B followed by a number.

Melissa-from the Wave, Dalton's party, and my heart. Once she went to NYC for college I lost track of her. The Brockingtons didn't have any family on the island and once they moved, as far as I know, nobody on our little island ever heard from them again. I wish I had, I wish I could tell you more. I can't.

David-Graduated from UNC and became a successful town manager in a large southern city. He contracted HIV/AIDS during a blood transfusion (he was a hemophiliac) and died in 1993, age 34.

Dani and Mandy-from Woodstock. Dani and I wrote each other intermittently during our formative years and she called me a couple times. We exchanged pictures, news about notable life events, and seemed to have a real connection. The communication just kinda stopped once she went to college at Ohio State. I didn't hear from her for over a decade. While I was working as a newspaper reporter and radio DJ in Virginia Beach at the end of the 1980s, Dani and her family (husband, one little girl) were coming into town for a vacation. She heard my voice on the radio, made her husband drive to the station and well, that was one of the biggest and best surprises of my life. She was simply stunning, having grown into a beautiful young woman. She'd become a nurse. Her husband was cool and asked me a ton of questions about Woodstock, what Dani was like back then, and lots of other music-related stuff. She said Mandy was already on her third marriage and had a couple of kids. They all still lived in Cleveland. Our families met for supper their last night at the beach and of course, we promised to stay in touch. We didn't.

Eggs-Last I saw Eggs was at the county jail at the end of the 1970s. I was doing weekends for being an idiot (drunk and disorderly-I was brawling on the boardwalk) and Eggs was there because he was acting up after being without his medicine (for PTSD) for a while. There were no big revelations. I was running the elevator as a "trustee" (inmates that are trusted to do menial labor while they are in the joint). I said "Hi Eggs". He never looked up just "mumble, mumble, raff, snaff" the whole elevator ride. As the deputies led him out of the elevator into booking he stopped, turned his head, looked at me, and clearly said "Lenny". I tried to visit him when I was released, but he had already been shipped off to the state mental hospital. I don't know what became of him.

Leslie and Hitch-Leslie and Hitch stayed together, lived mostly happily on the island into the early 1990s. They never married and had no kids. Leslie worked at various industrial plants on the mainland and Hitch became a wildlife rescue guy. He was really great at his job and loved helping animals very much.

He and I drank a few times in the early 1990s on the boardwalk when I would come to our little island to visit Mom. When I told him in late 1993 of my plans to attend Woodstock 1994, he said he was in, and then he said he would have to ask Leslie. Somethings never change. She gave him the o.k. to go. He was still the same fun, free spirit despite losing his mom the year before in a house fire that also claimed Henrietta, his beloved (our Woodstock wagon) VW van and most of he and Leslie's possessions. They were living with his mom at the time. Leslie was at work and Hitch was at a wildlife conference when the fire started. Hitch's mom had fallen asleep smoking a cigarette. Sadly, all members of Hitch's immediate family died tragically and he wouldn't escape that fate. Less than a year later, just before he was going to join me on another epic Woodstock adventure, disaster struck. Hitch had stopped to help a stranded motorist along a major roadway on the mainland. Hitch was returning from a wildlife rescue call when he was struck and killed by what the authorities concluded was a drowsy trucker. The trucker, Hitch, the stranded motorist, and the animal Hitch was rescuing all perished.

Track 29-Radar Love-Golden Earring (5:04) Highway to Hell-AC/DC (3:27)

Whew, not a lot of joy there, so let's shift gears and head back to me and Darlene trying to make curfew after our night of "boinking", laughing, and dealing with the cop as we tried in vain to make her 11:30 curfew after our first "official" car date in the Duster. I careened through unfamiliar roadways and streets, desperate to save every second I could.

"Slow down jackass," Darlene yelled, punching me on the shoulder. "It won't do us any good to be a few minutes early in Hell."

She was somewhat serious but laughing nonetheless. Danger made her hot, I knew it, and I always played to it. I slid the Duster into her neighborhood, almost on two wheels. "Radar Love" by Golden Earring blasted from the eight-track. I grabbed at the back of her head pulling her towards my lap, she softly slapped my face.

"I want to have tons more sex with you," she screamed. "But not right this second. Please don't hit that tree!"

I swerved to miss a giant oak that stood between me and my turn. Made it, barely. A few moments later I barreled closer to her street, screeching the tires around the last turn. We could see the lights in the front room still on as we pulled onto her street. I stopped fifty yards or so away.

She looked at me. I looked at her. We made out for a few seconds as hard and fast as we ever would. She pushed me away with both hands. My head hit the driver's side window.

"You'll be the death of me," she said trying to brush her hair.

"I know," I said. "And you mine. But we both know that's what we signed up for."

I slowly brought the Duster up the drive and pulled around back. The light over the kitchen sink was on. Crap, they were probably all in the living room. This wasn't going to be too much fun. The clock above the eight-track said 11:55. We looked at one another and of all things, giggled.

Even with the giggle, Darlene was in a bit of a panic as we approached her house. I had seldom seen her rattled, but she was definitely a bit undone.

"What are we going to do?" she asked as she frantically tried to align her clothes and work on her hair and face.

"It'll be ok," I lied. "We'll say we got caught in the storm."

I do come up with a good one every now and then, don't I? That little pearl brought her some much-needed peace.

"Damn Lenny," she said snuggling up close as we slowly inched up the drive. "That might just save us."

The rain had relented. The back deck light was on as the Duster crept by. If anyone was asleep I damn sure didn't want the Duster's 340 Turbo Jet to wake them up. Darlene once again looked in the rearview mirror to check her face.

"Thank goodness for that storm," she laughed a bit. "For a number of reasons."

She smiled at me and kissed my shoulder as the Duster came to a stop by the picnic table. The car clock said 11:57. The dining room light was on as well.

"Look, they're probably sitting there playing Rook," I said. "So let's just be cool and matter-of-fact, bad storm, movies, worse storm, got it?"

"Got it," she said sliding out of the driver's side after me.

We walked hand-in-hand up the deck steps, Darlene holding her strappy sandals in her other hand. She went in just ahead of me. Our moms were sitting there at the big old oak table having coffee. Ms. Winter moved her wheelchair slightly to get a better look at us. No dads in sight.

"Oh hi honey, hi Lenny," Ms. Winter, who was now facing us, said. "Did you have a good time? My, you're a bit of a mess."

"I know," Darlene started. "Storm was so bad we didn't make it to the party. We went straight to the movies since it was much closer. We got caught in the storm leaving the theatre."

"Oh, I know Desiree missed you," her mom said. "You can take her to lunch or something tomorrow. We're about to call it a night anyway. The guys are in the basement working on my old recliner. Lenny, I put some sheets and a pillow on the couch for you."

"Thank you," I said.

"Is it ok if we watch TV for a bit?" Darlene asked her mom.

"Sure, sure," she said. "Just don't stay up too late. I was hoping you two would take us to church in the morning."

Darlene smiled and nodded yes. She also squeezed the crap out of my hand.

"I'm going to go change," Darlene said. "Why don't you go grab your bag?"

I nodded and headed toward the door, pausing to give my mom a quick peck on the cheek. I didn't take time to think what I might smell like. My mom gave me a little knowing smile.

"Goodnight Son," she said.

Damn, I'm a stupid dumbass. I'm sure I smelled like Dwight and Connie did all those years ago when they helped rescue me at Woodstock. I couldn't make the smell out at that time since I was just 11, but I was damn sure what it was on me. I hurried to the car to grab my bag. At least the men were busy in the basement. I damn sure didn't want to get near them. I quickly opened the trunk and just as hurriedly started to close it. Then I heard my father's voice, it was close. I paused and began to lower the Duster's white trunk much more slowly.

"You catch much of that storm?" my father asked looking down at the Duster from about 10 yards away.

I glanced down as well. I hadn't noticed when the copper had us stopped or when Darlene and I got out of the car a few minutes earlier that the Duster was quite a mess also. Her beautiful white paint and black vinyl roof covered with mud, debris, and who knows what else.

"Yes sir," I said. "But no big problems."

Thankfully, the two dads stopped about five yards away from the car. They were both a little wobbly, beer cans in hand.

"Got to give it to the boy," my father said to Mr. Winter. "Best foul weather driver I've ever seen."

My dad gave so few compliments, I was stunned. He had ridden with me through a few storms, but probably not enough to make that kind of long-term assessment. But I took it, and I treasure it. I guess he really meant it because he repeated it several times over the years to family, friends, and co-workers. It was the best compliment my father ever gave me, and the only one he ever said more than once.

"Good to know," Mr. Winter said. "Heard a lot about this car Lenny boy, mind if I take a look and fire her up?"

Oh boy...

If I smelled like you know what, imagine what the inside of the Duster must have smelled like after two teenagers did mostly naked wrestling for two-plus hours? Mr. Winter and my dad both came a couple steps closer. Man, I knew I was about to die. They say your life flashes by you when you are about to check out, well mine actually did. I had a quick few seconds of video speed play. There were holiday images, ballgames, Woodstock memories, tons of Darlene, Melissa, and B memories, and Bluto. What the hell was Bluto doing in my "Greatest Hits" about to die video?"

"Darlene took the keys in the house," I quickly lied.

The devils on both my shoulders smiled. Damn, when I'm good, I'm good and when I'm bad, well you have borne witness, guess luck might be a lady after all, they do love me. You see, no lie, right then, no, right that second, it began to rain cats and dogs.

The guys did a quick about-face and drunk jogged to the house. I stood there for a second, regained my composure, and then locked the car. No way in hell were we taking our moms to church in the Duster.

Track 30-Right Place, Wrong Time-Dr. John (2:55)/Black Diamond-Kiss (5:14)

Sooo, remember my skewed rational for ruining our rival's prom? I know pretty screwed up, right? Well, my history of screwing up was already legendary. Despite my flawless execution of "Boom, Boom, Out Go the Lights", Darlene remained distant and silent. No answer to two letters and four failed attempts to contact her by phone over a couple weeks. Lexi wouldn't speak to me either. I figured I had screwed up for good. I was close to right. I'm often close to right, just not right enough, enough of the time.

The last time I had screwed up enough to tick her off big-time was the year before, during our 11th grade spring semester when I repeatedly put myself into situations destined for disaster. We had been through a lot over those last 16 months; her moving, her mom dying, me getting into trouble all the time. The distance thing was rough. They moved from the beach to Durham in late September of our sophomore year. Her mom's rapidly declining health, our ages, and a host of other factors made maintaining an intense relationship extremely difficult, but we seemed to manage, well, most of the time anyway.

Over those 16 months, our relationship was a roller coaster ride with great highs (the summer after 10th grade) and extreme lows (her mom's death). We tried, we tried damn hard, but when you're a stupid teenager it's so hard to stay focused. If I'm being honest, sometimes I didn't try as hard as I probably should have. Case in point, Antoinette Royal.

Mine and Darlene's "New Deal" had started after the holidays a few months after her mom died fall of our junior year. You know her Super Bowl date that January of our junior year was the end of our beginning. Well, my first foray into New Deal territory was more substantial and probably the real beginning of the end.

We were intrigued by one another from the start. She was new to our school, starting her sophomore year. I was a junior. She was on the junior varsity cheerleading squad and the first time I saw her she was with a group of other JV cheerleaders by the fountain on the promenade practicing for the first football game of the season. I was leaving my last class of the day and heading to the parking lot. I wanted to just stop and stare, but thankfully Anson, my soccer teammate you met at Ike's party in Disc I, grabbed me by the arm to talk so I had an excuse to do exactly what I wanted. I didn't hear a damn word he said.

She was about 5'6", just the right curves for a girl her age, light ebony skin with a beautiful, fluffy afro, and dazzling white teeth behind a spectacular face. My thigh muscles tightened and many others did too. She smiled at me. I smiled back. The girls had just finished a cheer and were talking excitedly with each other as I passed by as close as possible without getting in their space.

"Hey, hey," Anson yelled, jogging to catch up with me.

I'd left him standing in the middle of the quad.

"Damn Lenny," he said. "So what do you think?"

"About what?" I asked.

"All that crap I just asked you about!" he said, none too happy at my obvious indifference.

"Tell me again," I said. "But first, who is that sophomore with the pretty fro?"

"Damn dude," Anson continued. "You suck. You never let it rest. Her name is Antoinette Royal or Royals. She's in my biology class. I was talking about going to see Kiss, they're coming to Charlotte, right after Thanksgiving!"

"Oh wow," I said. "That's cool. Yea, let's make that happen. Who else is playing?"

"Styx, Mott the Hopple," Anson said. "I'm trying to work it so we can stay at my brother's house."

"That would help a bunch," I noted.

I was psyched to hear Kiss was coming within striking distance, no one great had lately. This was the first Alive! Tour, so yeah I got to experience the fellas in all their youthful debauchery. Seeing Kiss live at the beginning of their careers helped change my life in ways I can't even begin to explain. Most importantly, it shifted my focus from sports to music. They were the first band to use pyrotechnics on a wide scale and the explosions, the fire, the flashing sirens made it seem as if Zeus (Paul) had stepped down and the real devil (Gene) had stepped up to become rock stars along with one spaceman (Ace) and one cat (Peter) to round out the band. It was one of the most exciting and profoundly impactful nights of my life.

I was even more excited to meet Antoinette. I would see her at JV football home games and around school, but she had a different lunch period and after about a month she eased from the forefront of my mind. Besides, at this point, Darlene and I were still good. Darlene's mom's death that fall, a somber holiday season, and our New Deal had me in the dumps.

All that began to change when junior year spring semester started in late January. I was heading to my last class of the day, Stagecraft II. Yep, kinda the same one (Stagecraft I) that served as the starting point of Disc II the previous fall. I wandered in and saw a few familiar faces. I had missed the first day of class because, well, you know that story. This was my second go-round with the drama kids, but this was still kinda new stuff to me. This, my second semester delving into the theater arts definitely steered my life off its previous course. It was a combo class (Drama and Stagecraft) taking up the size of two normal classrooms with a stage on one end. We had some traditional desks as well and I quickly slinked into a good spot in the left rear. I had also been in this classroom a couple summers before as it served as the "book learning" classroom for driver's education.

My soccer and football teammate John (yep, the one that would rescue me after prom the following spring) strode into the room, spotted me, and made a beeline for the desk next to mine. John's brother was one of the drama stars of the school. Our instructor, the legendary Charles Foss, lumbered into the class and bellowed some lines from Hamlet. He was one of the best teachers I would ever encounter, and he made my last two years of high school way more fun than any kid deserves. He was a giant of a man, who almost always wore suspenders over his quite rotund physique. Coupled with his big dark glasses he created quite the memorable physical character surpassed only by his giant intellect. An encyclopedic knowledge of the arts, a keen wit, and an acerbic tongue kept you on your toes. He called me Prince Charming. I was so happy he was my teacher. I was about to get even happier.

Who walks into the room? I know you will guess this easy lay-up question, the softest of softballs I will toss your way. I expect 100 percent correct answers now...of course, Antoinette Royal. She said sorry to Mr. Foss as she entered after second bell, but Mr. Foss just bowed and said: "Welcome my lady, please choose a seat".

We had about 20 or so students and almost all the desks were taken but one right in front of her, and the one in front of me. She quickly scanned the room, smiled, and headed my way. What a lucky boy am I!

She was wearing jeans and a brown baby doll top along with big copper hoop earrings. She flashed her perfect smile and sat down right in front of me. Her hair was in cornrows flowing to the bottom of her shoulder blades. She had a tiny little mole on the back of her left ear lobe. She smelled like an earth goddess with a soft scent of cinnamon and apples. I didn't hear another word Mr. Foss said.

When the bell rang, I waited for her to get up. John smiled and wagged his finger at me. She rose and I moved slightly to her left to pass her, bumping her ever so softly.

"Hi, I'm Antoinette," she said. "You're the only face I recognized in here, from sports and stuff."

"Yea, hi," I said. "I'm Lenny."

We small talked it up and I just simply followed her to her next class, talking away. Of course, I was done for the day and since I didn't play school basketball, I would have usually just headed out to the Duster and on to our little island.

"This is me," she said, nodding her head toward Ms. Ellis' Human Studies classroom.

I followed her in.

"You have this class too?" she asked a little too excitedly.

I started to tell her no, but Ms. Ellis (another one of my favorite teachers you'll hear more about later) beat me to it.

"Ok, Lenny," Ms. Ellis started. "I can see why, but you know better. Keep that mouth shut and just leave, you took this class last year, so just vamoose."

I kissed Antoinette's right hand. I bowed in Ms. Ellis' direction and backed out of the room head lowered like you do when leaving the presence of royalty. Everyone laughed. Antoinette just shook her head and took a seat.

We began a school-based friendship from that day forward. We talked before, during (when the drama kids were practicing), and after class. She got assigned to the set design building crew and as you may remember, John and I were in charge of sound and lighting.

Darlene and I were working through our "New Deal" and I hadn't really planned to take advantage of my new, somewhat limited freedom quite so quickly, but Antoinette was just too spectacular a person to not make an attempt.

We kept it on a friendship level for almost two months, but the mutual attraction was strong and despite the obvious barriers of the time, we seemed headed for more than a cool friendship. Antoinette was fully aware of Darlene, our circumstances, and our "New Deal". Antoinette had ended a five-month relationship just before the holidays (got to save on those presents when you can) and wasn't looking to jump into anything despite being asked out numerous times by tons of guys of her race at our school, our cross-town rival's fellas, and guys from her community.

I enjoyed watching her in her role as a JV cheerleader and attended JV basketball games for the only time in my life. The first time we socialized outside of school was at a cast and crew party after our late February production of Arthur Miller's "Death of a Salesman".

"I was going to ride with Sabrina," Antoinette said as the party was winding down. "But, I'd love to ride in your car. I've heard so much about it from everyone if you wouldn't mind?"

"Sure, no problem," I replied, trying to hide my excitement. "You ready to roll?"

She nodded that she was and we took our leave, catching several sideways glances from our friends and classmates as we exited.

You see, there was zero, zilch, and nada interracial relationships in the open at our school. There was a rumor here or there about one couple hanging out on the sly, but no one dared to be open about it way back then. Our area, along with most of the rest of the nation had undergone several years of racial unrest, riots, and overall uneasiness not totally dissimilar to what is going in this day and age except back then, in the south in general, and our town in particular, race-mixing was verboten! You simply did not see a mixed-race couple on the streets, much less in high school.

"Oh wow," Antoinette said as the Duster roared to life. "That's a sweet sound."

The 340 Turbojet engine rumbled in perfect harmony to Dr. John rocking his Cajun/Creole blues. I think it was "Right Place, Wrong Time". Read into that what you will.

We talked about the play and the plans for our upcoming grand spring production of "Taming of the Shrew". I drove Antoinette into her neighborhood, a place I was more familiar with than most white teenagers because of taking some of my football and baseball teammates home over the last three semesters. We pulled up in front of her house which had a big front porch looking out over the street. The yellow porch light was on and I could see her father rocking in one of the chairs on the porch. She turned to face me.

"Hey, I know this is short notice," she said. "And I'm sure you've probably already been asked, but if you haven't, would you like to go to the Sadie Hawkins Dance with me?"

I didn't hesitate. Her smile was so beautiful, her brown eyes sparkled.

"That would rock," I said. "Looks like your dad is standing up, so you better get on in. We can discuss at school next week."

She clapped her hands together and leaned over and gave me a peck on the cheek all in one motion. Her dad was halfway down the steps when she raced to meet him, giving the giant of a man a big ol' hug. I swung the Duster around and headed back to our little island. I was so excited I wanted to gun it really bad, but I didn't.

For those of you unfamiliar with high school dance etiquette of the time, the Sadie Hawkins dance was one of the most anticipated high school events of the year. The dance was usually held in March. It gave the girls a chance to ask a guy to a dance. While many couples were already a given that they would be going together, there were always some surprises. Unattached guys often got to feel what girls must go through all the time, the waiting, the wondering, is she going to ask me? Is ANYONE going to ask me? A couple of girls asked me already, but I begged off, using Darlene as my crutch despite having the freedom to invoke the New Deal. I know, not super cool, but man I was excited Antoinette asked. At the moment she asked, I gave zero thought that she was black and I was white in a time when everyone else did.

B and I were washing the Duster and his Jeep at my house that Sunday when I brought up the events with Antoinette.

"Yea man," B said. "She's super fine. Prettiest sophomore there is in all of school, hell, maybe the prettiest girl in school period. Big leap though."

"I know," I said. "I don't give a crap about all that. I know what may happen."

B looked over the roof of the Duster from the passenger side as I was cleaning the driver's side window. He gave his signature left eyebrow raise as if to ask "you do?"

"Let's get a beer," I said.

Dad was working. Mom and Lil'sis were cleaning the beauty shop. B and I strolled under the house below the back deck and grabbed a couple of cold ones from my cooler that was sitting on the old china cabinet. We popped a top and leaned up against the ancient cabinet. My sister now has the family relic in her kitchen. She got it when Mom passed in late 2012.

"You know me," I said. "I'm just going to run with it."

"Yep," B said. "Figured as much. You know there are going to be some fights, with both black and white."

"Yea," I said. "But not right to start, I hope. It's just one dance."

"It's never just one dance with you," B said.

Antoinette was not in Stagecraft class Monday. Naturally, my mind wandered all over the place. Had her dad said something? Was she sick? Was it something worse?

Nah, none of that, praise Elvis. It was just a dental appointment she forgot to tell me about.

"Sorry I didn't mention that Friday night," she said Tuesday afternoon outside of class just before the bell rang.

"Sure," I said. "You didn't miss anything important."

I didn't want to seem too involved or concerned. The old Tao of Steve McQueen again (be cool, be excellent in her presence, be gone). As we entered the class I put my right hand on the small of her back. She smiled. Damn if I know what we discussed in class that day. I had baseball practice after and the last JV basketball game of the season was at 6:30.

"Are you coming to the game?" she asked as we headed out of the classroom.

"Yea," I said. "I think I'll just chill in town after practice then head over."

"Want to get some ice cream after?" she asked.

Wow, asking me out a second time in less than four days' time. This girl was bold with a capital B.

"Sounds good," I said. "Will your pops be there?"

"Yes, both him and Mom," she said. "They know who you are from sports, but they want to meet you. I told them about the dance and all."

She said it matter-of-factly, but also while searching my face for some kind of response.

"Yea, yea," I said. "That'd be great."

Of course, I didn't think that was great. Why do I always get the girls with the super imposing pops? Is that a life rule for me or something? I just did a quick scan through my "dads of girls I've dated" databank and found it to be true. Oh, the stories I could tell just from that sector, someday maybe, but anyhow back to our regularly scheduled program.

"Oh," she said as she turned to head off in a different direction. "My dad wants you to sit with him at the game."

Oh boy…

So I made it through baseball practice without pooping my pants. I almost got beaned at third base because I wasn't paying attention during batting practice. I split my time that year between playing third base, left field, and a few innings on the mound. I have always had a knack for being able to talk to folks, but this was one time I was a bit concerned. I could just focus on sports stuff talking to Mr. Royal. Can't go wrong there, right? I hoped anyway. I didn't have many other options. I knew Antoinette was an only child (sense any other pattern here?) so family talk would probably be limited. I knew better than to discuss politics or religion, but what if the Royals wanted to talk about those things?

I showered and put on some baggies and a Rolling Stones big bright red tongue logo black t-shirt. I know, not the best first impression for meeting the parents, but I didn't know all this was going to be going down when I stuffed it in my bag that morning.

"Hey Lenny," my teammate Eric said as we left the fieldhouse. "Can I catch a ride?"

"I'm heading to the b-ball game in a bit," I said. "I'm meeting Antoinette's folks tonight."

"Antoinette Royal?" he asked. "Damn that's the white, err, black whale at this joint man."

Eric was basically part of our family. He and I'd been baseball teammates since seventh grade and my dad gave him a ride for years. His family lived near Seabreeze, the black community just before the bridge to our little island. Eric would often joke that he was more "Melton than me".

"I know, right?" I said. "Do you know her folks?"

"Dumbass, not every black person at this school knows every other black family," he said with his great open-mouth laugh that was one of the best ever. "You might have bitten off more than you can chew this time Casanova."

"Could be," I said. "But dude, she asked me out to the Sadie Hawkins Dance. Would you have said no?"

"Hell no," Eric said. "But I ain't white."

Eric laughed some more and punched me on the shoulder as he ran toward our teammate Mark to try and catch a ride. He stopped after securing his ride, yelling back at me.

"Don't bring up politics around old man Royal."

That bastard! He knew stuff and was just going to let me suffer. He laughed, waved, and smiled.

"At least he probably won't kill you in public white boy," he yelled laughing even louder.

Track 31-Before the Next Teardrop Falls-Freddy Fender (2:34)

Sofia and I danced and danced. I was pretty exhausted, a little drunk, and getting sleepier as the party kept rocking. Rigo exited at some point after his little impromptu vocal showcase with Camila.

"Sofia, are you ready to go?" Camila asked.

Sofia shook her head no and they began a heated conversation in Spanish, only a little of which I understood. Something about religion, Catholic stuff I think.

Camila turned to me.

"We really must be going," she said. "Our parents are very strict with her and she still lives at home."

I just nodded. Last thing I needed was a bunch of angry Mexican dudes after me or even worse an angry Mexican mom.

"I'm done," B said strolling up and putting me in a headlock. "I'm grabbing a brew, want one?"

I started to joke and say "Does the Pope wear a funny hat?" but considering the present company and the recent discussion, I chose to just nod yes instead. I looked at Sofia, soft and so lovely, really compassionate eyes I could see really wanted to spend more time with me. I chose to make it easier on us all. A choice I rarely make. I looked at Camila while still holding Sofia's hand as more dancing erupted all around us as the jukebox roared to life with some more of Rigo's music.

"Tell her I'm tired and I'm going to hit the hay," I said.

Camila looked at me quizzically.

"I want to go to sleep," I said.

Camila relayed my sentiments and Sofia just smiled a little-disappointed smile and spoke to Camila.

"She says she will see you tomorrow," Camila said. "We'll come by at lunch."

Sofia gave me a nice kiss right smack on the lips, smiled, and walked away with Camila. I joined B at the cantina's bar. The two lap-sitting ladies were just down a few stools from us. B raised his left eyebrow. I sighed and shrugged my shoulders. Well, you didn't think I was going to be THAT good, did you?

We stayed around Matamoras for several days, B doing some work with Rigo's security people who also served as construction crew for one of Rigo's other business interests. I hung around the cantina, working in the kitchen by day (damn I washed a lot of dishes) and playing the drums at night with Rigo's rhythm guitarist (now playing lead) and a female singer. We made decent money and Rigo sent us a bonus envelope besides our regular pay from the big concert.

B and I decided we had enough money to head home. We picked Thursday for our departure. We decided we had enough hitch-hiking for us and made the command decision to walk back into Brownsville and take a Greyhound home. We found out we would have to get to New Orleans first by car. We caught a ride from Brownsville to The Big Easy where we almost got killed in a stupid-ass car wreck when our driver ran a stop sign and we got t-boned by a pick-up. It hit the driver's side and both drivers had to go to the hospital. B and I escaped with little damage, a few scratches and busted heads. Our next ride got us to New Orleans safely.

I was trying to play it safe with my new Mexican friends as well. Sofia, with Camila in tow, stopped by each day at lunch. She even tried a bit of English and I tried a bit more Spanish. She also popped in Wednesday night. I had told her we would be leaving early the next morning. After my final set of the evening, I said my goodbyes to the guitarist and singer and sat at a table with B, Camila, her husband, and Sofia. B had been keeping regular company with one of the limo girls and they kept me awake a night or two with their shenanigans, but I was happy for B. She showed up and the two of them disappeared to our sleeping area.

"Sofia would like to walk along the river with you," Camila started. "But we need to be going in about an hour. We'll wait here for you. Please don't be late."

She smiled a serious "don't screw up if you know what's good for you" smile at me as Sofia took my hand and led me away. We walked to the Rio Grande's southern bank, turned right, and walked toward the Gulf of Mexico.

We didn't do much but hold hands and star gaze with some kissing here and there. We smiled at one another a lot. It was a great walk. We started heading back after sitting on the shore for about 10 or 15 minutes. When we stood up we kissed quite passionately.

The moon was at half and a few lazy clouds ambled by pausing to gaze at us for a bit. The Rio continued its dance toward the Gulf of Mexico and we just watched it roll. Sofia put her head on my shoulder and sighed.

"I want to give myself to you," Sofia said in very broken English. "But you must stay."

She made a drumming motion and I knew what she meant. She wanted a relationship and figured if I stayed we would have one. Rigo had stopped by earlier and made an ultra-generous offer for me to become a permanent member of the band as he had alluded to the night of the big concert. He made a sweet package for B a part of the deal as well. We had politely declined.

It probably wouldn't be right for every dream to come true...

I smiled at her.

"I can't," I said. "I would love to be with you too, but."

I made a kicking motion.

"College, football (meaning soccer)," I continued. "Also baseball."

She lowered her head. I gently lifted her face and kissed her on the forehead. We walked back to the cantina without speaking, just holding hands.

Track 32-In the Heart of the Night-Poco (4:54)

On the way back, despite the accident, I slept most of the way to New Orleans. Our second, much safer driver let us out a block or so from the bus station, but we both had two pockets full of money so guess what happened? Yep, you guessed it, we missed our bus because we were drinking and shooting pool in a bar. We got a room in the French Quarter near where we had stayed on the way down a few weeks before. We even ran across a couple of regular drunks we had met on our first pass through town. Lots of true pros in New Orleans.

After we had left the Yankee girls in Destin at the end of June, we thumbed along the gulf coast hitting a bunch of great little seaside villages and towns and a couple bigger cities. Our first ride was with a trucker hauling crab pots who took us to Pensacola. He made a bunch of lame jokes about having the crabs, but was a pretty cool guy who burned one with us. After switching loads, we rode on with him to Mobile, Alabama. He was going to be heading north, so we decided to spend a night in Mobile. We had a good time at a few bars and got a cheap motel room.

The next day we hitched a ride with a traveling salesman who took us to Biloxi, Mississippi. We set up shop in a campground and caught a ride into town for some food and fun. We met a lot of cool people and discussed blues music, Elvis (from Tupelo, MS of course), and one of Mississippi's favorite sons, William Faulkner. *The Sound and The Fury* author is held in high esteem in most places, but none more so than his home territory. We had a great time debating the opaqueness of the book, its funky timelines, and of course, its connections to Macbeth.

The next day on the road took us to the northeastern shore of one of the country's most beautiful bodies of water, Lake Pontchartrain and the town of Slidell, Louisiana. We absolutely loved Slidell. We stayed two nights with some people we met shooting pool. We spent a lot of time hanging out with locals, playing rack after rack of eight-ball, and drinking along the shore of the Pontchartrain.

We learned Slidell was named for John Slidell, the Confederacy's Ambassador to France and also for a short time home to JFK's accused assassin, Lee Harvey Oswald. We went to a great bonfire party of the shores of the Pontchartrain the second night, dancing under the stars with some Slidell girls and getting absolutely blasted on local moonshine. The Slidell crowd was a fiercely independent lot and told all kinds of tales of pirates, the War of 1812, and the Civil War.

We were so drawn to the people and the place. I hope if you haven't, that you get to visit someday. It is hands down one of the most fun communities I have ever visited. The gang we hung with begged us to stay and we almost did, but NOLA beckoned.

One of our Slidell buddies, Hector, was taking a load of creosote to New Orleans the next day and we tagged along. He dropped us off along the banks of the Mississippi on the other side of the

Pontchartrain. We caught a ride into the French Quarter from a hotel worker who said he could hook us up for cheap, a clean $12 a night room with a shared bathroom. We took him up on his offer and soon found ourselves wandering one of the most debauched neighborhoods in the world. But oh what fun!

Now I got to say, I love New Orleans, I visit regularly for the Jazz and Heritage Festival in late April, early May many years and of course, Mardi Gras is a blast, but man visiting in July is far from optimal. If Hell is more oppressive than the heat and humidity in New Orleans in summer damn, I feel for those in that joint and hope I get to take the up elevator when I check out.

We still had fun, just stayed in bars most of the time. We hit the sights as well and visited several places claiming to be the site of the brothel/women's prison/other location made famous by the Animals' legendary hit "The House of the Rising Sun". Most were so bogus we had a hard time keeping a straight face, but a few, especially the former site of the women's prison made a compelling case. We staggered back to the French Quarter unconvinced, but pleasantly entertained, and quite intoxicated.

I'm not really sure how long we stayed in New Orleans, neither of us can remember. We did spend a lot of money there despite the $12 a night room. A fellow guest said he was heading to Lake Charles, Louisiana one evening and we just left with him. We stayed in Lake Charles for a night and of course, we asked about "Bessie" from The Band's "Up on Cripple Creek". We got a lot of laughs, but no info on Bessie. We had a night of too much Tequila. We left the next day a little worse for wear and headed southwest to Houston with a little cutie we met at a restaurant the next morning. She heard us talking about our traveling plans at a diner counter while wolfing down some pancakes.

"I'm heading to Houston," she said. "You guys are welcome to tag along. It would help if you could pitch in for some gas though."

She had a nice smile, gorgeous deeply tanned long legs prominently displayed in her tiny Daisy Dukes-type Levi short shorts, and radiant dark hair trimmed into a super cute pixie cut. She looked to be about 25 or so. We thanked her for the offer, discussed it briefly, remembering our old school plan was to head up the Mississippi River to Memphis then Kansas City. Instead we just went with the flow.

"Sounds like a deal," I said.

We strolled out of the restaurant and she pointed to her ride. Uh, we had an obvious problem. Her ride was a mini-car, sky blue, two-seat 1974 Triumph Spitfire 1500. This was a spectacular car, just really small. The saving grace was we no longer had much of our gear, just our travel bags. We had traded the other stuff for some marijuana just before we left Slidell. Still, we had an issue, we thought.

"Hope you can drive a stick," she said flipping her keys to B.

She took my hand and led me around to the passenger side. Of course, B could drive a stick. He had the 1944 Willy's Army jeep since he was 15.25. B loved driving the car so much he bought an almost identical one a few years later. We tossed our two bags in the compact trunk. She then directed me to sit and proceeded to plop down on my lap. We rode the I-10 with a few stops, including Beaumont where we hit a bar, had a few beers, and met some cool cowboy-type dudes who asked us for some dope. We burned one with them behind the bar, shot some pool, did a few shots, and hit the road.

Elle told us she was going to visit her folks and we could crash in their basement if we wanted. We had a fun ride in the little convertible listening to Little Feat, Pablo Cruise, and some Buffett along the way. Her parents were really cool. They both worked in the oil industry and took to us right away, asking tons of questions about our trip, and our plans for what was next.

"We're not sure," I said.

Her dad grilled us steaks and her mom tidied up the basement for us. We liked them so much we stayed for three nights, all five of us catching a Houston Astros baseball game one night. The Astrodome was unreal, so big. If I remember correctly, Houston's centerfielder, the diminutive Jimmy Wynn, the "Toy Cannon" blasted a couple of homers and the Astros beat the Mets by a bunch.

Elle was fun to hang out with, and yep, you guessed it, she was an only child. When we felt the urge to move on, she offered to take us "somewhere cool". We didn't even ask and agreed. We once again loaded up the Triumph and began heading back east, slightly southeast in fact. Houston was as far west as we would make it.

Elle started singing the words to the decade-old Glen Campbell monster hit "Galveston".

"That sounds like a cool place," I said.

It damn sure was. We spent a couple of nights in Galveston with a couple in their 30s. The dude was Elle's first cousin. They rented a little yellow cottage near the gulf. We played in the water and on the sand for a few days. Elle was one of the coolest girls I've ever met. There weren't a lot of questions, no exchange of numbers, we just enjoyed the time we had together, and that was it. When she said she needed to be heading back to Lake Charles, B and I had a bit of a dilemma. We could catch a ride with Elle back to Lake Charles, begin trekking elsewhere or start to head back home another way.

The second night in Galveston we all hung out around a bonfire on the beach during a party the neighbors were having. One guy we were partying with told us all about the "Great Storm of 1900" that killed between 8,00-12,000 people and is still to this day the deadliest natural disaster in United States history. Even after Katrina hit, all the hurricanes that have struck the US have a combined death toll lower than the one that struck Galveston in September of 1900.

The storm also obliterated what was a prosperous town and left up to 90 percent of the population homeless. We told him about Hurricane Hazel and our little island as we burned a few around the bonfire. He said he was going to be heading south to Brownsville in the morning if we wanted to roll that way and maybe venture into Mexico.

B and I discussed our options and decided, why the heck not, we may not ever make it back this way again (we haven't). So we took off toward Mexico. Our party friend Dave pulled up in front of Elle's cousin's house around 10 the next morning in an old green VW bug. Elle and I hugged for a bit as B loaded our bags.

"Bye Elle," I said from the edge of the road. "We had a blast, take care."

"Have a great life wild and crazy Lenny," she said. "Bye B, Dave."

And off we went on another Crazy Beach adventure, albeit far from home. The ride was outstanding down South Padre Island and on to Brownsville, so scenic and breathtakingly beautiful. Tons of shorebirds and other wildlife played, sang, and danced to the rhythms of life along the Gulf Coast.

Dave was just going to be in Brownsville for the day. We bought his lunch and said our good-byes. B and I got a room in an old boarding house near downtown and started making ourselves at home, which of course meant finding a bar with a pool table.

We partied and gambled in Brownsville and in quite the reversal of fortune for once we were the ones that got hustled by some locals.

We should've known better, but we were into day two of a three-day rum binge. We had played some pool with a couple of guys the night before and they were pretty good or so we thought. We broke even and when we encountered them the second night we thought we would raise the stakes a bit.

What dumbasses! They took us to the cleaners. We were really good at pool, but these guys were pros. After slow-rolling us for a half-dozen games as the stakes climbed higher, they put the hammer down once we were playing for $100 a game. They won a couple of tight games at that level and once we got into a double or nothing bet, they ran the rack, twice! Well, we sure shot a lot of hard-earned money down the drain quick, and learned an important lesson, don't think too highly of yourself or your skills. Ok to be confident, but…what the hell, we were suckers.

Like the great French author and director, Jean Cocteau said: "A little too much is just enough for me."

We were able to laugh about it enough that the guys that took us bought some more drinks and invited us to a poker game. Well, common drunk sense should have made that an automatic no, but you are quite familiar with my decision history, so it was off to play cards.

Thankfully poker has a high degree of luck involved and I caught a bit, but only after dropping a couple more hundred dollars. B excused himself from the game and hung out at the bar behind the card room, but where he could keep an eye on me. I managed to pull back even on the prior poker losses, recovered some of our pool losses, and decided it might be time to quit. B nodded. We headed back to our flop house tired, drunk, much closer to broke, and alone.

The next morning we asked around about some work, but most of the folks we talked with had seen our drunken behavior for days and said "no thanks". We tried one other part of town, but no luck either. We found ourselves standing on the footbridge looking over into old Mexico.

You've already heard that discussion, so that's how we ended up in Mexico…

On the return trip home the bus rides were pretty uneventful. We slept a lot. There was not anyone there to meet us when we got back to the bus station on the mainland. We hitchhiked back to our little island, our final time doing so.

College started on Monday.

Track 33-Beer Drinkers and Hell Raisers-ZZ Top (3:28)

Another ride back was way more fun for me. Darlene and I had a great ride back to our little island that June once 10th grade was completed just after seeing the Eagles' show in Greensboro. Darlene was so excited to go back home she could hardly contain herself. She talked excitedly about getting to hang out with Lexi, shoot pool at the Rec Hall, and tons of other beach related fun.

"I bet I won't have a hard time talking her into a Marguerite or two!" she exclaimed. "We're going to have so much fun."

I debated whether or not to tell her about my discussion with her dad. I decided to wait until later, I didn't want to dampen her enthusiasm. We rolled down highway 421 south and were about halfway to our little island when she spotted a sign.

"Lenny, Lenny let's pull over up there and get some ice cream," she said, pointing down the highway a bit to a couple of giant oaks by the road.

Nestled under the tall trees, which were in full summer shade mode, was a small wooden shack. I pulled the Duster onto a dirt path near the old building with a tin roof. Some lazy moss drifted down settling on the windshield.

She was out of the car before I knew it and had already raced to the combo fruit/veggie stand quicker than I could close my door. She had ordered us two cones by the time I caught up with her. There were two old rocking chairs on the far side of the stand under the taller of the two trees. We plopped down in them and begin tearing into the ice cream, peach for me, and chocolate for her. We swapped cones a couple times making a sticky mess. Even with the shade, it was a pretty sweltering June day and ice cream was dripping everywhere.

"Mind if we use some of that water to wash our hands?" Darlene asked the middle-aged lady who was wearing an old, shop-worn linen dress, and minding the business.

"Sure, honey go right ahead," she said.

"Thank you," Darlene said.

A large aluminum pitcher about half-full was sitting on the counter. We used as little as possible to try and wash the stickiness off of our fingers and hands. A younger guy, we took to be the lady's son had begun fussing with his mother over the music playing on the small black portable radio which had an antenna covered in aluminum foil.

"Why don't you turn that crap off?" he said. "And put on some real music, some country."

The guy, tall, heavyset and around 20 or so was clad in some dingy overalls and work boots. He looked at me. This dude really looked like a Hee-Haw reject.

"Don't you think she should?" he asked. "Country's the best, right?"

Before I could even get a breath out, Darlene had grabbed my hand and pulling me toward the car yelled back over her shoulder:

"He refuses to have a battle of the wits with an unarmed person," she said laughing.

The laughter got louder as I wheeled the Duster back onto the main road and sped off. Darlene scooted over close to me and changed the radio station with her right hand while clutching my right knee with her left. Once she found some rock suitable to her liking she turned to me and flashed her naughty girl smile.

"Find us a spot," she demanded.

Well, I knew US Highway 421 like the back off my hand as my family traveled the exact same course up and down it several times a year to visit relatives in the Piedmont. I knew where the farms were, the cemeteries (for playing the count the cow game of course), towns, bridges, and monuments.

Thankfully we were near a little creek that had a nice place to pull over under a small bridge just below Spivey's Corner. Spivey's Corner is where they have the National Holler'n (pig calling) Contest the first Saturday each June near Midway High School.

It was a great isolated spot and Darlene and I made good use of the picnic table under a couple of maple trees near the creek. We made sure and faced the top of the dirt trail leading down to where we were, in the unlikely event someone else was heading that way. My family had picnicked in the same spot several years before. Yep, right on that same picnic table. It was a good time. I had much more fun my second visit.

Darlene was always such a fierce, independent spirit she pretty much ran the show once we became "official" boyfriend and girlfriend. She also had few inhibitions once we started becoming intimate. She was up for about anything I could think of and hell, she came up with a lot of really great ideas that had never crossed my mind.

"Where's our next stop?" she asked, kicked back in the front seat with her bare feet in my lap and her hair blowing out the open passenger window.

She hadn't bothered to put her shorts or panties back on and was attired in just the Eagles t-shirt. Her shorts were on the floorboard. I glanced down, checking to see where her panties were. Her undies were nowhere to be seen.

"I left'em," she said. "I never really liked that color (green) on me anyway."

This continued a pattern that would become our custom. Darlene left panties all over the place. The girl had to buy a lot of drawers because she damn sure didn't like putting them back on after doing the "happy dance".

"So, the next stop?" she asked again as ZZ Top's "Beer Drinkers and Hell Raisers" came on the radio. "This is one of my favorite songs!"

She cranked up the volume as I managed to get us a bit farther down the road with the next place I could think of being a rest stop in a deserted rural area of Sampson County. There was only one other car there when we pulled in and no trucks. The Duster's mighty engine, much like Darlene did in times of ecstasy, made the sweet noise I loved most, an elemental sound, somewhere between a rumble and a purr as I glided to a stop at the far end of the parking area.

"Put your sandals on," I said.

"Why?" she asked.

"The woods," I said.

"Oh," she said raising her eyebrows.

As the great Mae West once said, "You only live once, but if you do it right, once is enough."

After fun stop number two, I managed to get us back to our little island without the loss of any additional clothing or more collateral damage to the eyes of young woodland creatures. Darlene wiggled back into her shorts and put her bra back on as we traversed the big bridge leading to our little island. She leaned her near-perfect body and gorgeous face between me and the steering wheel just as we reached the apex of the tall bridge that signaled we were home. She leaned out my window and taking in a deep breath, proclaimed the magnificence of the salt air. All was right with the world. For a second anyway, a town cop car pulled behind me from Killing Floor Road. I hadn't been back on the island one minute and I was getting pulled. As I pulled over, I could see it was Big Bob behind the wheel of the patrol car.

"What the hell?" Darlene asked.

"I have no idea," I said. "It's Big Bob, so it should be alright."

Big Bob approached my window. Big Bob and every other copper on the island and the city on the mainland knew the Duster by now. Word was that the narc that would bust me and my buds the next spring for public urination already had a picture of the car posted on the city's police department officers' meeting room with "known juvenile delinquent" scribbled across the Duster's white paint job. What great geniuses, huh?

"Hey Big Bob," I said. "What's up?"

"Not much Lenny," he said. "Oh, hey Darlene. How's your mom?"

"Thanks for asking Big Bob," she said. "She's a very tough lady, but it's pretty bad."

"Me and Nicole's prayers are with you all," Big Bob said. "We have her name on the prayer list at church."

Darlene nodded.

"Thank you so much," she said.

"Lenny," Big Bob continued. "Your right rear is a little low and oh yeah, tell B he has to get that window on the jeep fixed before he drives it on the road again."

"Thanks, Big Bob," I said. "Will do."

I promised you in the first book I would tell you the story of how Big Bob saved my life. I guess this is as good a time as any. It was the summer after my first year of college. I was partying upstairs on the deck of the bar that anchored the far northeastern end of the boardwalk (where a Hampton Inn sits today). I had been jamming pretty hard for several days in a row and was feeling no pain. None of my crew was around. Big mistake.

I thought I made friends with a couple of guys and gals, did a few shots, and invited them to walk out on the beach and smoke one. Once we got down the beach a bit, the two fellas lit into me about dancing with one of their girls. I trashed talk back to him and he took a swing at me. So, all hell broke loose.

Next thing I know I am trying to fight two guys and taking a pretty good ass whipping. I got my shots in, but would have lost easily on points if it was a scored boxing match. Well, it was two on one. After what seemed like forever, one of the girls screamed the cops were coming. The beating continued. I saw one guy pull a knife so I focused on him and knocked him back with a side kick. Pleased with the result I just stood there. What a dumbass.

Next thing I know I am being tackled from behind by the other guy and we wrestle for a bit. I manage to get on top and as I was pummeling him pretty good I was suddenly whisked into the air like I was snatched by a giant crane. Well, it was a giant all right, just not a crane. It was Big Bob. I found out later from the other cop on the scene the guy I had kicked to the sand had regained an upright position and was about to stab me in the back when Big Bob yanked me away and promptly knocked the guy with the knife out cold with one punch while still holding my drunk ass a couple feet off the ground.

Big Bob was something else. A true gentle giant. But someone you damn sure did not want to mess with. Thanks Big Bob. He is gone to the great flatfoot beat in the sky but will always be fondly remembered on our little island as a true servant. Now back to the regularly scheduled adventure with Darlene.

"Where we going first?" Darlene asked. "Lexi's?"

"In a bit," I said. "I need to pop by the house first."

Darlene was messing with her sandals as I pulled onto our street and eased the Duster in behind some other cars.

"Why are all these cars here?" Darlene asked.

"Family game night switched to Saturdays now," I lied.

Darlene nodded and we held hands going up the 12 steps to the front deck. Upbeat soul music was playing from the old clock radio on the bar as we approached the screen door. I opened it for Darlene and let her go in first.

"Surprise!" a crowd of friends and family yelled as she entered.

Darlene went over and hugged Mom and Lil'sis. Lexi grabbed her, gave her a bear hug, and a kiss on the cheek. The party was on! Darlene turned and wagged her right index finger at me.

What a crowd. I could see my pops manning the grill outside with a bit of help from Uncle Ed. Of course, all of this was Mom's idea. Lexi was co-party planner and helped a bunch with friend invites and setting up, tons of balloons included. The whole gang was there as were Granny, the great aunts, Aunt Monty, her daughter Danielle, Uncle Wes (Monty's husband and Danielle's dad) and all kinds of assorted friends, and Crazy Beach people. The biggest crowd we ever had. A perfect peaceful riot.

We all heard the old Scout rumble up outside, severely misfiring as Hal attempted to shut her down. Hal bumbled in with Bluto on a leash. Mom immediately got Bluto some water and told Hal to let him rest on the back deck.

"Damn, I missed the surprise?" Hal asked. "That's the best part."

"Nice to see you too Hal," Darlene said giving him a hug.

Hal's face turned red. We all laughed as Lil'sis and Danielle took Bluto and his water to the back deck. A nice ocean breeze was coming in via the spot usually occupied by the two big double glass doors.

"He can't ever get anything right," Lexi laughed.

"He doesn't need to," Darlene said patting Hal on the shoulder as she wrapped her arm around her best friend's waist.

The party was great. Darlene was so surprised and touched she just kept hugging people for a bit. She was so happy to be back on our little island. The party lasted for several hours. There was great grilled stuff my pops had made, tasty coleslaw from Mom and potato salad courtesy of the great-aunts, along with several mouth-watering deserts. After everyone had their fill, Lil'sis brought out the board games. The party split between a game of Life on the bar and a Monopoly contest on the table. Dad, Uncle Ed, and Uncle Wes chose to sit on the ocean side deck and have a few drinks.

"Oh yea!" Hal exclaimed as he polished off the other competitors in the game of Life.

Lil'sis and our eight-year-old cousin Danielle along with a quite tipsy Aunt Pat were his foes. Still, a win is a win, so Hal celebrated by pulling Lexi's hair as he headed out to join the older fellas on the deck.

"I'm going to get you," Lexi said throwing a hamburger bun and doinking Hal on the head just as he exited the room.

The whole crowd just busted out laughing.

"I think they should kiss," my little cousin Danielle said.

More laughter filled the room. Our Monopoly game resulted in three or four of us just saying let's call it a tie after a few hours. Mom and Aunt Monty got the youngsters cleaned up and off to bed, the great aunts and Uncle Ed headed home, and the teenagers hit the beach.

"That was so much fun," Darlene said. "Your mom is the best Lenny."

I smiled. There were nods and yeas all around. We all just strolled down to the pier. Hal brought Bluto along and let him play in the ocean some. The great song classic "Under the Boardwalk" by The Drifters blasted from the pier's outdoor speaker system.

"How long has your family been doing that game night stuff?" Lexi asked. "I remember playing one time, a long time ago, before Darlene even moved here."

"Ehh, a reallll long time," I said. "I think ever since Aunt Pat and Uncle Ed moved here to run the campground, maybe summer after fourth grade?"

"That's about right," B said. "I remember playing one time right after you guys moved into the house."

"Oh hell yea," I said. "That was when those two starting busting on each other."

I, of course, was pointing to Hal and Lexi. There infamous one-sided feud had started (we think) one night when we all about eight years old at a party for my lil'sis. It began when Hal pulled on Lexi's pigtails. She, of course, hated it. Hal never stopped and you've seen how the ensuing years' events only enhanced the ongoing drama between the two.

"I won game night then too!" Hal boasted as he claimed another win.

"Yea," Lexi chimed in. "But it was only Chutes and Ladders and the rest of us had pretty much quit to watch Lenny's Uncle D try to make it up the back steps."

We all laughed at the good, fun memory.

"Darlene, I told my parents we wouldn't be out too late," Lexi added.

"Ok," Darlene said. "Lenny, you ready to take us over?"

Of course not, but I did. Hal offered, but Lexi turned him down despite the fact they only lived four houses apart, right across from the state park near the buffer zone. B and Hal decided to go camping. They asked me to join, but I had a baseball game away the next day I needed to leave early for and was pretty beat from all the traveling and other stuff. Other stuff, man I love other stuff.

"Get some rest," Darlene smirked as I dropped them off in front of Lexi's family's modest two-story white frame house with a lone maple tree in the well-manicured front yard. "I'll see ya when you guys get back from Scotland County."

I pulled the Duster up to the pool table and headed up the front steps. Everyone else was gone. Mom was cleaning up around the bar while looking at an old picture album.

"You know, someday we'll all just be faces in old photographs," she laughed her beautiful wispy light southern drawl laugh. "And someday, today will just be a real long time ago."

"I know Mom, I know," I said. "I got the rest. You go to bed."

"Ok, thank you Son," she said giving me a peck on the cheek.

I finished up what little bit was left to be done and started to head to the bathroom to brush my teeth before bed. I noticed a tiny green Monopoly house had escaped detection under the table. I reached down to pick it up and return it to its rightful place in the game box under the couch. It was the last time I would touch the game box for many years.

Game night just kinda died out after that summer and never returned as a regular staple of our family and friend time. We, the teens, were getting older, and were spending more time away. Great-Aunt Pat and Uncle Ed moved deeper into the mainland after the campground they ran on just the other side of the bridge sold. Great-Aunt Nina returned to her roots near Randleman in Randolph County. The other cousins didn't come every summer anymore as their lives all changed with age and the passage of time. The game just simply died out. It was fun, for a very long time, seven years or so. A core institution in our household, but as the great George Harrison once sang "All Things Must Pass".

Track 34-Walk Away-James Gang (3:34)

I was sure ready for our time with the Yankee girls to pass. I was on pins and needles as we made our way to their grandma's farm and was constantly trying to figure out a way to avoid Emmy while keeping up appearances.

The farm was a large one, over 100 acres of orange groves that had been in the family for over a century on the girls' mothers' side of the family. We spent a lot of time helping some of the farm hands. Picking season for the Valencia variety gown on their trees had finished in April so it was prep time for the next season. We toiled for a week or so helping the migrant workers with their chores.

The girls' grandmother, "Ms. Stout", was exactly that. She had a short, fire hydrant like physique, with an ample grey bun of hair piled high on her head that was almost perfectly round. She always wore dresses down to her ankles. She ran a tight ship and offered us paid work for the rest of the summer. We politely declined but gladly accepted room and board for the time and effort we put forth along with the same pay the migrants received. The work kept us away from the girls for about eight or nine hours a day, but we had lunch each day at "The Big House" as the impressive old two-story green farmhouse was known.

During lunch, we would sometime encounter the girls, but it was always in a group setting as we chose to eat with the migrants out back on the half-dozen or so picnic tables set up for their use. The girls would invite us in on the days we crossed paths, but we would beg off noting our hard work had made us hygienically unfit for mixed company. We also stayed in the migrant shacks lining the southern rim of the property near a large fish-filled pond the workers made good use of. They offered to share their bounty with us on multiple occasions.

Finally, after we'd been there for a few days, Sasha made a point to see me right after super.

"You want to get together tonight?" she asked. "I can sneak out my window."

She nodded toward her second story window. Of course, I should have said that was too risky. Of course, I didn't.

"Sure," I said. "About what time?"

"Let's shoot for 11," she said. "Gran goes to bed with the chickens, but I don't want Emmy tagging along."

"Me either," I sighed.

We managed our late night rendezvous and hooked up under an orange tree fifty or so yards into the grove. If you ever get the chance to do that, make sure you do, one of the best experiences of my life. Intimacy mixed with the powerful smell of citrus is a pleasant experience you'll never forget.

Sasha was able to sneak back in undetected via some latticework covered with vines at the back of the house. I returned to my quarters only to hear B's rumbling freight-like train snore that had run all the girls into mine and Sasha's room in Savannah. I decided to sleep outside in a worn out old hammock strung between the shanty's front porch post and a weeping willow tree. The old willow hung low over a smaller pond whose shore approached the back of our end of the row shanty.

While we were having breakfast bright and early just after dawn the next morn, Grandma Stout came out to give us some new marching orders for the day. She directed the migrant fellas to various tasks and asked B and I if we could drive a stick.

"Yes mam," we responded in unison.

"I need you boys to go into Destin and get some supplies," she said. "I made a list and you can just put it on my account at the feed store. Take the flatbed over there."

She pointed to a WWII surplus rusted green Ford flatbed that had four wheels on the back axle and those huge side mirrors work trucks sported back then. It still had faded US Army stars on its side.

"Store will be open time you get there," she said. "Oh, I almost forgot, take Emmy with you. She has a dentist appointment at eight right across from the feed store. They'll put that on my account too. I'm keeping the other girls here to help me can. Shouldn't take long, I made sure she was first up at the dentist when I called yesterday. I expect you boys back by 10 or so, no goofing off now."

Oh boy...

Just when I thought I might weasel out of my sticky situation with Emmy, her grandma dumps her in my lap, literally. The old truck's front bench seat was crushed in the middle like some 600-pound guy sat there for a long time. Two ancient seat springs were exposed and Emmy said she wasn't sitting on those rusty coils. I know, I could have driven, but B was way more experienced with the stick than I was, since he had the Willy's Jeep and all. It was a big damn truck and well, Emmy was so fine...I know, I know, she was young, but nothing was going to go wrong just going into town, right?

Track-35-Street Fighting Man-The Rolling Stones (3:16)

Talk about things going wrong. I've blown so many great relationships with so many incredible women. I have to appear on some all-time idiots list somewhere, though I should appear on each and every one. Now I'm the kinda guy that will take his vitamins all right, but I'll wash'em down with beer. You know we make our decisions then they make us and man have I made a whopping ton of bad ones.

I was trying not to make any more the summer after 10th grade. I was trying to keep my promise to Mr. Winter and the first week went ok, mainly because due to a rainout the week before, we had three baseball games that week and they were all away. So, I was simply, mostly gone.

Aunt Monty was the back-up driver had something happened to Darlene's mom while I was away that week. Her job allowed her the flexibility to be available for an emergency trip had it happened. Thankfully, as you know, it wasn't necessary.

That summer and sometimes since I've often thought I wanted to start some kind of revolution, but often settled for starting a riot. This is how I started a small one that summer.

I had come so close to being so good the whole time Darlene was there. We had a magical month, almost too good to be true. After that first week of intense baseball action, we were together almost every day, save for my one away game each week.

We did all the great fun summertime beach things, spending tons of time on the beach, the boardwalk, and Rec Hall. I still worked and hustled just as much, but this time Darlene was a much bigger part of my everyday life like never before and never again. Outside of sleeping in two different houses, it was as if we were married. We loved it! With a car, the freedom to roam our little island and go to the mainland was unbounded. We made good use of the time and seldom a day went by that we didn't do "the happy dance" as she called it, multiple times.

We had just finished up another fun session and were supposed to meet the gang back at the Rec Hall. We were about to enter through the glass double doors when I heard a familiar voice yell.

"Let's play for some real money Lenny," a very drunken and/or stoned Heath screamed at me as he approached from the boardwalk side of the Rec Hall.

Nathan and a couple other guys were with him. Darlene tugged at my arm trying to pull me inside. It didn't work. She was the best brakes my runaway train wreck of a life could have ever had. They worked almost every time, but not today.

What ensued is told many different ways by many different people. I'm the villain in a few of them because Heath and one of his buddies ended up in the hospital. This is the way it went down from my perspective, and yes, this is the first time I went through the giant plate glass windows at the Rec Hall.

I turned to face Heath and his mini-gang. They were upon us faster than I thought they would be and were even more toasted than I anticipated. I was perfectly sober having taken my promise to Mr. Winter quite seriously. Darlene was a little high as she had smoked with Lexi some a couple of hours or so before all this went down.

"I got $100 says I can beat you two out of three at eight-ball and arm wrestling," Heath boasted.

He pulled a wad of crumpled up tens and twenties out of his pocket.

"I could use a hundred bucks," I smirked.

Darlene again tugged on my left elbow. I ignored her physical plea.

You see Heath always had a bit of a problem with me, and I had no love lost for him. It had started when he moved to the island in sixth grade. He had been a big shot at his previous school on the mainland and strutted into our world thinking he was going to take over. I quite unintentionally squashed that plan the first day of school when we boys were playing a game of pick-up football in the schoolyard. I continually smashed his butt into the ground each time he had the ball. I also ran right over him a couple of times as a running back when my team was on offense. He never got over it and things just escalated over the years. We had a couple of shoving matches and I had taken him down three or four times arm wrestling. He couldn't stand it. This would be our second "real" fight.

The first happened near the end of the eighth-grade school year. We were riding the bus back to our little island and were almost to our stop at the old post office. Heath was picking on a little seventh-grade girl. He said a couple of disparaging things about her hygiene and her parents. I was sitting with Lexi a couple of seats ahead of them in the middle of the bus. I turned around in my seat, my feet in the aisle.

"Cut it out Heath!" I yelled at him.

He turned my way. Yep, you guessed it.

"Whatcha gonna do about it if I don't pretty boy?" he leered.

"Just quit, will you?" I asked at a reasonable decibel level.

"Why?" he asked. "You screwing this stinky skank here too?"

I was upon him before he got halfway out of his seat. Now Heath was strong, don't get me wrong. I had no illusions this was going to be a cakewalk. He had already been working a few years as a carney on the south end rides each summer and helped his dad with construction work in the winter. He was taller than me by a bit, wiry, and mean. He was a bully's bully. He constantly badgered girls both verbally and sometimes physically. I heard the stories. He never took it too far when I was around. This incident on the bus was the last straw.

I had the advantage of first strike and I used it well. I was rising as I reached him. I grabbed both his shoulders and pushed him violently back over his seat. I could see B stand and place his hand on a rising Nathan's chest in the seats a couple rows back to keep him from jumping in.

I placed my right knee between Heath's legs on the seat as his feet wildly flayed in the air. I used my left leg as leverage and as Frank Costanza said on the "Festivus" episode of *Seinfeld*, "I rained down blows upon him".

George's dad Frank was beating up a guy in a toy store over a doll for his kid. My cause was a wee bit more just. Heath had no chance that day. The odds were a bit more in his favor outside the Rec Hall two years later.

"Well," Heath slurred. "Let's see if you can take this $100. Oh, and I'm going to fuck your girlfriend too."

Needless to say, we never played those games of pool or arm wrestled. The great Bruce Lee once said if you know you're going to take an ass whipping, at least get in a great first punch. I did, on both counts.

I was facing the four of them. Heath straight in front of me, Nathan directly behind him, and the two other guys I didn't recognize on each side of Heath. I correctly assumed my fellas were inside, but the windows were tinted...so...here we go...

I threw the hardest punch I ever landed, a strong straight out left right across Heath's right eye and nose. His smug smirk evaporated as quickly as his hair would in a few years. He crumpled to the ground. Knockout!

No time to celebrate though as the other two guys both solidly whacked me pretty hard. Nathan reached to grab Darlene to keep her from calling in the cavalry but he was just a bit slow, kinda like his mental capabilities. He and Heath stayed carnies their whole lives till Heath got them both killed while driving drunk in 1985. Thankfully, they didn't hurt anyone else.

The two guys and I punched at each other for a few. I could see Heath face down on the sidewalk, blood pouring from under his nose. It never looked right after this night. I had broken his nose, his jaw, and his right eye socket. He had to be hospitalized for a few weeks.

I was giving ground and now had my back to the plate glass window, which had a small brick ledge jutting out a few inches about butt high that people often sat upon. I was trying to protect my face and throw punches. I was definitely getting beat up. I could see out of the corner of my eye B and Hal emerging from the doorway where they encountered Nathan. B knocked him back into the street with a powerful roundhouse kick. Just as Hal reached to grab the brawler on my right, it was too late, the three of us went through the plate glass window. Hal was left grasping for air.

Shards of glass blasted everywhere as the three of us landed on the old thin green carpet near the foosball table. Startled Rec Hall partiers scrambled backward as we combatants began to rise and continued our fight. I was getting pummeled mercilessly. B had Nathan in a chokehold outside the broken window. Hal climbed through and pulled one of the fighters off of me. Blood was everywhere. I hadn't bled this much since my encounter with the animals in the woods at Woodstock. I was getting hit pretty hard by the remaining fighter, but at least it was one-on-one now and I was coming back at him with a flurry of left-right combos. He had pieces of glass all over him stuck in both body and head. I cut myself more punching his glass covered face than I had by flying through the window.

Hal was getting the best of the other guy when we heard police sirens approaching. I violently shoved my sparring partner back over the window and onto his back on the sidewalk right near Heath's still motionless body. His head hit the pavement with a sickening thud. He was out cold as well.

B landed a couple of more punches to Nathan's face while still holding him tightly in a headlock. When the cop cars pulled up B shoved him to the ground and ran through the double doors. Hal disengaged from his rival by body-slamming him and we three bolted out the back of the Rec Hall and into the alley.

We left a substantial trail of wreckage behind. The broken big ol' plate glass window, a ruined carpet (it was already pretty ruined), a sidewalk littered with fight debris, not the least of which were two guys with a significant amount of blood loss out cold on the pavement. Dutch had stepped forward from behind the bar when I went through the window and helped push me along to the back as he moved to encounter the cops.

B ran left across the street behind the old gas station that recently become a sporting goods joint (where Fork and Cork is today). Hal clamored up the fire escape and entered the second-floor landing. I turned right and went up the alley towards the Sugar Shack. I hopped over the alley-side counter. Sabrina was the only one working and thankfully no one was at the boardwalk-side front counter of the open air snow cone and milkshake stand.

I gave her the shh sign as I scooted into the small back area and even smaller restroom. I locked the door with the tiny hook latch and turned to look at my face in the greasy old mirror. Oh boy... my teeth were all still there, but I was bleeding from a bunch of places. I feverishly worked to clean myself up. Thankfully none of the cuts were too deep, but it took me a bit to get all the glass out of my elbow and hands.

"Lenny, Lenny," Sabrina whispered from just outside the bathroom door a few minutes later. "I cleaned up the blood. What else you want me to do?"

"Get somebody we trust to go tell Darlene where I am," I said.

"On it," she said.

Track 36-Rebel Rebel-David Bowie (4:26)

I was definitely trying to be on it when I met Antoinette's folks. My time with Antoinette's parents at the JV basketball game went surprisingly well. I was a little nervous, a pretty foreign feeling for me. Her mom was pleasant, kind, and sweet. Her dad really didn't say much, we mostly just talked sports and school stuff, but only during timeouts and halftime. The most important thing was he asked me for a favor.

"Lenny," Mr. Royal began. "Antoinette just turned 16, so if you can drive to the dance, I would appreciate it. I have to work and Ms. Royal doesn't drive."

"Yes sir," I said. "No problem."

There was one awkward moment. Antoinette's ex-boyfriend came and sat on the other side of Ms. Royal for the second half.

Oh boy…

When Antoinette went out to cheer during the first break of the second half she saw Roman, her ex sitting with us. You could tell she was concerned. Much to my surprise once again, Roman didn't cause a problem. He was even cordial. As the game came to a close, he stood and hugged Ms. Royal and shook Mr. Royal's hand.

"Lenny, I'll see you Monday," Roman said. "Want to warm up together?"

"Sure thing Roman," I replied. "You're pitching, right?"

He nodded yes and walked down the bleachers to speak to Antoinette. Mr. Royal kept an eye on their exchange as Ms. Royal and I talked about my college choices. At the time I had narrowed my choices to in-state schools offering me a scholarship.

Mr. Royal began to make his way down the bleachers just as Roman was leaving the court. Ms. Royal and I followed.

"Everything ok?" Mr. Royal asked his only child.

"Fine, fine," Antoinette said smiling. "He just wants some of his albums back. Mom, Dad, is it ok if I ride home with Lenny? I'd like to get some ice cream across the street."

"That'll be fine," a beaming Ms. Royal said.

She answered so super-fast, Mr. Royal was left with his mouth partially agape. He just nodded.

"Home by 10:30," Mr. Royal said hugging his daughter. "We're going to visit your aunt in Winston-Salem for the weekend. So we'll be leaving early tomorrow morning. We'll see you next week Lenny."

"Yes sir," I said. "Have a safe trip and a great weekend."

Antoinette and I talked with some of her cheer squad friends and their boyfriends as we made our way out of the gym. The couple ahead of us were holding hands as we descended the few steps from the promenade to the front sidewalk. Antoinette smiled at me as she took my right hand in her left. We could feel several sets of eyes upon us. We didn't care.

We slid into a booth at the ice cream shop and talked about what to order. A few minutes later one of Antoinette's squad members and her boyfriend stopped by to say hi.

"You guys want to join us?" Antoinette asked Cindy, pointing to the vacant seat across from us.

"Sure," she said sliding in.

"Ah, I gotta tell Richard something," said Thomas, Cindy's dude, motioning with his head and shoulders to the counter area.

There were about a half dozen of our classmates and kids from the academy seated at the counter.

"I'll order for us over there," Thomas continued.

Cindy gave him a quizzical look. Thomas just walked away without speaking to Antoinette or me. Yep, you guessed it, he had a problem with me and Antoinette being together. This was a kid I had known since seventh grade and helped on multiple occasions from getting his butt beat.

"Sorry," Cindy said. "That was rude."

Antoinette smiled and didn't say anything. I just sat there. Cindy, obviously uncomfortable, stumbled through some attempts at conversation but gave up after Thomas and a few of our classmates continued to glare over at our table. Cindy started to slide out of the booth.

"I guess I better go get my ice cream," she said as she left kinda shaking her head.

The group at the counter continued to stare. No one had come to take our order.

"Do you want to just go?" Antoinette asked clutching my right elbow and smiling.

"Nah," I said. "I'll go order at the counter.

"Do you think that's a good idea?" she asked.

I was already up.

"Want to split a strawberry shake?" I asked.

Antoinette nodded yes. I made my way over to the counter. The two white guys working behind the counter paid me no attention and stayed at the other end of the long Formica-topped serving area.

"So Lenny," James started. "How's Darlene?"

James went to the same academy as Darlene attended when she lived on our little island.

"She's doing great, James," I replied. "I'll tell her you asked."

He stepped toward me.

"She know about your love of chocolate?" he continued in a threatening manner.

Two of his classmates and Thomas inched closer.

"Not that it's any of your business," I said quite sternly. "But Darlene and I have agreed that we can see other people. And if you don't step back, all you're going to be seeing are the ceiling tiles!"

Just then, Cindy grabbed a hold of Thomas.

"No Morehead Scholarship if you get arrested," Cindy said loudly, grabbing Thomas by the arm quite forcibly, and jerking him back. Plus, you know Lenny's half-crazy. No disrespect Lenny."

I smiled a wild-eyed smile at Cindy.

"I'm sure you big bad boys can take me," I said. "There are four of ya, but I'm going to fuck at least one of you up real bad."

I said the last part slowly turning my head to glare into the eyes of each one.

"Lenny," Antoinette's sweet voice beckoned from directly behind me. "I'd like to go now."

"Lenny!" one of the counter guys who graduated the year before said as he approached the about to be a brawl crowd. "Lenny, get out of here! Don't come back either."

I lurched my head and shoulders forward at Thomas. He leaned back.

"That's what I thought," I said. "Any of you racist assholes want to try me sometime you know where to find me. Hope you got a good doctor."

I turned and grabbed Antoinette's hand and left. I fired the Duster up and did a doughnut right in front of the ice cream shop entrance creating a wall of smoke from the Duster's Michelin tires. I gunned it big time leaving the parking lot. The Duster roared.

"Well, I expected some problems," Antoinette said as I tore down the main drag back to her neighborhood. "But Lenny, you got to take it easy, you can't fight the whole world."

She slid over close to me and laid her head on my shoulder.

"I know you would, but don't," she said. "My parents will step in if you get in trouble because of us. Anyway, slow down. I don't have to be home for another hour and a half. Let's just go be alone, together."

Antionette was the epitome of a young lady; innocent, a little pouty, and girlish at the same time, but also about as fiery a combo of will, intellect, and physical beauty as I would ever run across.

Track 37-Thunder Road-Robert Mitchum (2:58)

The Duster was one fiery combo as well and a seriously mean machine. It deserved a better owner. By most accounts, I had three significant accidents driving it to an early grave. As a team, we acquired countless other tickets, a horrible driving record, and enough other incidents that would fill an entire dossier. It was impounded twice and torn apart by the mainland coppers once in a fruitless search for something to pin on me. Thank goodness, I never physically hurt anyone but myself with my reckless driving. Emotional turmoil, now that's another story.

There were a couple of fun things the Duster was involved in as well. Of course, the times with Darlene will always remain number one. My brief time with Antoinette is second. And tied for third? A slew of happy insanity, here are a few.

1.   Eleventh grade, spring semester. They opened a new bank a few miles from our school. During lunch period one day, Hal got the brilliant idea to open an account, but not just any account. He told me his stupid plan. I agreed. Hal sat behind me with Anson up front that day. We approached the drive-through. I rolled my window down.

"Hello," I smiled. "I'd like to deposit, a moon!" Hal had dropped his drawers and pressed his big ol 'butt up against the Dusters' driver's side back window. I sped off. "You're going to clean that window," I laughed.

2. The first time I significantly damaged the Duster I was running from the law during the holidays 10th grade year. Back then, several of our little island's side roads were still dirt between the two incorporated areas. I knew them well, the highway patrol didn't. I was just 16, had a car full of drunk and stoned teenagers with me and decided it would be a wise choice to try and run from the coppers who attempted to pull me for speeding. What an idiot. I had managed to elude them thus far this particular night, but the three cars giving chase (that I could see) were beginning to gain on me. So I whipped it down one of the dirt roads from the main drag leading back to Killing Floor Road. Their lights and sirens were screaming and dancing behind me and so were a couple of my passengers, including Lexi, Sabrina, and Donny. I knew this particular dirt road had a substantial "gulley" about three-quarters of the way down. The coppers didn't. No way could they have seen it with the dust I was kicking up, the beautiful pure blackness of a dirt road night, and the absence of any streetlights. They were right on me as I quickly swerved right up a slight embankment to avoid the trench. The first cop car barreled right into the gulley, the second plowed into him and the third ran into the woods and hit some trees. My bent tag, coupled with the mud and dirt saved me from paying the immediate price. The Duster hid in Hal's garage for two weeks. Dad bought the story I was having my Keystone rims reset. Of course, the downside was I began to think the Duster and I were invincible. Like I said, what an idiot.

3.   Road trips and concerts would have to be right up there as well. I drove down to Myrtle Beach one summer night after 11th grade with a car full of buds to see the Doobie Brothers. I drove back in a damn tropical storm. Lucky that night as well. Great show, they were right at the height of their powers, "What Were Once Vices, Are Now Habits" tour. How true, how true. Also, a great trip to the Underground in Atlanta to see the original Lynyrd Skynyrd. Shook my soul, to say the least. Damn, Cassie Gaines was fine! She was one of Skynyrd's back-up singers, The Honkettes. Both she and her brother Steve, who played guitar in the band, perished in the infamous plane crash that decimated the band the next year.

4.   I could go on and on, if I see ya around, I'll tell ya some more, but it's about time to wrap up Disc II, so this is the Duster's last ride. Anson and I had been to a party at Knotty Beach and were heading home the back way, the same way Hal used near the end of Disc I. Anson lived on the Intracoastal Waterway about halfway between Knotty Beach and our little island. The NC Department of Transportation has changed the road significantly over the years due to the fatalities in or around an area known as the cliché "dead man's curve" for our county. It was a bad, bad curve. I had traveled it many times and never had any problems. Of course, I was going near the speed limit all those times and mostly sober. This night I was flying in more ways than one. Paul McCartney and Wings' "Jet" from the LP *Band on the Run* in eight-track form was rocking us down the highway. This particular dead man's curve was actually two bad curves back to back. I made the first, a hard right, barely. The rear

end fishtailed slightly to the left, I corrected just right to get the Duster back square but didn't have time to make a clean, hard left the second curve required seconds later. I pulled the wheel too much and she fishtailed hard right as I exited the second curve. Made it through! Opps...I dumbassedly (don't you love it when I invent words?) overcorrected and we went up on the two left wheels slamming the passenger side into a giant oak about 30 yards past the exit to curve two. The car tagged the old oak and bounced off, fishtailing hard left. The Duster, briefly back on all four tires, careened east across the road and promptly began mowing down a wooden fence with the left rear quarter-panel. A light pole stopped our sideways progress as the driver's side door clanged against it. Whew! When the chaos came to a close, the damn thing was still running. I looked at Anson. He looked at me. He had a little scratch on his right cheek. Me? Nothing...I instinctively hit the gas. The Duster roared forward, fishtailing slightly right, but I got her straightened back up and off we went toward Crazy Beach. The windshield was mostly gone, as were the side windows. Both doors and most of the rest of both sides were crumpled in some. Anson's side of the roof was crushed a bunch. The engine sounded fine. We blazed on down the back road.

"Holy Shit!" Anson exclaimed. "You're insane!"

I laughed, a little in shock I think. We got to his road and I slowed the Duster to a crawl. The DaMino's had a huge tract of land along the Intracoastal Waterway and I came up with the bright idea to try and hide the Duster as far into the woods as I could get. I was able to ease her down a narrow dusty path near a shed to her almost final resting place about 150 yards or so from the DaMino's waterfront home. A small forest of trees provided great cover.

Fast forward to the weekend of our 10th high school reunion. Anson was hosting a little shindig for about two dozen of our classmates at his parent's waterfront home.

"How you still alive, Lenny?" Big Will laughed.

Several nods all around from the peanut gallery.

"Lenny," Mr. DaMino said. "You ever going to get your car out from behind my shed?"

"You got to be kidding me," Big Will said. "That's where the Duster is? I got to go see it. Damn, I had some fun in that ride."

So almost the whole crowd, with the exception of Ms. DaMino, a few of the girls, and Chico the old Dachshund, walked out to the dilapidated shed. And sure enough, there she sat, just where I left her 11.2 years before. A few exclamations, expletives, and gasps were heard. Everyone standing there was familiar with the Duster. Almost all of them could tell their own story or stories about their time having some big fun in which the Duster played a major part.

It was my first time seeing her up close since the night of the wreck. I pulled and pulled with no luck trying to open the driver's side door. I looked over the left side of my first car. The left rear quarter-panel was destroyed, the frame severely compromised, and roof bashed in above the passenger-side door where it had struck the oak tree and the driver's side where we finished our crash up against the light pole. I walked around the front, the right headlight was gone, and the whole hood area and right side a general disaster. The only glass left intact was the rear window. The ol' Duster looked like she had been ganged up on by several much bigger, heavier cars at a Demolition Derby. Anson struggled with the crushed passenger side door for a bit but finally managed to get it partially open.

"Unreal," Anson said. *Band on the Run* is still in the eight-track."

I walked to the door reached in and pulled the tape out. I also pulled the keys out of the ignition and began to walk back toward the house. The key fob was a MOPAR logo on one side and the Duster decal (a swirling tornado with eyes) that also adorned the trunk on the other.

"Oh man, you got to tell that story Lenny," Big Will said. "What the hell happened? We figured you just traded her for the Monte Carlo."

That's what I told my dad.

Track 38-Rambling Gambling Man-Bob Seger (2:25)

I was just finishing up polishing the Duster's Keystone mag rims when my father approached from beneath the front deck. I rose and started to put my polishing rags back in the trunk. Dad put his hand on the right rear quarter panel in a manner that kept me from closing the trunk. He looked down at its contents. Thankfully, I had sold most of the goodies the day before as my friends loaded up for the big Sadie Hawkins dance. Still, there were a couple of pints and one fifth somewhat exposed, partially covered by a beach towel.

"Just saw your report card," Dad said. "That's strong. You're going to need to keep that up if you're going to get in Duke."

Duke was and will always be my favorite school. I was fortunate to be able to do some post-grad work there about 10 years ago and enjoyed every moment. You've already heard the circumstances that led me to pick our local school's scholarship offer over the half-ride scholarship offer Duke pitched me back in the day. But at that moment when I was talking to Dad, I was 100% going to Duke.

"You can't screw up either," Dad said, looking down at the booze. "Your mom doesn't know, but I do. Some of the other stuff too, but you've always made A's, played sports, and worked hard, so..."

He walked away. He got to the third step and turned around as I closed the trunk. He came back about halfway to me.

"You did make that one C," he said, a little smile crossing his face.

He turned to go inside.

Well, I did make one C. I had always made straight A's. The C came in Biology the very first six weeks grading period of ninth grade. The reason? Yep, you guessed it, a girl, Joanie Chiconconie. Joanie had been my classmate for five years and had perhaps the prettiest face I have ever seen. She was of Italian heritage with high cheekbones and a gorgeous smile, but she had always been a real skinny little tom-boy with short jet black hair and we had never really talked much. At the start of eighth grade, she had begun to let her hair grow some.

The first day of ninth grade, I walked into my Biology class and guess who got their "boobies" over the summer. Yep, Joanie Chiconconie and they were perfect, showcased exquisitely in a skin tight short sleeve red top. She had on black pants just as tight. She sat down right beside me. I about swallowed my tongue. She also got assigned to be my lab partner. I was so mesmerized. Her gorgeous, shiny hair was now half-way down her back. The next six weeks were the only time in my life up to that point that I didn't know what to say or do around a girl. I was the stereotypical geek mumbling and fumbling all over himself trying to find a way to communicate with this suddenly goddess of a girl I had known forever. I failed, and I almost failed the class. The only reason I didn't? Joanie and her family moved before our final six weeks test. I was able to recover enough to earn a very generous C. When I had to take that report card home, I knew my only hope was to tell the truth, the whole truth, and nothing but the truth, I swear to Elvis. So that's what I did. My dad gave me a pass, little light chuckle included. My mom didn't think it was funny, serious negative headshake included.

The day I was polishing the Duster's rims, I could tell by the look on my dad's face he still found it funny too. Over the years, when things in life were going a little too good for me, he would always, at just the most perfect moment around family, friends, or just when we were alone, say: "You did make that one C".

So, another bullet dodged with the booze in my trunk. I went inside to get ready for the dance. I hate dressing up, black t-shirts, and shorts for me, please. But I dressed up in a nice dark blue suit, dark blue shirt with a black tie, and came out of my room.

"Now that's a sharp looking fella," Great-Aunt Pat said from the bar, where she and Dad were having a cold one.

Mom turned from the stove and displaying her beautiful, charming smile came over to meet me by the end of the counter. She put her hands on my shoulders.

"Not everyone thinks like we do Son," she said. "React the way Jesus would."

She kissed me on the cheek. My dad gave me a little-downturned smile and took a big gulp of his brew. Great-Aunt Pat raised her beverage with her left hand and mouthed the words "kill-em all" as she made a pistol firing motion with her right hand. I gave Mom a kiss back and headed down the stairs.

The Duster roared to life and the radio blasted some Temptations' music into the cool spring evening air. I took a deep breath of the salty mist and headed to the mainland.

"Antoinette will be out in a bit," Ms. Royal, basically a couple of decades older version of her daughter said. "You two have a good time."

She walked past me and out the front door. I thought it was kinda curious she left. I saw her walk down the street toward her sister's house. Mr. Royal appeared from Antoinette's room.

"She's coming Lenny," he said. "You know how girls are. Let's you and I sit on the porch a bit."

Oh boy…

I thought here comes another "talk". Except for this time, I knew I needed to hear what was about to be said. We settled into two old unvarnished rocking chairs on the right side of the porch facing the street. A black couple walked by, Mr. Royal waved. They waved heads down and quickly walked past. Antoinette and I were already the talk of her neighborhood, our school, and my little island.

"Lenny," Mr. Royal started. "I been watching you play ball since you were a real young fella in Little League. My nephew has played against or with you quite a few times over the years. I guess I seen you most years, all but soccer, and I hear that might even be your best sport."

I just sat there nodding and smiling a little. So far, so good. I knew the tone was about to change.

"You're a hard-working young man by all accounts," he continued. "And like I said, I seen with my own eyes what a fine ballplayer you are, but Ms. Royal and I, we've been having some talks about this, about you and our Antoinette liking one another. Well, you can't help who you like, and from our talks with our daughter, she likes you plenty. Ms. Royal says I should just let you two make your own way that you'll figure it out soon enough."

I knew this is where the next but, the critical but would come in. There's always a critical but in these type conversations, right?

"But," he said.

Damn, sometimes I hate being right.

"The time for this ain't come yet," he said looking me squarely in the eye.

I just sat there leaning over, my forearms resting on my upper thighs with my hands lightly clasped together. I tried to remain expressionless. I probably failed.

"Now, don't get me wrong," Mr. Royal said. "The times coming for it, it just ain't yet. Some people will still be against it when the time does come. The loud-mouth ones will be the only ones to say anything, now and then. And they damn sure will have a lot to say."

Just then Antoinette walked out the screen door. Her father and I both rose. She looked like she stepped out of a painting. She had on a shimmery, mid-thigh length pink pastel dress with black Candies open-toe heels and a gold ankle bracelet on her right ankle. Her hair was full afro and she had on dangly onyx earrings. Once again, what a lucky boy am I!

"Well, I already told you how pretty you look," Mr. Royal said hugging his daughter. "But, I'm going to tell you again. You and your mom sure picked a lovely dress."

I just nodded in agreement with Mr. Royal and kept nodding, like an idiot. I may have drooled a little too.

Antoinette pinned a nice dark blue and white boutonniere on me and I gave her a pink and white wrist corsage my mom had helped me pick out. I awkwardly slipped it on her left wrist.

"Wait, wait," Ms. Royal called, hurrying up the sidewalk. "I had to get Latisha's camera. You kids stand by the car."

There were two spectacularly beautiful things in that picture, Antoinette and the Duster, both in full-flower of the optimism and shininess of youth.

Track 39-Runaway-Jefferson Starship (5:24)

Sabrina managed to get a hold of David who went to see Dutch. Dutch had sequestered Darlene and Hal from the cops in his office upstairs. Hal and Darlene got in David's car and parked behind Britt's donut shop. David told Sabrina the coast was clear and I quickly slid down the alley next to the shop and made my getaway. We picked B up at his house and went to Lexi's.

Lexi's folks were always very standoffish and I don't think I ever had a real conversation with either one. Her older brother had built her an enclosed treehouse when she was about eight and it was one of our "safe houses". You could access it from the woods behind her house. The six of us sat inside for the first time in many, many years.

"How about a game of spin the bottle?" Hal asked.

"What are we, 12?" Lexi smirked.

"Well, what are we going to do just sit here?" Hal inquired.

"For a bit," I said.

"Ok," Lexi said. "But you guys keep it down, Dad's home, and Darlene and I need to go in."

Darlene was pretty shaken from the earlier events. She kept brushing my hair back and looking at my damaged elbow. She laid her head on my shoulder until Lexi urged her to come with her to the house.

"I'll see you tomorrow," she said giving me a big hug and a quick kiss on the lips.

"I got to go guys," David said.

"Me too," Hal said.

They climbed down the makeshift wooden ladder and eased into the woods.

B and I just looked at one another.

"Crash here?" He asked.

I nodded, but we both knew we would have some explaining to do if anyone said anything to the police.

Luckily no one said exactly who was in the brawl. Heath, the big butthole that he was, never said a word to the cops, neither did Nathan or their flunkies, code of the streets and all. A couple of tourists gave the cops a little info and we were questioned separately a few days later. We all had a standard story to tell the coppers.

"We were camping by Boy Scout Lake," I told the Chief.

"You boys sure do camp a lot Lenny," the Chief laughed. "Someone almost killed that Heath boy. He's going to be in the hospital for a while. They just let the other guy out. But he's on probation up in the mountains and he went back up there without talking. I made them pay for the window to stay out of jail. You might want to tell anybody you think may have been involved not to mix with that crowd anymore."

"Will do Chief," I said rising to leave.

"Oh, Lenny," the Chief said standing up. "One more thing…how did you hurt your arm?"

"Sliding into home," I smiled.

I walked out of the Chief's office, put my sunglasses on, and strolled across the street to Vito's Bait and Tackle Shop by the marina. Vito's was also a locals' bar where my dad and others his age hung out. Darlene and Lexi were waiting for me. Darlene breathed a sigh of relief. Lexi shook her head.

"Let me get a coke Vito," I said sitting on a stool next to the girls.

"So?" Darlene asked, punching me on the shoulder.

"All good," I said.

"You're the luckiest person to walk this earth Lenny," Lexi said. "Anybody else would be under the jailhouse by now."

"I would ask you to promise to not do stuff like that anymore," Darlene said. "But I can't think of a bigger waste of time. Sometimes I think I should just run away from you."

We all laughed. Vito looked at my arm.

"You going to be able to play this week?" he asked. "But more importantly, are you going to be able to cut donuts? Tammy don't like working with nobody but you."

"Thanks for the sentiment Vito," I started. "My arm is fine."

"I'd ask." He said. "But I got a feeling I don't want to know. I got an idea. We all got an idea. What did G.R. say?"

"Bout the same thing you did," I laughed.

The last week of Darlene's stay with Lexi went pretty smooth. Darlene and I spent a lot of time on the beach, rode the Skyliner cable car out over the pier and the Ferris Wheel a couple times, and played several games of putt-putt. Our teenage lust ran rampant, which was a lot of fun. Most importantly, I was able to keep my promise to Mr. Winter, but thankfully didn't have to fulfill it in totality. There would be no fifth straight Fourth of July cookout for our families. Ms. Winter was too ill to make the trip down. Our American Legion baseball team was in the state playoffs so Lexi's folks took Darlene back home.

"You going to come up before school starts?" Darlene asked from Lexi's driveway.

"Yea, I should be able too," I said.

We kissed for a moment. She turned to go, and yep you guessed it, she gave me our little wave. I did the same.

Track 40-The Boys are Back in Town-Thin Lizzy (4:24)

Ok, to finish up our big road trip story for this Disc, we took Emmy with us and got her to the dentist without incident. She messed around with me some, but I let her have enough fun that she didn't spill the beans on what had transpired almost two weeks before. B and I picked up the supplies from the hardware and waited for Emmy's stuff to be done.

"I'm bout ready to roll on," I said.

B looked over at me as we sat in the ancient flatbed.

"Yea," he said. "Jema is a little crazy. I'm not getting tons of sleep and she likes taking too many chances."

I nodded. Oh boy...did I do some nodding.

"The other night she wanted to do it outside her grandma's bedroom door," B continued. "Old lady woke up, went to the bathroom while Jema was riding me right down the hall."

I laughed out loud. B did the same just as Emmy emerged from the small brick office. She had a wad of cotton in her right cheek. She looked sore and sad. She could only mumble. I understood they did something pretty harsh to her, dental-wise, but I couldn't make out just quite what.

To try and make Emmy feel better B told her a couple stories about our misadventures.

"This fool," he began. "He'd make me carry his soccer equipment on away games because his bag was full of booze."

Being my teammate had its perks.

"We were playing North Myrtle Beach one time," B continued. "After the game, our Nigerian coach, Coach Nwsou stopped the bus to get some gas. Now Lenny, realizing all the booze was almost gone, opens the emergency door, and strolls over to the Red Dot Liquor store next door. Don't ask how he got them to sell him booze in a high school soccer uniform."

Emmy raised both her eyebrows at me.

"Told'em it was a college jersey," I smiled. "Besides, I still got the fake ID for the hard stuff.

A quick side note about North Myrtle Beach. It is the hometown of Ms. Vanna White of Wheel of Fortune fame. She was a cheerleader for her squad the day we played her team in North Myrtle. I think she was a sophomore that year. North Myrtle produces some unreal looking girls with Vanna of course, being one. That day she was just a real skinny kid with a gorgeous face. Several of her teammates got most of the attention from us as they were upperclassman and physically more mature. One of our players, Alex, and one of the North Myrtle girls, Dusty, even connected enough that they are still together all these decades later.

B continued his Lenny history lesson.

"We lost one game 2-1 to a small rural school," B said. "Coach Nwsou was sooo pissed. In his thick Nigerian accent, he said 'I never had a team play drunk on me before'."

Emmy laughed and immediately grabbed her jaw.

"He got our buddy Hal into big trouble last year in Coach Nwsou's Sports Lit class," B said as we approached the farm. "We were having an oral pop quiz. He and Hal were in the very back row side-by-side. Now those two had been smoking a lot of weed and Hal was asleep with his head on the desk. Coach called on Hal for the answer. Hal woke up and asked Lenny to help him. Lenny said the answer was D, so Hal told coach, "The answer is D coach". Now Coach Nwsou was furious. He took several steps in Hal's direction and pointed his finger at Hal and raised his voice. "Dobbins, Hal, you are a stupid ass. There is only A, B, and C for an answer. Go straight to the principal's office'."

Emmy again had to clutch her jaw as we pulled into the farm's long dirt drive.

We uneventfully slipped away that night.

Track 41-Vincent (Starry, Starry Night)-Don McLean (4:38)

"Maybe I'm a painter for people that haven't been born yet."-Vincent Van Gogh

Antoinette and I battled for one another, but the forces of the times swept us apart. The dance, well you can imagine. I wish I could say people were more open-minded. They weren't. Now don't get me wrong, we got some support. Just not very much, and not out in the open by hardly anyone. The most support we garnered came from the least likely source.

We managed to make it through the dance without a riot breaking out, barely. We made it in the gym without too much hassle and of all people, Lexi was the one who hung out with us the most. She was well aware of mine and Darlene's "New Deal". She and Antoinette knew each other a little from cheerleading camp and had a history class together. My fellas were nowhere to be found. I don't think they got asked. Lexi had invited a senior transfer guy that we knew zilch about. He seemed ok and didn't hassle us about being together. He was a bit suspicious Lexi and I had something going on. Well, we had been friends since third grade, we have that, and always will.

"I got to go," Lexi said to Antoinette motioning for her to come along.

Oh boy…

I don't remember Lexi's date's name, of course, he probably doesn't remember mine either.

"How long you two been going out?" he asked.

"Just started," I said.

"Oh," he said. "She's really pretty and seems cool."

"Yea," I said. "She's something special."

"Well, I don't know you man," he said. "But I got to give it to you. It's pretty ballsy."

I nodded just as a group of black guys approached.

"Hey Lenny," Donnell started. "What's going on man?"

"Not much," I said.

"No man," he continued. "I mean with my cousin, Antoinette?"

"We're hanging out," I said. "She rocks."

Donnell nodded his head up and down a few times. His three buddies, two of which I had played sports with or against for years stepped closer.

Donnell extended his right arm to block a couple of them from coming closer.

"Look man," Donnell said. "You always been alright with me. But this isn't cool. Something bad going to happen y'all keep it up."

"I appreciate the concern," I countered. "But I'm a lucky kinda guy. I'll take my chances. I think Antoinette is well worth it."

Just then Bossy Mossy stepped in.

"Alright boys," he said.

I could see the girls approaching. Lexi's date walked toward them and began speaking rather loudly.

"Going to be some trouble," he said. "We should go."

Lexi pushed away his attempt to take her arm and walked toward me hand in hand with Antoinette.

The staring contest between me and the fellas eased off.

"Why don't you boys go get some punch," Bossy Mossy said pointing to the other side of the gym. "I got to talk to the King of the Zeroes."

They waited a few seconds, then backed away. Lexi and Antoinette were right beside me. Antoinette took my hand while still clutching Lexi's with the other.

"Damn it Lenny," Bossy said. "You're not going to make it to 30 boy. Hell, you probably won't make it to 25. Anything else happens I'm going to suspend you. I knew I should have last week, but Coach Hall talked me out of it. Those scholarship offers can go away pretty quick if you're in jail."

When he said the anything else happens part, he glanced over at Antoinette. Just then a slow song came on and I pulled Antoinette out on the dance floor. Bossy just shook his head. We danced to Don McClean's "Starry, Starry Night", a hauntingly beautiful ballad about Vincent Van Gogh.

Antoinette placed her face next to mine and whispered:

"Let's just go after this. We can go down to the beach, it's still kinda early."

I held her tight and danced. It was the best slow dance I ever had.

Track 42-Show Me the Way-Peter Frampton (4:04)

The crowd slowly trickled into the small, brick Presbyterian Church across the river. It was my dad's church. It was late February 2006. Dad had moved across the river after he and Mom divorced in the early 1990s. He married my step-mom in 1992. They had a nice house, in a nice neighborhood. She was one of the best things that ever happened to my dad. Like June Carter deserving to be in the Country Music Hall Fame multiple times, one for her musical career, and another induction for helping keep Johnny Cash alive many more years. My step-mom filled the same role with my pops.

This day was my dad's funeral. I stood at the front and watched my dad's church friends, his old friends, beach people, and family come through the doors. Most of my old gang of fellas was there. I was supposed to give the eulogy. I had nothing yet. Thankfully, I still had a few more minutes. I took a seat in the front row. The pastor asked me to go to the back and enter with the whole family. My mind wandered off.

Mom had left Dad in 1990 for another dude and they stayed together until her death. She had her reasons for leaving. No one knows what goes on behind closed doors as Charlie Rich sang. My dad never physically hurt my mom, but he hurt her plenty. Having your parents divorce sucks, even when you're grown. Mom kept the house Dad and Uncle D had built almost 25 years earlier. Of course, she didn't keep it long, as noted in Disc I. Hurricane Fran washed it out to sea in 1996. Mom lived in a small condo two blocks from her beloved ocean the rest of her days until passing peacefully in 2012. My step-mom made clear my mom wasn't welcomed at my father's funeral. My father would not have wanted her there. My mom didn't attempt to come.

My mind kept wandering…oh the places it went, but still, nothing was coming to me except the usual cliché eulogy stuff. B took my arm. Of course, he was going to sit with the family.

"You got this man," he said firmly, looking me in the eye to make sure I did. "She's here."

I nodded. Well now, things just got even tougher. Still, not quite as tough as our last few days together decades before. It all started with a phone call.

I heard the phone ring, yep same old cream colored phone in the same old place by the calendar above the bar. I just happened to be home, I hadn't been much lately since I had gotten back from Mexico.

"Lenny," she said. "It's me."

"I know it's you," I said.

"Both mine and Dad's schools have fall break next week and we're coming to the island Friday," Darlene said. "Our dads are going fishing, golfing, and stuff. We're going to be staying with you guys for the week."

Oh boy…

It was the first time we had talked since she had moved again. Four months, at least. We had exchanged a few letters. It was like she was a million miles away. It was the fall of our freshman year of college.

"Oh, wow," I said. "That's cool. What time are you guys getting here, about?"

"We're leaving super early," she said. "So probably suppertime?"

"Ok," I said. "We have a home soccer match that night at seven, so I'll see you after."

"No, no," she said. "I want to see you play. I'll make sure we make the game."

She did.

When I looked up in the stands before the match, for the briefest of moments, it was like no time had elapsed, like there was no geographical separation, and like nothing bad had happened to either of us. Mr. Winter and my dad were sitting side by side like always about halfway up the bleachers with Darlene next to her father.

The night air was a little cool and the autumn sky dark blue, almost violet, like Darlene's eyes. The nighttime canvas was covered by a host of light white, cotton soft clouds with sparkling stars hanging between them like tiny beacons in a beautiful storm. The night had the feeling of a setting in a story involving magic and the forces aligned against it.

Darlene had on jeans, small black boots, and a big white sweater with her hair in a ponytail with a golden ribbon. When she saw that I spotted her, she stood up and did our little awkward half wave. I did the same.

I played decently, had an assist, and we won 2-1. Darlene rode back to our little island with me. The last time she would do so.

"This car's no Duster, or Monte Carlo even, but its damn fine," she said.

I had sold the Monte Carlo the week before and bought a Petty-blue 1974 Pontiac LeMans Sports Coupe with black louver windows on each side of the back seat's tear-dropped shaped windows and a huge rear window with the same black louvers. It was a sweet ride. I wrecked it running from the law a year later. I didn't get away that time. I had to do more than wash police cars. But those are tales for other days.

We talked mostly about her school, the Shenandoah Valley, and Lexi.

"I don't know what she's going to do," Darlene said. "She's late, real late."

"Who's she seeing?" I asked. "Or was it just a hookup?"

"I'm not supposed to say," she said looking out the passenger window while Frampton's "Show Me the Way" played on the radio. "His name is Ricco. He's on the football team there at UNC."

Lexi and several of our friends and my classmates had left for Chapel Hill for college a couple months earlier. Lexi had made the cheerleading squad. But it sounded like she might not be on it much longer.

"Her parents are going to kill her," I said.

"Well, your parents didn't kill Jane," Darlene said.

"Yea, but my parents aren't silent closet psychos like hers," I said.

Lil'sis had gotten pregnant the year before at 16 by a 27-year-old carney she later married. That didn't last long. There is a whole book in Lil'sis' story, but that's a tale for another time as well.

"Oh," Darlene said. "I know you won't care, but her family will. Ricco is black."

After a few minutes of silence, except for more Frampton, I changed the conversation.

"I don't have any Tuesday/Thursday classes," I said. "So we can hang out those days if you want. I'll have practice though and an away game Wednesday."

"Where is the away game?" she asked.

"Campbell," I said.

"That's pretty close isn't it?" she asked.

"Yea," I said. "Less than two hours."

"Well, maybe we can all go?" she asked.

"Nobody goes to our away games," I said. "Not even my dad."

"Oh," she said. "Well, I just might."

I wheeled the LeMans into the carport behind the Winter's vehicle.

"This should be interesting," I said as we made our way up the front steps.

I opened the door for Darlene like I had done so many times, funny how stuff like that strikes you sometimes. But I thought about it right then. You don't think about it each and every time, but that time I did.

The dads were on the back deck. Mom was reading at the table. "Only the Good Die Young" by Billy Joel was playing on the ancient AM/FM clock radio on the bar. It would give up the ghost during the Winter's visit. It had been a part of my whole life playing the soundtrack of my youth. I can still hear its alarm, an unpleasant reminder it was time to go somewhere. It had been a wedding present to my folks from Mom's best friend. Dad tossed it in the garbage like supper leftovers. Dad wasn't the sentimental type.

"Oh hey sweetie," Mom said rising to give Darlene a big ol' hug. "It's so good to see you."

"I'm so happy to see you too," Darlene said kissing Mom on the cheek.

"I've already set your dad up in Jane's old room," Mom continued. "You'll take Lenny's room. Son, you'll be on the couch."

Darlene and I just looked at one another. Mom smiled.

"You want something to eat honey?" Mom asked.

"No thank you," Darlene said. "We stopped in town before the game."

"Oh, ok," Mom said. "Your father said your team won and you made some good plays."

"Yes ma'am," I said. "I passed it to Iwan and he scored. I helped stop them from getting a couple of shots."

"Well, that's nice," Mom said. "I think I'll go read in my room. I'll see you both in the morning."

She gave us both a kiss on the cheek. I looked over at the couch. Mom had put a bed sheet over the cushions and tossed an extra pillow at one end.

"You want to go for a walk?" Darlene asked. "I'd love to see the boardwalk."

"Sure," I said.

"Let me go tell my dad," Darlene said and turned to go outside.

You ever have that feeling when you know something feels so right, but it also feels like a dream?

"It's a little windy out there," Darlene said. "Let's walk down the boardwalk side. You think anybody is at the Rec Hall?"

"Maybe," I said. "We can go check it out."

We headed down the front steps and walked past where the old steel pier and Skyliner cable car ride used to be. A hurricane had taken it all out the year before.

"That's so sad," she said. "Remember the last time we walked up there?"

I laughed.

"Yep," I said. "That was the last time we pulled the old jump from the pier bet bit."

She punched me on the shoulder.

"It's so deserted now," she said. "That was where we had our first kiss. It was my first kiss period."

I nodded. I would have bet $100 she was going to say that in almost that exact order. Of course, she was alluding to the fact my first kiss was with Dani at Woodstock. A story she knew well. Remember what I said in Disc One about her always remembering every important date, firsts, and stuff like that? Man, that girl could pull up anything, like a damn computer does.

When the pier fell and several other businesses were damaged, the boardwalk fell into a funk it took 20 plus years to recover from.

It really rocks now, mostly renovated, with a few gaping holes still, but definitely headed in the right direction. For a very long time, it wasn't.

The only things open on the south end were the Silver Dollar, Loretta's, and the Rec Hall. We strolled into an almost empty room as was often the case in late fall and winter. Two guys were shooting pool on one of the middle tables. Dutch was sitting behind the bar counting the money. He didn't see us until we were right near him. We sat on two corner stools.

"Let me get two of the usual," I said.

"Well," Dutch said looking up. "I'll be, if it isn't the long lost Queen of Light on high come home to reclaim her throne."

We laughed.

"Hi Dutch," she said. "Nah, just visiting ol' Lenny boy for the week during fall break."

Dutch asked her about her school, her dad, and life in the Shenandoah Valley. Darlene quizzed Dutch about the Rec Hall, Mirna, and the Cubs.

"Ok, if I take Lenny back here for a minute?" Dutch asked.

She nodded in the affirmative.

I walked back to the end of the bar by the bathrooms. Dutch told me about a meeting he was supposed to have with some people from the mainland on Sunday. He wanted me to be there. I said I would.

"All yours," Dutch said smiling as he walked me back up to the corner of the bar.

"Oh, he's never all anybody's," Darlene laughed.

Everyone was asleep when we got back to the house. Mom left the kitchen light on for us. Darlene went to the sink to get some water. I went to the bathroom to brush my teeth. I came back out and she was sitting on the couch. I went over and sat down beside her.

"Do you want to talk about it now or tomorrow?" she asked looking at me with a sideways glance. "Or later?"

"Is there another choice?" I laughed.

She punched me on the shoulder pretty hard.

"I'm trying to be serious," she said. "I think we need to talk about some things."

"Well," I countered. "In that case, let me get another beer."

She lowered her head as I walked past her to grab a brew. I popped a top, took a big chug, and sat back down.

"Ok," I said. "Fire away."

"Look," she said. "This is important. It's important to me anyway. Despite everything, I still love you more than you will ever know, and I always will. I know a lot of people say crap like that, but I damn sure mean it. Whatever happens you will always be the love of my life and I'm pretty sure I'm yours. We've been mostly together since we were little kids and shared so much. I don't think it would right to let something that special and long lasting just drift away and die without fighting for it. Do you?"

Oh boy…

I wasn't expecting all that. I thought she was going to ask me about my hitchhiking adventure or school, or anything else. Had turning 19 made her more introspective? I knew she had dated some fellas. I'm sure Lexi had kept her abreast of what she knew about my lust life. Man, I wish I'd been better prepared for what all she said. Once again timing, damn timing, for at that precise moment, my normal abilities temporarily left me. Ms. Ellis, my Human Studies and Sociology teacher had, just before graduation, given me a "talking to" after class about my blessings.

"Lenny," she started. "You have that rarest of abilities to say the most appropriate thing at the most opportune time. Goodness knows why He did, but the Good Lord blessed you with so much, you better use it to help people and protect the vulnerable. Now get out of my class and go do some good."

Well for a few moments that night with Darlene on the couch, they all left me, just plain left. Where they went and why they picked those precious, critical moments of my life to go AWOL, I don't know. I only had the one beer at the Rec Hall and two swallows of the one in my hand. I hadn't smoked any dope in a week. How long I sat there I don't know.

"Well?" she asked. "Lenny, are you going to say anything?"

I just sat there. I know, I know, I'm an idiot, a dumbass idiot. The weird thing is, for once I was trying, and I really was. I was trying to find the right sequence of words to tell her I felt the same, but that I knew I would just repeatedly hurt her, and her life would be a roller coaster of disaster and joy if we tried to go forward. Of course, I didn't say any of that. What had come naturally to me my whole life was simply gone. Maybe, it was the only real moment I have ever had my entire stupid life. Maybe it was the only time I ever examined myself and was honest with myself. It sucked.

She raised her hands to her shoulders palms facing inward. She shook her head.

"You better have something to say in the morning asshole," she said shoving my right shoulder as she rose.

She stormed off to my room and slammed the door.

Track 43-It Don't Come Easy-Ringo Starr (3:02)

Before I wrap mine and Darlene's story up, I want to tell you what became of Lexi. She was in fact pregnant. And while Antoinette and I had a very tough time a year and a half before, we only went out for a few months. School let out, summer came, and after another heart-to-heart with Mr. Royal, he and I decided I wasn't going to do anybody, most of all Antoinette, any good if I was dead or in prison. She wasn't happy. She called me some names, later apologized, and we were even able to become friends for my senior year and her junior year. She went to UNC and then to Medical School, where I have forgotten. She became a pediatrician in the Piedmont.

Lexi decided to keep the baby. Ricco and she kept their secret through the first semester freshman year, but when his parents found it out, they forced him to abandon Lexi. Her parents did as well when they found out the kid had a black father. Lexi dropped out of school after her first semester of college.

My parents helped her with an apartment on the mainland. Uncle Ed got her a good job. The kid, a beautiful, healthy little girl named Priscilla was born the next summer on the fourth of July. My mom watched the baby while Lexi worked. By this time my poor sister was such a mess, my mom and Dad were raising her kid as well. I look at my nephew like a little brother.

Anyway, Lexi struggled for a few months, then, I don't know if you believe in miracles, but a miraculous thing happened. Who stepped up to the plate? Not too hard, huh? Yep, you guessed it. Good ol' Hal. Hal stayed at it, despite years and years of rejection he kept chasing her and loving her. At first, it was gifts for the baby. Then gifts for Lexi and the baby. Lexi's car broke down, Hal fixed it. Lexi got behind on her bills, Hal fixed it. He finally fixed her cold ass heart too.

She finally melted on her birthday two years later when we were having a party for her at the house. Hal, a little late, as usual, lumbered in with Bluto and B2, who was then a tiny pup. Yep, you guessed that one too. B2 was a gift for Lexi. There was something else, tied around B2's cute little brown neck was a yellow ribbon holding a tiny yellow box. Yellow was Lexi's favorite color. She opened the box, pulled out a diamond ring, and screamed. Hal dropped to one knee and asked Lexi to marry him right in the middle of our living room, the site of so many joyous events. This may have been the most joyous.

They're still together, three kids, all grown, and leading great lives. Hal has his own auto repair shop and Lexi does medical coding work. They were all there for Dad's funeral. B5 was in the truck.

Track 44-Kiss and Say Goodbye-The Manhattans (4:15)

I woke first, early, real early. I opened the double doors and walked out on the deck. What a morning. The crispness of fall was ripe with the scent of the briny sea. The sun was just peeking over the horizon and the gulls were squawking at the trawlers to slow down so they could get their breakfast. I decided to go surfing. The last time I would do so. I hadn't been in quite a while and although I still enjoyed it, I had never been hardcore about it, and for me, it just left me, or I left it, like comic books, cartoons, and treehouses.

As I finished my last ride and started to jog back up the beach, I saw Darlene sitting on the deck looking my way. She had on a long white bathrobe tied at the waist. I peeled my wetsuit down to my midsection and doused myself with some fresh water from the shower head halfway up our walkway. It was so cold! I bent over and shook my head really hard, rapidly stood up, and pushed my hair back. I sat my old board in its usual spot by the china cabinet and went up the steps.

"Good morning," I said. "Hey, I'm sorry about last night."

"Shut-up," she said. "You suck at apologies and anybody can tell when you're lying."

She laughed a little at the last part while placing her right palm on my bare chest.

"I brought you a coke," she said handing me the red and white can.

"Thanks," I said.

"You had a couple decent rides," she continued. "That last was real sweet."

"Yea, one of the best I've had in a real long time," I said.

"Breakfast is ready," Mom called from the living room.

I had left the double doors open and the house smelled as good as it ever would. Darlene and I walked in and it all hit me, the powerful aroma of coffee, bacon, the rest of a fresh-cooked breakfast, the fall ocean air, and Darlene's scent.

I wish I could stand there again.

"The guys got an early tee time," Mom said. "So they are already off to the mainland. I've got to get to work at the beauty shop. Stop by and say hi to Gail later."

She was already heading out the door. Our plates were on the bar.

"Let me take a two-minute hot shower," I said.

"You're going to need more than two minutes," Darlene laughed.

I flipped her the bird and headed to the shower. I brushed my teeth and got in. Damn, the hot water felt good. I was washing my hair when I heard the bathroom door open and then close. I opened my eyes and Darlene was standing just outside the shower's opaque door. She dropped her robe and shimmed out of her dark colored panties. I opened the door.

"Let's just let this week be what it will be," she said as she stepped inside.

Track 45-Lucky Man-ELP (4:36)/Time in a Bottle-Jim Croce (2:29)

The family walked into the main seating area. It was standing room only. Folks lined the back of the church and some of the side aisles. I caught many familiar faces as the processional made its way to the front. Of course, I saw her. I got a quick glimpse of her as we passed. She was sitting about three-quarters of the way to the back sandwiched in between her father and another guy, who I later learned was her husband. I couldn't see her face. She had on a black dress and her hair was much shorter, just above her shoulders, still radiantly shiny.

I had to concentrate on what I was going to say. I still had nothing. Was I going to get a repeat of the night on the couch, when my usual gift of gab just disappeared? Thank goodness, there was the usual funeral stuff before my turn to speak came just before the benediction. I don't remember any of it up to this point.

"And now Lenny will say a few words and deliver the eulogy," the old pastor said.

I just sat there. B nudged me. My three children and their mother, my ex-wife, all looked my way. I slowly stood. I felt I had the weight of the world on my shoulders. Those few steps from the front pew up to the pulpit were the most difficult of my life.

I stood there for a moment. I grabbed ahold of the pulpit with both hands, not for emphasis, but support. I could have used a cold one. I could have used several cold ones. I looked out over the sea of faces. It briefly made me happy to see so many people my dad cared for and those that cared for him. I tried to smile.

"My father loved golf, the Washington Redskins, Carolina, Ford, the St. Louis Cardinals, and all of you," I began. "Except maybe you Hal. Bluto messed Dad's tiny patch of grass on the side of the house he called a yard up more than once."

Everyone laughed.

"Just kidding Hal," I said. "You know my father loved you. Just like the rest of you. You may have never heard the words, heck I never heard the words, but you knew he did. My father was a man's man who let his actions define him for good and for all else. He served his country, his community, and his family well…"

I said some other stuff that people seemed to be touched by or laugh at. Stuff I think Dad would have been ok with. Then I saw her face. I tried not to focus there. It was difficult. She was still just as lovely as the day we met. Different, of course, but time had treated her extremely well. Then the finish came to me, how or why I don't know.

"When I think of my dad," I began the end. "And how best to describe him or honor him, a passage from my favorite book, *To Kill a Mockingbird* is what resonates. You probably know the scene. The little heroine of the book, nine-year-old Scout Finch has snuck into the courthouse to watch her father, Atticus, defend a black man accused of assaulting a white woman. It's the last day of the trial and Scout has managed to slide upstairs and sit in the colored section. She's on her knees peering through the rails mesmerized by her father's intelligent, impassioned pleas for a not guilty verdict. You know that didn't happen. The courtroom begins to clear out and Atticus gathers his papers and is the last to leave downstairs. As he begins to walk by below, all of the black people upstairs slowly rise. An elderly black man, a pastor, puts his hand on Scout's shoulder and says.

"Stand up Miss Scout, your father's passing."

Track 46-Love Reign o'er Me-The Who (5:49)

From *Requiem for a Nun*- "…the past is never dead. It's not even the past."-William Faulkner

We held a gathering in the church's reception hall afterward to feed everyone and give people a chance to talk. I got to speak to most everyone, old friends I hadn't seen in ages, family members from the Piedmont I only saw on Christmas Eve, and at funerals, and my friends from nearby Elizabethtown and White Lake, where I had lived for the past 17 years.

My dad loved that lake. He went to the FFA (Future Farmers of America) camp there while in high school in the early 1950s. His love for the place meant it was our vacation destination for much of my youth and the reason I ended up spending a big part of my life there and raising my family on its beautiful shores looking out over its crystal clear water. But those are tales for another day.

It was so heartwarming to hear story after story from folks about how Dad had helped them or what he meant to them. Some I knew about, most I did not. I could see the Winter family approaching. There were just a few people in line ahead of them, Lexi and Hal included.

"You got so many people here Lenny," Hal said. "We'll just catch up with you back at your dad's house."

Lexi was hugging me as Hal was talking. Of course, he kept talking.

"That'll be great Hal," I said. "Will you make sure the garage door is open? I want people to be able to see Dad's golf workshop out back if they want."

"No problem," Hal said.

"Be sure and close that gate, so B5 can run around," I said as he hugged me.

Lexi and Darlene were talking as Mr. Winter shook my hand. Dad wouldn't have expected him to say much. He didn't.

"Fine looking family you got there Lenny," Mr. Winter said.

"Thank you, sir," I said.

He turned to go.

"Mr. Winter," I said.

He turned back to face me.

"I have a set of golf clubs I think Dad would want you to have," I said. "If you could stop by the house?"

He nodded that he would. I found out later he and Dad had stayed in touch over the years and even played golf a few times. Dad never said anything to me about it. Interesting guy, my old man. I seriously doubt Mr. Winter ever said anything to Darlene about it either.

I turned back to the line. There she was, right in front of me. It had been 28 years since I had seen her. It was the day she and her dad pulled out of our driveway after visiting for that week during fall break our freshman year of college. Her cheeks were moist. Her face still soft and lovely. Her violet eyes were still stunning.

"Lenny," she said, hugging my neck tightly and then quickly stepping back. "Your dad was some guy. What you said, there wasn't a dry eye in the place. Oh, this is Arie, my husband, and this is Colette, our daughter, and Rich, our son."

They looked to be about the same age as my two youngest children, mid-to-late teens. I caught a glimpse of Mr. Winter talking to B.

"Sorry for your loss," Arie said shaking my hand. "Heard a lot about your father. Would love to have met him."

"Thank you, thank you," I said. "That's very kind."

I said hi to her kids. Rich looked like both of them, and yep you guessed it, Colette was the spitting image of her mother. So much so I was shocked. I thought my mind was playing tricks on me for a second. I snapped back to reality. Darlene had been talking to my kids.

People stayed and talked and talked and talked. Finally, things started to ease off and the fellowship hall was emptying. Darlene had got away before I could say good-bye. We made our way out and over to my dad and Step-mom's house. A crowd of about two or three dozen ambled in and around the house and the fenced-in back yard. Another spread of food and leftovers brought from the fellowship hall filled a couple tables on the screened-in back porch. The kids were all playing fetch with B5. I saw Darlene's kids talking to my kids. I saw my 19-year old son talking to Colette.

Oh boy...

"Lenny," Mr. Winter said. "Hal said these were the ones you wanted me to have?"

"Yes sir," I said.

"You sure?" he asked. "These were his favorites."

"I know," I said.

"Thank you," Mr. Winter said. "Thank you so much Lenny."

"Dad, it's time to go," Darlene said smiling from just outside the detached garage that also served as my dad's golf workshop. "Bye Lenny."

"Bye Darlene," I said.

I watched them all get in their big black SUV. Arie was driving and for the first time I ever saw, Mr. Winter got in the back seat. The kids got in on the driver's side. Darlene got in on the front passenger side. I turned around and B started talking to me about something. Damn if I know what it was. A second later, he tapped me on the shoulder and motioned with his head for me to turn around. I did.

Darlene was standing outside of the SUV. She was crying. Yep, you guessed it, she gave our stupid little awkward half-wave one last time. With tears running down my cheeks, I did the same. Darlene smiled while wiping tears from her eyes. I smiled. She quickly climbed back in the SUV and it slowly disappeared from sight. B5 chased it to the gate.

I stopped by to see Mom later, out of respect. I knew it was a tough day for her too. They were married 33 years. Plus, the grandkids wanted to see their grandmother. We had a good visit and I told her who all was at the service that I could remember. Mom seemed to be ok. You could tell she'd been crying. She was pretty tender-hearted. I'm sure that's why I am as well. Back in the day if I had a problem with someone we might be brawling, but if that person's pet died, I'd probably help them bury their friend and mourn the loss with them. Hugs and kisses were exchanged and the kids began making their way back outside.

"Oh," Mom said. "I have something for you from the Hermit, err, Mr. Robert. Years ago, he stopped by, it was a month or so before he died I think. Aunt Pat gave him a beer."

I gave her a quizzical look. She walked over to the old china cabinet and opened one of its tiny top drawers. The cabinet, which had always been under the carport, survived Hurricane Fran because it was on loan to my sister. Mom pulled something out and walked over and placed the item on her dining table.

"I've almost given it to you a couple of times over the years," she said. "I asked Mr. Robert when I should give it to you. He said I would know. I'm sure today is the day he was talking about. Oh, and he said to tell you it was from him and Captain Thompson."

Made in the USA
Middletown, DE
14 June 2023